LOVE & REDEMPTION

THE LOVE & RUIN SERIES BOOK THREE

J.A. OWENBY

CHAPTER 1

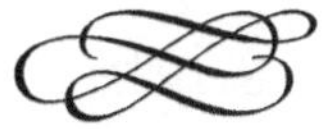

"My father admitted he's sexually attracted to young ladies," I said. My pulse raced while I stared directly at Jack Wilson, my father's defense attorney. It was the first time I'd stated this information to anyone other than my friends and the police.

He paused. "The term *young lady* is a bit broad and doesn't necessarily mean a minor."

"He specifically said fourteen," I replied.

"When did you learn about this, Ms. Thompson?"

My chest tightened with the memories of my father's twisted confession. The same night he almost killed me.

I glanced over to Hendrix and Mac who sat in

the audience along with multiple reporters. Our little town of Breaux Bridge, Louisiana, made headlines across the country a few weeks ago when the news of a secret society of men who raped underage girls was brought to light.

Hendrix nodded slightly, his piercing blue eyes filled with love and support. He was the reason I was alive today. Him and Ada Lynn.

"March 5th."

My attorney, Marcus Johnson, had advised I keep my answers as short as possible. So far, I'd succeeded. But the longer I was questioned, the more I was afraid I was going to lose control of my emotions. Not only was I testifying against my father, but it would be the last time I saw him. I was going to move on, and he would rot in jail.

"And what happened on March 5th?"

The courtroom was silent while I collected my thoughts. I cleared my throat before I spoke.

"On March 5th, my father admitted to me that he had arranged for Carl Roberts to rape me when I was fourteen."

Although the jury wasn't supposed to show emotion, someone gasped. The defense attorney's gaze traveled toward them, his brows knitting together.

I took a shaky breath and continued. "And in

exchange, Mr. Roberts arranged for my fa—my father to have Carl's niece. To rape Carl's niece." My voice quivered with anger. "We were both fourteen at the time."

"Was he sober when he divulged this information?" Mr. Wilson asked, placing his hands on his hips.

"I don't know. I hadn't seen him in weeks."

"Does your father have a drinking problem?" Marcus had mentioned the defense would push the issue that Kyle hadn't been coherent or in his right mind when he'd admitted the trade.

"I'm not a professional who can make that decision," I replied. Thank God Marcus had coached me well. I'd never seen the inside of a courtroom before. Not to mention the sight of my father was enough to unnerve me.

I peeked at my father a few times during my questioning, but his expression never changed. He remained deadpan and aloof.

After what seemed like an eternity, I was excused from the box. My legs wobbled as I stepped down and made my way to the seat between Hendrix and Mac.

"You were amazing," Hendrix whispered in my ear. He planted a gentle kiss on my cheek and took my hand. Mac took the other one. I stared at the back of my father's head. This was it. I was minutes away from eliminating him from my life forever.

"Let's take a fifteen-minute recess," the judge said.

Hendrix released my hand and stood. He straightened his red and black tie and buttoned his suit jacket. I wasn't sure if my heart was pounding because he looked so hot or that I was finished in the courtroom. Maybe a little of both.

"Let's get the hell out of here," Mac mumbled.

"I don't ever want to see another courtroom for as long as I live," I said.

Mac nodded in agreement. Her brown hair flowed past her shoulders, and she wore a navy-blue fitted dress. She looked amazing, and it was a nice contrast from her usual braids and plaid flannel shirts.

I stood and smoothed my black skirt and emerald green blouse. My father glanced over his shoulder at me and our eyes locked. I stood motionless and held his gaze. Then I tilted my chin up and turned away.

"I need some fresh air and fast," I said softly to Hendrix and Mac.

We hurried out of the courtroom and through the front doors. The fresh spring air greeted me as I stepped outside the courthouse. We made our way to the side of the entrance, and I removed my ponytail holder, shaking my hair free. Marcus had wanted to make sure I looked young and angelic for my court appearance. Apparently it would make a positive impression on the jury. I'd have worn a chicken suit if it helped put my father behind bars for the rest of his life.

I leaned against the wall and inhaled deeply while Hendrix removed his suit jacket. Mac discarded her heels immediately. I couldn't help but smile. We were both more comfortable in jeans and tennis shoes.

"Gemma," Marcus Smith didn't look anything like the bulldog he was in the courtroom. He was on the short side, probably five foot nine, and skinny as a rail with a receding hairline. "You did great. You're free to go. I'll keep you updated on the trial. I'll be here every day until the jury comes back with a verdict."

"That would be great, Marcus. I can't go back unless I have no other choice." I wrung my hands together at the mere idea of seeing my father again.

"Just make sure she doesn't have to come back," Hendrix said, slipping his arm around my waist.

"That's my goal," Marcus said.

"You did super awesome, bestie," Mac said. "I'm so proud of you. I don't know if I could testify against a parent. Not to mention having to talk about the whole sex trade deal. It's so fucked up. Like who even thinks like that?"

"Mac," Hendrix said gently, "not now."

Mac nodded. "Sorry." She peeked up at me. "I think I should just get that word tattooed on my forehead."

I couldn't help but laugh. "I appreciate your support, but I sure as hell don't want to do it again."

"Hopefully you won't have to, but stay near your phone," Marcus said.

"We have the concert tonight," Hendrix reminded him.

Mac bounced on her toes, excitement filling her face.

Hendrix and I were opening with our song, "Couldn't Love You More." Although I had the jitters, it was a good thing. I desperately needed to have some fun after today. We all did.

"That's right. It's in Baton Rouge, correct?" Marcus asked.

"Yeah, it's a quick trip. We'll be back late tonight," Hendrix said.

"Sounds good."

We said goodbye to Marcus and walked toward our cars.

"It's only ten-fifteen, so I have a few hours to jump Jeremiah before I get ready for the concert," Mac said, wiggling her eyebrows at us.

"Whatever you need to do is fine but be ready by three. I'll pick you up in front of your dorm," Hendrix replied, grinning at her. Nothing seemed to faze him when it came to the outrageous stuff that flew out of Mac's mouth.

"Okay. I'm so excited!" she squealed as we arrived at her Kia.

"I couldn't tell," I teased. "Thanks for coming, too. I don't want to be alone while Hendrix is performing."

"But you're still singing with him, right?"

"Yeah, just the opening song."

"For now," Hendrix said, rubbing my back. "We're going to write some more together."

"Omigosh! I can't wait to hear the new material. Okay, seriously, I have to go. Jeremiah isn't always in the mood for a quickie because, ya know, he likes to take his time. I just don't have a lot of that today. Gotta go!"

She gave us a quick hug and got into her car.

Hendrix led me to his Lexus a few spots down

from Mac's vehicle. We settled in, and he started the engine.

"How are you?" he said, his thumb gently rubbing my cheek.

"Honestly?"

"Always," his expression filled with concern as he searched my face.

"I'm not sure, but I'm going to say I'm leaning toward the *fucked up* end of the scale."

"Understandable. Let's consider tonight our new beginning. We're singing for the first time since we got back together. I've missed singing with you, Gem." He leaned across the console and gave me a gentle kiss. "And don't forget, you and Mac are meeting Billy tonight, too."

There was no way I could fight the grin that spread across my face. Billy Raffoul was my favorite singer other than Hendrix.

Hendrix shot me a look and then frowned. "Should I be worried about introducing him to you?"

"What?" I asked, shock lacing my words. "What are you talking about?"

Hendrix pulled out of the parking lot and headed toward our house.

"Gem, you're beautiful, genuine, and your

voice is amazing. There's not a guy on earth that wouldn't want you."

Oh my God. Was Hendrix jealous? Between his money and singing career, girls hit on him all of the time. I should be the one in our relationship that was worried.

"Babe, it's business, that's all. You said it yourself: we're meeting with him to discuss music opportunities, right? Just because I'm fangirling doesn't mean I'm going to run off with him. There's no one else for me except you." I took his free hand in mine and kissed it.

"You're my everything, Gem. I don't want to lose you again. I guess the residual effects of what Andrea did still lingers inside me. I've never felt so helpless and devastated before. All of a sudden, someone else had the power to ruin my life, and it fucked me up. I'm still working through it."

"I know, me too. But I told you when I came back that nothing would get in the way of us again. Not even music."

"You're right. I'm sorry. It's been a crazy morning, and my mind is still reeling from your testimony in court," he said and squeezed my hand.

"For the record, I'm totally over this entire shit

show. I just want us to be free to move forward." I leaned my head back against the seat and stared out the window for the rest of the ride home.

Hendrix pulled into our driveway and parked.

"I need to check on Ada Lynn," I said, getting out of the car.

"Do you want me to go with you?"

A chill shot through me when my eyes landed on my father's empty house across the street. My childhood home. It was the house I hid myself away in after I was raped, and the place I left behind to find myself in Spokane, Washington. It was also the last place I saw my mother alive. The majority of my life had happened within those walls, including the nearly fatal evening when my father broke my ribs. Phantom pains still stirred inside me from the repetitive impact of his foot. It would most likely haunt me for the rest of my life. I wondered what would happen to the house when he was sentenced.

"It's okay. It will give us a few minutes alone before you come over to meet the nurse," I said, approaching him. He pulled me to him, kissing me tenderly.

"I know he's gone, but I'm still watching you cross the street," he said, leaning his forehead against mine.

I smiled up at him. "Thank you." I stepped away and walked toward Ada Lynn's house, my heels clicking against the pavement. Turning to peer over my shoulder, I waved at him, and then knocked on her front door.

CHAPTER 2

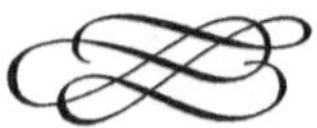

"I was hoping to see you before you went to Baton Rouge," Ada Lynn said, motioning for me to come in.

"Yeah, I wanted to see you, too. I wouldn't have left without visiting first, anyway."

She nodded and sat down in her favorite recliner. I sat in my regular place on her black leather couch.

Ada Lynn looked damn good for an eighty-three-year-old woman. No one would have any idea she'd recently had a heart attack. Not to mention this tiny woman was a badass. Her fierceness had saved my life when she held Kyle at gunpoint.

"Did you testify today?" she asked, her gaze intense while she waited for my answer.

"Yeah," I tugged on my skirt and crossed my legs.

"How was it?"

"Hell," I muttered, looking at her. "It was really hard. Especially seeing Kyle."

Ada Lynn's lips pursed together.

"I've noticed you no longer refer to him as your father."

"I hate him," I whispered.

She reached for my hand. "Let me tell you something. There's nothing wrong with hating him. Don't let anyone tell you different. Healing is a process. You'll hate him one minute and grieve the loss of him the next. Don't try to convince yourself you shouldn't feel one way or the other, just go with it. Over time it will get better. Nothing pisses me off more than people telling you how you *should* feel. How would they know unless they've been in your shoes?"

"Really? I can hate him?"

"Of course, you can. Hell, *I* hate him. Most days, I think about the horrible crimes he committed, what he did to you and those other girls, and I wonder if he's even human. He has a dark soul and no conscience. Something inside that man is severely broken."

"What if..." I paused, afraid to verbalize my thoughts. "What if I'm like him?" My voice faltered as I spoke.

Ada Lynn's chuckle filled the living room.

"My blue-eyed girl, you're everything beautiful and good about this world. Don't you ever think otherwise."

"Thank you," I whispered, swallowing down the ball of pain and grief that had lodged in my throat.

"Now you go have fun tonight. Ya'll deserve a good time."

I smiled. "Yes, we do! Your nurse is scheduled to arrive in another hour. Hendrix wants to meet her before we leave."

"He sure is a good young man. Someone taught him well."

"I suspect it was Mac's mom. After Kendra's death, Hendrix moved out of his dad's house and went to live with her and Mac. Franklin, his dad, has only been back in his life for the last few years, but he's trying hard to make up for his absence. He seems to really love Hendrix and Mac."

"I don't think you've ever mentioned what

happened to Mac's biological dad," Ada Lynn commented.

"Oh geez. In all of the crazy, she's never mentioned him. I only know that her mom married Franklin and they divorced after a couple years."

"As much as that girl talks, I suspect she would have told you by now if he were in her life."

"Yeah, but now I feel bad for not asking her. Or maybe she prefers it that way."

"Sometimes, the past is better left alone."

"Yeah, I know. Maybe I'll ask Hendrix if I should bring it up to Mac or not."

Ada Lynn nodded and took a sip of her iced tea.

A loud knock at the door startled me from my thoughts about Mac.

"I've got it," I said, jumping up from the couch. I opened the door as much as the chain would allow and grinned. "It's Hendrix," I called over my shoulder. Even though we'd just seen each other a little while ago, he kissed me as soon as he stepped inside.

He gave my hand a squeeze and sauntered over to Ada Lynn.

"How's my favorite lady?" he asked, placing a kiss on the top of her head. He'd changed from his suit into Levi's and a black fitted polo. I was ready to change my clothes, too.

Ada Lynn smiled, "Oh you know me, I'm just over here causing trouble."

We all laughed.

Another knock sounded at the door, and I cracked it open. Hendrix stepped up behind me and protectively slid his arm around my waist. Kyle was no longer living next door, but we were all hyper-aware of our surroundings. It had only been a few weeks since he'd nearly killed me and was afterward arrested for child pornography. Hendrix still blamed himself and was taking extra precautions to keep me safe.

The lady flashed her ID and a warm smile.

"Hi, I'm Kim. I'm your nurse for the evening."

I scanned her spikey bleach blonde hair, stepped away, and allowed Hendrix to talk to her. She had an ID and was wearing a white polo shirt with the blue star logo, but I still thoroughly inspected her when she stepped inside and spoke with Hendrix. Having a nurse stay with Ada Lynn was the only way I'd go to the concert tonight. Granted, it was only a forty-five-minute drive from home, but if she had another heart attack, one minute away was too far.

"Don't you worry about me. Everything is going to be fine," Ada Lynn assured me.

"How did you know I was worried?" I asked her.

"The look on your face made it pretty clear," she said, squeezing my fingers.

"Babe," Hendrix said. "Kim is from the best agency around. Ada Lynn will be in great company."

I nodded, then turned to Kim. "Thank you."

"Oh hon, don't you worry one bit. Ada Lynn and I've got this. I also have your number and your boyfriend's if anything happens," she said, patting me on the back. She moved past me and straight to Ada Lynn. "Hi there, it's so nice to meet ya."

"You too," Ada Lynn said, eyeing her cautiously.

They continued to chat while Hendrix and I watched their interaction. If Ada Lynn seemed uncomfortable at all, I wouldn't even hesitate to stay home and miss the concert. I was nervous about leaving her with someone new, but I also wanted it to work out. Moving forward, it would allow me to travel with Hendrix.

Ada Lynn chuckled, and the tension eased from my neck.

"I think they'll be fine," Hendrix said.

I nodded and smiled as Kim flitted around the living room and into the kitchen.

"How are you feeling about this?" I asked Ada Lynn.

"She'll be alright. It might be nice to have someone new to beat at cards. You two get out of here. I know how to use a telephone if I need you."

Hendrix chuckled and checked his watch. "We need to get back to the house and get ready."

I nodded. "I love you," I said, kissing Ada Lynn's cheek. "I'll be over tomorrow."

"Sounds good. Drive safe, Hendrix." She nodded and arched her eyebrow at him for emphasis.

"Always," he said, flashing his beautiful smile.

"By the way, Kim, if you and Ada Lynn play cards tonight, don't get fooled by her sweet old lady routine. She's a card shark at poker," I said.

Kim laughed and gave me a warm smile. "Oh don't you worry, my grandpa taught me how to play at the age of five. We'll see who's really the shark." She winked at Ada Lynn.

Hendrix chuckled.

"Bye, Kim," I called, feeling a little better about leaving.

She stepped out of the kitchen with a Diet Coke in her hand. "Ya'll have a great time! I'll be here until ten tomorrow morning so don't you worry 'bout a thing."

We waved goodbye, then hurried across the street to our house.

The second the door closed behind us, Hendrix pinned me against the wall.

A giggle erupted from me.

"I thought I'd never get you alone," he said, placing kisses along my neck. "You look so sexy in your skirt."

"Hendrix," I laughed. "It goes to my knees, how in the world is that sexy?"

He leaned his hips into me, and I moaned softly when I felt his erection press against my stomach.

"Oh," I said breathlessly. "I guess you weren't kidding."

He pulled me away from the door, leading me to the living room. "It doesn't matter what you wear, you're always sexy." He palmed my ass and grinned.

Even though we'd been together for several months, I still blushed with his words. I'd never considered myself pretty, much less sexy.

"I have to admit, you looked hot in your suit. I

think I'll have to take you out more often." I placed my finger against his lips. "Thank you," I said softly. "Thank you for hiring someone for Ada Lynn and thank you for staying with me in court. There's no way I could get through this without you." I moved my finger so he could speak if he chose to.

"There's no way in hell I would let you go through this on your own, Gem. I love you." He leaned down and kissed me gently.

"I love you, too," I replied. "So much."

His hand moved up my back and caressed my neck. Our mouths parted, his tongue gliding over mine.

Hendrix flipped open my blouse buttons and slid the silk fabric over my shoulders. A smile eased across his face as his eyes landed on my black and red lace bra.

"You've been shopping," he said, his tongue darting across his lower lip.

"Do you like it?" I stepped back and unbuttoned my skirt. In one quick motion, it was on the floor. "It's a set," I said, turning around slowly for him to see the matching G-string.

"Jesus, Gem," he said, unbuttoning his jeans. "It's my new favorite on you."

I giggled. "Don't say that yet. I bought more."

He growled, and in two steps grabbed my waist with both hands and pulled me against him. He walked me backward to the couch and eased me down onto the cushions. I leaned over to slip off my heels.

"Nope, those stay on." He kneeled between my legs and pulled the lace cups of my bra down, exposing my breasts. My nipples hardened as he gently pinched them. I ran my hand through his hair and watched, while he placed soft kisses down my stomach and to the inside of my thigh. Heat swirled through me, and my core throbbed with anticipation.

His hands traced down from my ribs and tugged on my G-string.

"This is in my way," he said, hooking the thin satin strings with his fingers and pulling it down my legs. He nipped at my ankle as the material slid over my shoes. "You're never taking these shoes off again." I shivered at the sound of his husky voice.

Hendrix didn't waste any more time, his head quickly dipping between my legs, his mouth making contact with my sensitive flesh. My fingers threaded through his hair and I arched my hips upward, as he lifted my legs over his shoulders and worked his magic on me, my heels slightly digging into his back.

"My God you taste so damn good," he groaned. "Stand up."

I eagerly did as I was told. The look on Hendrix's face was pure lust before he turned me around and gently nudged me to bend over and grasp hold of the back of the couch. The sound of his zipper echoed through the room. I glanced over my shoulder and our eyes locked as he rubbed his hard dick against my wet folds. A gasp escaped me when he entered me with a firm push. He remained still for a moment, allowing me to adjust to him in this position. Hendrix moved slowly inside me as I held onto the furniture in order to keep my balance.

His front plastered to my back, I felt his arm sneak around, and his hand move between my legs to tease my clit.

"Does that feel good, Gem?" he whispered against the side of my neck and picked up the pace.

"Yes," I whimpered, shivering with pain and pleasure.

But when he grabbed my waist and thrust inside me, memories rushed back like a dangerous tidal wave. My attacker's rough hands, Kyle's words about the sex trade, and Brandon's evil sneer all blasted through my mind.

"Hendrix," I said, my tone filling with panic. He stopped immediately and turned me around.

"I'm here." His warm hands cupped the sides of my face and tilted my head, so we were eye to eye. "It's okay, it's me, Gem."

I nodded, taking deep breaths. "I'm sorry."

Hendrix pulled me to him, wrapped his strong arms around me and kissed my forehead. "Don't ever apologize."

"I'm okay to keep going, just not in that position. I need to see you today," I said, chewing on my bottom lip. The memories of my rape and reliving the profound betrayal by my father in court today had twisted my insides into knots. I wanted to be with Hendrix, but I needed to see him. Even though Hendrix was muscular and a trained boxer, nothing about him frightened me.

He nodded, took my hand, and led me to our bed. I lay down and scooted toward the top. Hendrix balanced over me, then slipped inside me again. We lay still, our gazes locking.

"Are you sure?" he asked.

"Yes," I whispered. My fingers trailed down his muscular back to his ass, my hips lifting to meet him.

"You feel so good," I groaned.

His tongue darted across my sensitive bud, and our bodies rocked together. He trailed his hand up my side and cupped my breast, gently stroking my nipple. I leaned up to kiss him, his pace quickening. The familiar sweet sensation swirled inside me, and I bucked against him.

"Faster, baby," I said, my hands grabbing onto his shoulders.

He moaned into my mouth, and I linked my legs around him, my shoes digging into his ass.

"Shit, I forgot you had those on," he said, panting.

He leaned back and pushed my legs up. Now, he had a full view of me and the heels. He smiled and slid deep inside me.

"Ohh," I said. "Oh my God." My eyes fluttered closed while I took in every single, beautiful inch of him. This position, my legs straight and toes pointed to the ceiling, was one we'd never tried. I was so tight, it felt as if Hendrix couldn't possibly fit, let alone move inside me. I clutched the bedspread as he continued.

"Don't stop, Hendrix, please," I whimpered.

"Gem," he said.

The sound of his gravelly voice sent me over

the edge. I yelled out his name as my core tightened around him.

"That's it," he said. "That's my baby."

Panting, I opened my eyes and focused on him.

"You're so deep inside me," I said softly. "You have no idea how good you feel."

With one more thrust, his body tightened and shuddered with his release.

He lowered my legs and relaxed on top of me. We remained silent, holding each other.

"Thank you," I said, kissing his cheek. "I needed you."

"Me too," he replied and kissed the tip of my nose. "We should probably get out of bed and shower. If it were up to me, we would stay here all day, but we're singing together at a concert tonight."

CHAPTER 3

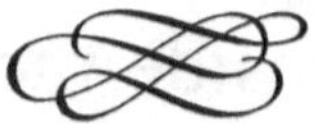

I waved to Mac as Hendrix pulled the car up
to the sidewalk of her dorm. She hopped
into the back seat and flashed a silly grin at
us. Mac had left the braided pigtails behind
tonight, and her brown hair fell past her shoulders in soft waves. Surprisingly, she'd also
ditched the typical flannel shirt in exchange for a
soft pink one that brought out the natural rose
color in her cheeks.

"Soooo excited," she squealed. "Oh, and proud
of you too, Hendrix. I mean, I should have said
that first, but Billy Raffoul is *not* my brother and
he's hot as hell. That factor alone gets him mentioned first."

Hendrix chuckled. "He'd probably think that was funny, actually."

Mac leaned forward as much as she could without crawling into the front with us.

"You and he talk and hang out and shit, don't you? It's not like, you had a drink together in a big group and raised your glass kind of thing. I mean, how else would you know he would think that was funny? I'll tell you, you fucking *know* Billy. You're friends!"

I cringed at her volume and laughed. She'd been this loud the first day I'd met her on campus in Spokane, too. While I was super happy living alone with Hendrix now, sometimes I missed living with my bestie, including our late-night talks, her Starbucks coffee runs, and even her constant chatter.

With Hendrix and I back together, rooming with Mac again at college was off the table. Plus I was taking online classes. It didn't matter, anyway. She and Jeremiah were busy planning their upcoming nuptials. I'd tried to talk to Mac about not rushing into marriage, but she had her mind made up. A part of me understood, and I wanted her to be happy, but I hoped they would wait a while longer. Besides, Jeremiah planned to enlist in the military soon. Mac would most likely end up living wherever he was stationed. My heart sank at the thought of it. What I found interesting, was that she hadn't told her mom or Franklin about Jeremiah, let alone their plans. When I'd mention it, Mac would just shut me down. A part of me wondered if she was concerned that Franklin would pull her college tuition funding.

Hendrix pulled onto I-10 E, and we headed toward the concert venue. Butterflies fluttered in my stomach, and I reached over and grabbed his hand.

"Yeah, we've hung out some, Mac. He seems like a good guy so far. You always have to be careful in this business. People try to take advantage, or they want to use you for something, but I guess that can be said for anyone." He peeked at me and arched his brow.

I knew him well enough to understand he was checking to see if I was doing ok. It had been an intense day. A small smiled pulled at the corners of my mouth as I focused on Mac firing a million questions at Hendrix concerning Billy.

"What time do you two go on stage?" Mac asked, clapping her hands together.

"Six," Hendrix replied. "Gemma and I will sing first, then she'll join you while I finish the set."

"I'm so excited you're singing together again.

Omigosh, your voices are fucking amazing. I'll never forget the night you walked us back to the dorm room Hendrix, ya know after that fucker Brandon—shit, sorry. The night you two sang together for the first time. Gemma, I swear I watched Hendrix melt into a big ol' man puddle right there on the sidewalk. Girl, you snatched his heart right out of his chest."

Honest to God, I wasn't sure which comment to react to. Hendrix rubbed his chin and frowned. Mac never meant to bring up Brandon and the disturbing memories his name triggered, but her ADHD contributed to her brutal honesty.

"Mac, I know you're excited, but let's steer away from conversation concerning Kyle or Brandon tonight, okay?" Hendrix said gently. His patience with Mac amazed me. There'd been more than once I had chewed her out when she blurted inappropriate or insensitive things. But Mac was a package deal, and her heart and friendship outweighed her ADHD every time.

"I'm sorry, shit just flies right out." Mac's face twisted with regret and she sank into her seat.

"That night changed my life," I said softly, looking at her in the back seat. "Each moment, from the concert where I first heard Hendrix sing, to Brandon accusing me of starting the fight, to you encouraging Hendrix to sing outside our dorm—it all led to tonight. Mac, if those things hadn't happened, Hendrix and I wouldn't be together, and you and I wouldn't be as close as sisters. So yeah, you brought him up, but everything else about that night was amazing. Don't feel bad. I think the court case has made us all sensitive. We need a mental break and some fun tonight, too."

"You're not upset?" she asked, her tone perking up.

"No, I'm happy you're with us tonight. It's like old times, we're just in a different state. Those days mean a lot to me. You, Hendrix, and Ada Lynn are my entire world. I love you all so much," I said, my words catching in my throat. Gratitude and affection overwhelmed me, and I swallowed the tears back. Life could have gone in such a different direction, but I'd somehow managed to end up in a good place.

"I love you," Hendrix said softly.

"Bestie, you're going to make me cry. I would be lost without you, too."

Silence hung in the air while we all gathered our emotions. Court had taken its toll on each of us, but no matter what, we had each other.

The drive passed quickly and the next thing I

knew, Hendrix had parked behind Cane's River Center in the designated performer's area. The back of the building wasn't much to see other than a lot of brick, but it appeared massive. The parking lot was already near maximum capacity with cars and trailers.

A smile eased across Hendrix's face. I loved seeing him this excited about performing. When he was on stage, he was full of energy and a true performer who had the audience on their feet and cheering. Regardless of what he said, I would never want him to choose me over his music.

"Ten thousand seats and we're sold out," Hendrix said, getting out of his Lexus.

"Holy hell," Mac said.

"That many?" I asked, my tone climbing in pitch.

"Take a breath. I'll be with you the entire time," Hendrix said, walking around the car and slipping his arm around my waist. He gave me a reassuring kiss.

"And me, too," Mac said.

"I've lived in Louisiana most of my life, and I've never been here." My nerves and awareness were on full alert as I scanned the building. It wasn't just because we were performing. I'd spent five years shut away from the world, and I'd only just begun to live again, thanks to Hendrix and Mac. And I loved singing with Hendrix, but the last time we'd sung together...No, I wasn't going to allow my past to steal my happiness. Not tonight.

"Makes sense, though. When you were old enough to attend concerts, you weren't interested in leaving your house. But now you have us!" Mac said, bounding over to me and looping her arm through mine. "Like old times!"

I smiled. Mac talked a lot, but she had super Spidey senses when my anxiety was beginning to climb through the roof. She intuitively knew when I needed her.

A blue Chevy Silverado and a large trailer pulled in next to us.

"If you change your mind and aren't ready, say the word. We can perform together another time. I realize the trial was a lot for you today, and I want you to have fun tonight, not stress out."

I looked up at him. His expression was protective but gentle.

"You're with me, Hendrix, and it's all I need. I'm okay," I assured him. "Can we see the stage?" I asked.

"Yeah, I want to do a warm up with you, too."

Mac gasped. "Ohmigod!" She said, smacking

her hands over her mouth to contain any further outburst.

I turned to see what Mac was excited about.

"Hey, man. How the hell are ya?" Billy asked, approaching Hendrix.

Holy crap, I would recognize that sultry voice anywhere. It melted me like butter and made my insides all gooey. I'd listened to his song, "Forever," a million times. I must have gasped because Hendrix's low chuckle rippled through my body as he turned me around in his arms.

And there was Billy Raffoul himself, reaching out to shake Hendrix's hand. They slapped each other on the back like they were best friends. Billy was taller and thinner than I expected, but he still rocked it. His long dark hair was pulled back in a man bun, and most of the time I wasn't a fan of that style, but he made it work. He looked relaxed in his jeans and red Converse, his black T-shirt slightly big on him. This was a look I'd seen him wear often.

Tonight's concert was super casual, and there were five bands performing. I'd been relieved when Hendrix said we could wear jeans to perform in, or whatever else we wanted.

"Good, I'm pretty ramped up about tonight," Hendrix responded.

"Me too. It's going to be a good crowd." Billy extended his hand toward me. "This must be Gemma."

"Hi," I said, the dreaded flush traveling up my neck rather quickly. I shook it and grinned.

"This is Mac, my sister," Hendrix said, introducing them.

"Good to meet you, Mac." Billy grinned and extended his hand to her.

She dropped her hands from her mouth and flashed her toothy grin at him.

"Hi," she said breathlessly, holding onto his fingers a bit longer than usual. I wasn't sure if Mac or I would faint first, but I was guessing it would be me.

"I've heard you sing," Billy said to me. "You've got one amazing voice. I would like to talk with you and Hendrix after the concert."

"Thank you," I replied while Hendrix's arm tightened around my waist briefly. I looked up at him and gave him a soft, reassuring smile. "I'd love to hang out and talk. Hendrix mentioned some possible opportunities."

"Yeah, I think you guys would be great to work with. Listen, I've gotta get set up and ready for tonight, but I'll catch up with you later."

He gave a small wave and returned to the truck.

"Oh. My. God. Oh. My. God." Mac whisper-yelled, her eyes never leaving Billy as he walked away.

"Don't forget about Jeremiah," I said, teasing her.

"Who?" she asked a bit dazed.

Hendrix laughed. "I think both of my girls are a bit starstruck."

"Maybe a little," I admitted, holding my fingers apart a smidge. I stood on my tiptoes and kissed him.

"Let's go." Hendrix took my hand and led us to the arena. "John and Cade should be here, too."

I nodded while we walked toward the building. From the outside, it didn't seem as though it could hold that many people.

"Oh wow, it's been forever since I've seen John and Cade. It will be nice to see them."

"Cade grew a beard. Not like mine where it's trimmed and close to my face, but a long one." Hendrix laughed.

"Like, as in Duck Dynasty kind of beard?" Mac asked, her nose scrunching with the thought.

"Not that bad, but it's a bit rough. I'm going to

take you through the front of the arena so you can see everything."

"I would like that," I replied.

We approached the entrance. I eyed the floor to ceiling windows and large outdoor white columns. Hendrix held the door open, and security stopped us. Typically, performers used the backstage door, but once they realized who we were, they were cool and pointed us in the right direction. Our footsteps echoed through the nearly empty hallway as Hendrix led us to the back of the stage.

Mac and I remained silent and wide-eyed while the seating came into view. How in the hell was I going to sing in front of all these people?

No wonder the building had seemed empty, everyone was in the back. Every inch was filled with instruments and musicians busily buzzing around. Billy stood off to the far side, chatting with some guy I didn't know. He peered over at us and waved. I smiled and glanced at Hendrix. After everything Hendrix had done for me, I never wanted him to feel insecure.

"Hey," I said, tugging on his hand. Then, I looked at Mac. "Can you give us a minute?"

"Oh yeah, I'm just going to peruse the eye candy," she said, wiggling her eyebrows.

"Stay close," Hendrix said.

"I'm not twelve, dude." She rolled her eyes at him. "But I will."

Hendrix nodded, giving her permission to wander off.

"I need your full attention, please. Just for a minute." When his beautiful blue eyes locked on me, I melted on the spot. "I don't care about any of the celebrity musicians here or who might be interested in singing with us in the future. If it causes tension between us, I'm done. I won't sing. I'll walk off this stage right now and support you from the audience. You, Hendrix...Are. My. Everything. I love you so damned much. Nothing is worth the risk of losing you again," I said softly.

"Babe." He paused, his eyes softening while stroking my cheek with his thumb. "I love you. I want you by my side on this stage and many more to come. I want us to do this together. I've already done it without you, and it was agony." His gaze dropped to the floor and back up to me. "I trust you, it's the other guys I don't trust. I'll keep an eye on you and on them. I've let you down before, but I won't do it again. So, if I come off as untrusting or worried, it's not about us. It's about the other guys."

"Oh. I hadn't considered that."

"I've been in the business long enough to know sex, drugs, and women are all a part of it. Some guys aren't into it, me included, but a lot are. And the more you step into this world with me, the more you're going to see what I'm talking about. You're my main priority along with keeping you safe. You've lived through a lot of shit, and now it's time for us to create some happy memories—plan our future together."

"I want that, too. Thank you," I said, my heart pounding against my chest. "I still have my pepper spray and so does Mac."

"Good, but you'll be with Mac or myself tonight the entire time, and I feel good about it."

"I just want to make sure everything is okay between us. I thought you were getting jealous of me fangirling over Billy."

Hendrix laughed.

"Gem, *I* fangirled over Billy."

A giggle escaped me, and I peered up at him through my eyelashes.

"Shit, if you don't stop looking at me like that, I'm going to sneak you out of here for a quickie."

"Really?" I asked, wiggling my eyebrows at him. "How about we use one of the dressing rooms?" I bit my lower lip with the idea.

"The minute I'm done on stage, you're mine," he whispered in my ear.

My entire body tingled with his words.

"Maybe Mac can hang out with Billy while we're busy." A mischievous grin eased across his handsome face.

"Hendrix Harrington!"

We turned toward the stage manager who'd just barked out Hendrix's name. He spoke something into the mic of his headset, then motioned with his clipboard to follow him.

"Duty calls," Hendrix said, taking my hand and placing a sweet kiss on my forehead.

CHAPTER 4

The remainder of the afternoon flew by with preparations—sound checks, tuning instruments, props, and the lineup of all the performances. Hendrix and I were up first. Since I was only singing the first song, we decided Mac would wait for me back-stage, then we would grab our seats in the front and watch the rest of the performances from the audience.

"Don't be nervous," Mac said while Hendrix walked out on stage to a full house. The crowd went wild.

"How in the hell am I going to not pass out on stage?" I asked, covering my face with my hands.

"Oh good Lord, don't faint, Gem. Just focus on

Hendrix the entire time if you need to. Do you remember how we planned out every detail along with an exit strategy for your first date with him? I said, worst-case scenario, to start singing and he would join in, then you wouldn't be so nervous. It's the same way this time. Plus John and Cade are there with you, too. You're surrounded by friends."

I nodded and inhaled sharply.

"Good evening, Baton Rouge!" Hendrix's voice boomed through the arena.

I took Mac's hand and squeezed it tight, my legs turning to Jell-O.

"Girl, you're about to join your man on stage again, and I bet you guys will have mind-blowing sex tonight, so think about that." Mac giggled.

I laughed. I hoped she was right.

"I would like to thank everyone for coming out tonight," Hendrix began. "We've got an amazing lineup of musicians to kick off the first concert of the season for you, and I'm stoked to share the stage with them. But first—" The auditorium quieted as Hendrix paused.

"What's he doing?" I asked Mac. "Is something wrong? He just stopped talking."

She replied with a half-shrug.

"This past year has been pretty insane in my

music career and personal life. Things have taken off, but they've also come with some difficult challenges. But no matter what, over the last several months, one person has kept me moving forward. And, for the first time in my life, I've learned what love is all about."

I shot Mac a look, my eyes popping open wide.

"This person has carried me through the good and the bad times, and taught me how to open my heart. After I watched a car hit and kill my little sister several years ago, I never thought I'd let anyone in again. And then I met her, and my entire life changed. This first song is one I wrote for her. She had no idea because we hadn't even spoken yet." His chuckle filled the auditorium. "Eventually, I invited her to the studio to listen to it, and we collaborated on the song and finished it together. And tonight, you all get to meet the love of my life."

The audience's cheers split through the silence. My pulse sped into overdrive, and I took in some deep breaths, attempting to bring it under control.

"Holy shit, now that's an introduction," Mac said.

Words eluded me at the moment.

"Listen to the crowd, Gemma. They already love you. Well, maybe not the girls that want to get in Hendrix's pants, but the rest of them do."

I barked out a laugh and nodded. "Thanks for being with me," I said, giving her a quick hug.

"Please help me welcome Gemma Thompson to the stage!"

"Go get 'em," Mac said, slapping me on the ass. I yelped and entered the stage. The lights were so bright I could barely make out the audience at first. But I knew what I needed and made a bee-line for Hendrix. He kissed me and took my hand.

"I love you," he whispered.

"I love you, too."

Hendrix gave my fingers a squeeze and led me the short distance to the piano, sitting center stage. We hadn't rehearsed it this way. But if I was going to remain standing, laying my hand on the top of the lid and using the piano as a prop seemed like a good idea. I could easily sing from there.

Cade brought the mic over to me and grinned.

"Glad to have you back." He winked, then walked back to his place.

I looked at Hendrix and nodded.

He played a C on the piano, and the audience

cheered. "This is "Couldn't Love You More." I hope you enjoy it." Hendrix gazed at me, and my jitters calmed.

"I never knew, life could be so beautiful until the moment I saw you," Hendrix sang.

I joined in, my eyes never leaving his face.

"So much love," we sang in unison. "Between your heart and mine." The longer we sang, the more I relaxed into the music, and the more I fell in love with him. Everything and everyone simply slipped away while he stood and walked over to me. He took my hand as we turned toward each other and finished the song. Hendrix lowered his mic, and slid his other hand around my waist, pulling me into his body. Before I knew it, he laid a scorching kiss on me. The crowd roared. I was grinning like an idiot as we backed away.

"Gemma Thompson," Hendrix yelled over the cheers and whistles of the crowd. He leaned over and nuzzled my cheek. "I love you. Go find Mac, and I'll see you after my set is over."

"Love you too." I handed my mic to him and waved at the audience. Then I walked off stage, lightheaded from his kiss and our performance. The crowd's reaction had utterly stunned me as well.

A hand snapped out from behind the curtain and tugged me behind the stage. Mac tackled me with a bear hug. "Oh, my fucking gosh! That was amazeballs on so many levels!" She let me go and fanned herself. "And that kiss. Girl, I was back here fanning myself, and I guarantee you every girl's panties were wet in a flat second."

"Mac!" I smacked her arm, embarrassed by her words.

"You two are hot! You guys should do porn. And the song, I forgot how incredible you sound together. Once it's on the radio, everyone will be making babies!"

"Oh my God, Mac. Stop. I don't want to have that mental image in my noggin every time we sing that song." I placed my hands on my cheeks, willing the thoughts to go away.

"Let's go get something to drink, and I gotta pee."

I laughed. "Okay, I want to listen to Hendrix out front, too so let's hurry up."

Mac and I hurried off the back of the stage. I hesitated, the only way to the food court was up the stairs and through the crowd. Mac took my hand and led the way.

"Holy shit, you're more beautiful than on

stage. You can kiss me like that any time," a guy said, grabbing my arm as we passed by.

"Sorry, I'm already taken. You need to let me go," I said firmly.

"Listen up douche-bag, you don't get to touch someone without their permission, and you have one second to let go of her before I start screaming for security," Mac chimed in.

"Bitch, calm down. I'm just having some fun." He scowled at us, but he let me go. Anger shot through me. Why did people think they had the right to put their hands on someone without their consent?

I jerked my hand away and hurried up the stairs. The only thing that calmed me was the fact I could hear Hendrix singing.

"Let's hurry. I don't want to miss any more of his performance," I said while Mac and I stepped through the doors and into the hallway. We hurried to the food court. Thank God it wasn't busy. Mac ordered us some sodas, tapping her foot the entire time it took the guy behind the counter to make them.

"I can't hear Hendrix out here," I said.

"Yeah, the inside of the auditorium is sound-proofed," she replied.

My phone chimed in my back pocket, and I quickly pulled it out. I hoped it wasn't the nurse contacting me with bad news about Ada Lynn. It had been hard to leave her, let alone with a stranger. I knew I was being paranoid. Hendrix would have taken every precaution when he hired Kim. But my days of blindly trusting others was over.

I peered at my phone and froze. "Holy shit," I said, terror, coursing through me. This couldn't be happening.

I grabbed Mac's arm as the bright emergency strobe lights started flashing, and the blare of the warning sirens filled the lobby of the arena. Alarmed, I stared at the guy behind the counter, now suspended in wide-eyed horror, our drinks in his hands.

"We might have two minutes," I yelled at Mac. "We have to get to Hendrix."

"What's going on?" Mac yelled over the noise, panicked. I pulled on her arm and hauled ass back into the stadium. Hendrix had finished his song and had stepped over to the piano for his glass of water.

I sucked in a deep breath as a shaky voice rang through the PA system.

"We have an approaching tornado, please

move to the inside walls and take cover. Stay away from the windows."

"What the fuck?" Mac asked. People stared at me with dumb expressions on their faces.

"Hendrix!" I screamed, hurrying down the stairs. I had to reach him in time. I grabbed Mac by the shirt and pulled her behind me. Even though I knew she was talking, my mind wasn't grasping what she was saying.

"We have to get to Hendrix," I yelled at her.

People stood and pushed toward the exit doors. We moved against the flow of bodies, my heart racing with every step.

"Gemma!" Hendrix called over the mic.

"Get off the stage," I yelled, but the crowd had erupted into a panic, and he couldn't hear me.

"Gemma!" Mac yelled, our hands breaking loose from each other. The rush of people was too strong. Anyone who lived in tornado alley knew running wouldn't do any good, but I guess fear took over in situations like this, eliminating any common sense.

I turned away from the stage and elbowed my way back toward Mac. She was too petite. She would get trampled if I didn't get to her in time.

Finally, I grabbed her shirt and tugged her to me.

"Oh my God," Mac said, tears streaming down her face, holding onto my arm with a death grip.

"You're okay, we need to make our way to Hendrix, and we only have seconds left. Do. Not. Let. Go. Of. Me!" I yelled over the noise.

Once again, I pushed through the opposite flow of the people toward the band. I could no longer see Hendrix, and I'd assumed he was making his way toward us. Did he even know what to do during a tornado? He'd only been in Louisiana for a few months off and on. It probably had never even crossed his mind.

A massive roar pierced our ears as parts of the roof were ripped off like it was made of cardboard. With Mac in tow, I stumbled down the last few stairs to the main level. Mac and I watched in horror as chairs that were once bolted down to the floor began to fly around.

"We have to take cover, Mac!"

"Where?" she screamed.

I hauled her into a windowless corner where we had less chance of being run over. The structure had been built to stand up to a tornado, but nothing was ever guaranteed. Mother nature had a mind of her own.

I shoved Mac into the corner and then kneeled on the outside of her.

"Like this," I said, crouching down and covering my head. She did as I showed her, and I nudged up against her. If I could feel her next to me, I'd at least know where she was. But where was Hendrix?

CHAPTER 5

Time stood still as the tornado did its damage. I squeezed my eyes closed and covered my ears with my hands to shut out the screaming sirens and the roaring wind as I tried to focus on Mac's body next to mine. I'd heard of twisters picking up people and dropping them a mile away. No one survived something like that. I would rather squish Mac and keep her safe than lose her.

The sound of the destruction was deafening, and I continued to cover the back of my head the best I could. A scream ripped from my throat when a heavy object whacked against my back. The pain jolted me, and I peered over at Mac. She was okay from what I could tell. Even though I knew better, I looked up. The majority of the roof was now missing, and I stared directly into the tornado. Frozen in place, I didn't duck in time as a large piece of wood made contact with the side of my body, smacking me into the wall. My last thought was of Hendrix as my surroundings turned black, and I slumped forward.

"Bestie, oh my God, bestie." Mac gently shook me.

"Yeah," I said, my throat raw and scratchy. I reached up and rubbed my throbbing temples.

"You're bleeding," Mac said, panic in her voice. "Can you sit up?"

I nodded and allowed Mac to help me. The room spun, and I quickly leaned back against the wall. I glanced at my hand, now covered in blood, and wiped it on my jeans as I performed a quick survey of Mac.

"Are you okay?" I choked out.

"Only because you smooshed me in the corner. You took that for both of us, Gemma." She pointed toward a large piece of wood near us. It had splintered into pieces, leaving sharp, jagged edges.

"It could have speared right through you," she cried, tears streaming down her cheeks. "You're lucky you're alive."

"Hendrix!" My eyes widened while I scrambled to my feet, the adrenaline kicking in. "Oh my God," I gasped, taking in the scene in front of me. People called out, searching for their loved ones as others lay on the floor, unmoving. Debris covered the entire floor. Somehow, we'd managed to not get buried beneath it. But where was Hendrix? How in the hell were we going to find him? Panic twisted inside me.

"Let's go," I said, grabbing Mac's hand. I turned toward the stage and stopped abruptly. There was no stage left.

"Mac...It's gone," I managed to choke out. "What if he—"

"He's fine, Gemma. We just have to find him." Her voice shook with her words. "He's a state champion boxer, he's taken a lot of hits, and this won't take him down." She shook her head while she stared at the wreckage on the floor.

A quiet strength stirred inside me. I turned to face her, placing my hands on her shoulders. "I don't want to lose sight of each other. Got it? We need to try to stay together," I said, firmly.

Mac nodded, wide-eyed.

I slowly stepped forward, searching the rubble for anyone lying beneath it.

"Help," someone cried. I turned toward the voice and spotted a young woman. Her legs were pinned beneath multiple chairs. I carefully made my way toward her.

"Hi, I'm Gemma. What's your name?" I asked, kneeling down.

"Leann."

"Can you sit up, Leann?"

She nodded and sat up slowly. "That's good. Can you breathe alright?

She took a deep breath and nodded.

"I was in a tornado when I was younger, and the ambulance and trained professionals were there in a few minutes. Can you feel your legs?"

"Yeah," she said. "I can't find my son, though," she hiccupped through her tears.

My heart sank like a lead ball into my stomach. "I'm going to continue to move toward the stage. What does he look like? My friend and I will see if we can locate him."

"He's eight, light brown hair, green eyes. His name is Andrew. He's on the small side," she said, her words laced with fear.

"Okay, I'll be back shortly. Try to stay as comfortable as you can."

I stood and stared at Mac.

"Gemma, your face is covered with blood. Are you sure you can do this?" she asked. "Are you dizzy? Faint?"

"Mac, Hendrix is over there. I won't stop until I find him. And, now, we're searching for a little guy too. I'm fine."

I smiled at Leann, then Mac and I continued toward the stage.

Cries from the wounded and lost echoed throughout the arena. I tried to stay tuned in for Hendrix's voice, but it was impossible. There was too much noise.

"Hey, look," Mac said, pointing toward the front of the arena. Teams of EMT's were filing in and checking on people. A small amount of relief flooded me. Help was here.

Another ten minutes passed while we searched for my boyfriend with no luck. The wail of a child broke through my focus, and I turned toward the sound.

"Mommy! Mommy!"

I crawled over the pile of furniture as quickly as I could. Mac was right behind me.

"Hi sweetheart, what's your name?" I asked, trying to calm him down.

"Andrew," he said, wiping his runny nose.

"What's your mom's name?" Hope rose in my chest.

"Leann."

"Andrew, I know your mommy, and she's safe."

"She is?" he whimpered.

I nodded.

"She can't get to you yet, honey, because...because a bunch of chairs are on her legs. But she's alright. How about my friend takes you to her? This is Mac."

"Can you take him, so I can continue to search for Hendrix?" I asked, taking Andrew's hand in mine.

"I don't want to leave you, Gemma. You're bleeding and—"

I held up my hand to stop her.

"Take him to Leann. Please. I'll be moving in that direction, just catch up to me." I pointed out where the stage should have been.

She nodded and reluctantly took Andrew's hand.

"Come on sweetie, I'm going to take you to your mom," she said.

Andrew nodded, and Mac led him through the mess.

My hands fisted in an attempt to remain calm.

I'd just sent my best friend off in another direction, and I'd not told her how dizzy I really was. It would take her a while to make it back to me, too. I had no choice but to press forward alone. I had to find Hendrix. Fear crept up my spine, and multiple scenarios of him hurt—or worse—played through my head. Tears threatened my eyes, but I willed them away. I had to stay focused. Hendrix's life might depend on it.

With each careful step on top of the splintered wood, broken brick, and chairs, I continued to make my way toward where I thought Hendrix might be. My heart split in two with each person I saw on the floor, unmoving. There was no way to tell how many were still alive.

Finally, I reached the edge of where the stage had stood earlier. From what I could see, the entire thing had collapsed and split into a million pieces. If he was under there, he would have suffocated by now.

A cry escaped me, and I crawled over the chairs as fast as I could. My foot caught on the edge of the rubble, and I sailed through the air, landing with a thud. My head throbbed, and I grabbed my side where my ribs had been broken a few months ago. A sharp pain speared me and left me gasping for air.

I pushed up with my other arm and peered around, my entire world screeching to a halt.

"Hendrix!" I cried, scrambling toward him. "Baby." I dropped to my knees. My hand trembled as I reached toward a deep, bloody gash on his forehead. His face was unusually pale, and cuts were scattered across his cheeks.

"Hendrix," I cried. "Say something." Nausea rolled in my stomach when there was no response.

My heart pounded loudly in my ears as I leaned over and placed my fingers against his neck, feeling for a pulse.

CHAPTER 6

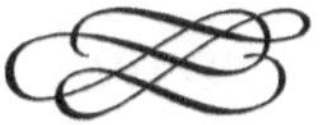

"Mac!" I screamed. "Mac!" I had no idea if she could hear me, but she needed to know her brother was alive. His pulse was strong, but he was unconscious. I called again for her while I attempted to move the pile of objects that had nearly buried him. My head spun as I tried to lift a heavy piece off him, but I wasn't strong enough on my own.

"Dammit!" I screamed. "I won't fucking lose you!" I searched the area. EMTs and firefighters were scattered across the auditorium, and I needed someone to help me. I couldn't lift all the shit off him by myself. And where was Mac?

"Help me!" I screamed, searching for Mac.

Arms waving madly in the air caught my attention.

"Gemma!" Mac said, waving her arms again. "I've got help!"

I stood and signaled her. She and a few EMTs slowly made their way toward us. Kneeling down with Hendrix, I took his hand in mine.

"I love you. Hang in there, baby. Help is on the way." I smoothed his hair away from his face and kissed his hand. "Just wake up."

"Hendrix!" Mac screamed when she saw him. She rushed to his side, crying.

"He's alive, Mac. That's all I know."

"Gemma."

I stood at the mention of my name. "Josh?" I asked, shocked to see him. "What are you doing here?" He was an EMT in our town and had been one of the responders when Ada Lynn had her heart attack a few months ago.

"When there are big events in the surrounding areas, they ask for additional EMTs to work. I was up the street when the tornado hit. Fortunately, it went around us, so we were able to respond quickly," he said, nodding to the other guy who was attending to Hendrix.

"He's breathing. Please, help me get all of this crap off him."

"Gemma," Josh said, placing his hand on my shoulder. "Let us take care of it. You're injured, too. Why don't you and Mac stand to the side?"

Logically, I knew he was right, but there was no way I wanted to leave Hendrix.

"I need you to keep a level head." Josh looked into my eyes and spoke calmly. It was comforting to see a familiar face, and I trusted him to do everything possible to help Hendrix.

"I know," I whispered. "Mac, come on. We need to move so they can get to him."

Mac stood, her eyes rimmed with red. She took my extended hand, and we made our way to the wall that was next to the back exit.

"I think something is wrong with me," I mumbled.

"What? Not you, too? I can't lose you both," she said, grabbing my shoulders.

"No, I don't mean my body, but...it's like I'm free falling in a dream and nothing is real. Why am I not in hysterics that Hendrix is unconscious, and we're surrounded by death and pain?"

"You went into fight mode, bestie. You took care of that lady and found her son, you protected me, and you got yourself hurt in the process. Your mind and body are in shock. I actually envy you. It would be easier to stay logical and not panic right now. But when you come down off that, I suspect it will be a shit show. I'll be with you, though."

The back exit doors flung open, and another paramedic rushed in with a gurney.

"Over here," Josh said, motioning toward him.

We watched in horror as they picked up an unmoving Hendrix, placed him on the gurney, and carried him out of the door.

"How do you know him?" Josh asked me.

"I'm his girlfriend, and Mac is his sister."

"Well you're family, and you both need to be checked out as well, so you can ride with us in the ambulance." Josh held the door open for us. "Watch your step, there's debris everywhere."

I stared at him, unmoving, as my mind went blank.

"Are you feeling nauseated? Dizzy?" Josh asked, releasing the door and stepping toward me. "You probably have a concussion. I'd put you on a gurney, but we're a bit short due to the need, and you're still able to walk."

"No, it's okay. There are others way worse off than I am. Thank you for helping us."

Mac held my hand while Josh pushed open the door again. My breath hitched. I had no idea what to expect when we stepped outside. The only thing I knew was that it was dark.

Josh flipped on a flashlight, illuminating our way. Mac pulled her phone out and turned the flashlight app on, and we gasped in unison.

"Holy shit," she said.

My mouth gaped open. Trees had smashed cars and blocked multiple paths in the parking lot. Chunks of the building and furniture were scattered everywhere. How had we survived?

"Let's go, ladies. We need to get Hendrix to the hospital."

Our attention turned away from the nightmare, and Josh helped us in, closing the ambulance doors behind us.

CHAPTER 7

For all the chaos going on throughout the city, the ER was a well-orchestrated operation. Not surprisingly, the room was filled to capacity, every chair occupied with injured people, and those able to stand were lined against the walls.

Mac and I watched as they rushed Hendrix away, my heart leaving with him.

"We need to get you looked at," Mac suggested.

"No, I'm fine."

"Mm, no you're not."

I stared at her blankly, the gravity of our situation not having fully registered yet.

"Hi, hon." A nurse wearing light blue scrubs

and pink Crocs smiled and flashed her clipboard and pen in my direction. "I'm here to take your information and assess your need for treatment."

"I'm fine. It's my boyfriend who's hurt." My voice cracked with my words. "He was singing on the stage of the arena…"

"Oh my gosh. Were you two there?" she asked, her focus bouncing between Mac and me.

"Yeah, he's my brother," Mac said, a tear spilling down her dirty cheek.

"He's in good hands, now. Try not to worry," the nurse assured us. Her hazel eyes looked tired. I could only imagine what she'd seen tonight.

"What's your name, hon?" she asked me.

"Gemma," I mumbled. Suddenly, exhaustion slammed into me, and my legs wobbled. I grabbed for the wall to stabilize myself, but only managed to drop to the ground.

"She obviously has a head wound," I heard Mac say before the darkness claimed me.

MY EYES FLUTTERED OPEN to find Mac's dirty face, filled with concern, staring down at me.

"You're in a hospital bed, so no sudden movements," she ordered.

"Huh?" I reached up and rubbed my pounding forehead. The strong smell of hospital antiseptic invaded my nose as my fingertips grazed over several butterfly stitches.

"You have a concussion, and your ribs got banged up, but they're not broken."

"Hendrix?" I asked, sitting up. The sudden movement caused my stomach to lurch, and the nurse shoved a container under my mouth just in time. Mac turned away. I didn't blame her. No one wanted to see someone hurl.

"Lie back down, hon," the nurse said, handing me a wet wipe.

I didn't argue.

"Are you all done, bestie? That was pretty rank."

"Sorry," I said, wiping off my mouth. "Any news about Hendrix?"

Mac's face fell as she pulled up a chair next to my bed. I wasn't in a private room, and everywhere I looked I saw the damage from the tornado. A shrill cry of a child echoed through the room while an adult attempted to calm him. Every single bed was occupied, and I'd seen how many more people were in the waiting room.

"You weren't out long, Gemma. They did a quick patch up on your head and checked you for other injuries, too. So, no. No news about Hendrix yet."

I shut my eyes, my hands clenching and unclenching in fists. How could life be so cruel?

"I just got him back, Mac. I can't lose him."

"I know. Me either. What if—" She stopped herself from verbalizing what we both feared. That Hendrix wouldn't live.

"If—if something happens. Please promise me, Gemma—promise me you won't leave me, too." Her hand flew to her mouth, muffling a cry.

For the first time all night, my own tears broke free. I couldn't lose him. We couldn't lose him.

"I swear," I said, grabbing her hand. "We're family," I whispered and then broke down, sobbing. Mac and I clung to each other as reality came crashing down on us.

"Ugh, I'm so not into public crying." Mac sniffled and released me, then pulled a few tissues out of the Kleenex box and handed one to me.

"Thanks." I carefully blew my nose. The pain in my ribs had lessened, but my side was still throbbing. I pulled up my filthy shirt and peered at the bruise.

"What time is it?" I asked.

Mac pulled out her phone. "It's a little after one in the morning."

I bit my lower lip. "It's too late to call Ada Lynn. I doubt she knows about the tornado, and I don't want it to scare her when she turns on the news."

"Here's your phone. I grabbed it before it got smooshed when they put you on the gurney." Mac handed me my phone. No calls. She would have contacted me if she'd heard. I set my phone alarm for six-thirty a.m. She'd get up around that time and turn on the TV. I would need to get to her first.

"I should call Franklin," Mac said. "I'd hoped I would know something about Hendrix before I called, and now I don't have a clue of what to say. I mean, the hospital is a madhouse, it stinks, and everything is fucked up. I don't think that would go over really well even though it's accurate." She frowned and stared at the floor.

"Just tell him to fly in, and we need him. His son needs him."

Mac nodded, her expression grim. "I'm going to step outside to call. I'll be right back. Don't go anywhere."

"Umm duh, where else would I go?" I rolled my eyes and watched Mac head out of the room.

Pursing my lips together, I willed this nightmare to go away. Life had already cheated me out of my teen years, my mother, and now my father. I would fight fate with everything I had to keep Hendrix. She couldn't have him.

Mac returned about ten minutes later, her eyes bloodshot from all the crying.

I looked at her, waiting for her to tell me how the conversation went.

"Guess who was at a convention in Dallas, Texas?" Mac asked.

"Really?"

"Yeah, he'll be here within an hour."

"What? How? How can he get here so fast?"

"Um, well." Mac took a deep breath. "I guess Hendrix hasn't told you Franklin has his own plane."

"What?" I asked, straightening into a sitting position. Grabbing my head, I fought down the nausea.

"It probably didn't occur to you to ask after all the shit with your dad."

"Kyle. He's not my dad," I corrected.

"Kyle," she said in agreement. "Remember when Franklin came down and met with you and Marcus the first time?"

"Yeah," I said, with a hint of impatience in my tone.

"You were too fucked up to think about how he got there so fast. He has his own plane."

My brows furrowed while I struggled to piece together what she'd said.

"Like a two-seater?"

Mac flipped her messy hair behind her shoulder and leaned forward. "More like a Gulfstream G450."

"I don't know anything about planes. I mean, I've heard about companies like Boeing, and I understand what a private plane is. Aren't those like super spendy?" I asked, my brow arching up.

"Mil-lions." She sank back in her seat and scanned my face for my reaction.

I chewed on my thumbnail and attempted to think through the brain fog.

"I've seen how nice Hendrix's house in Spokane is, and he mentioned it was paid for. He also drives a Lexus. Well, he does if it survived tonight. And he bought a house down here with cash, which means Hendrix also has money, but Mac...Hendrix doesn't talk about it. How much money does Franklin really have?"

Mac pursed her lips together and pretended to zip them closed.

"You're serious right now? Most of the time I can't shut you up, and you're zipping your lips right now?" I asked, exasperated.

"Billions," she said, her brows shooting up for emphasis.

I couldn't even wrap my mind around that word. My wound must have been worse than I realized. Maybe I'd misunderstood her.

"Don't tease, Mac. It's not funny, especially right now."

She stared at me, her expression stone serious.

"Besides," I said, "if that were true, Hendrix would be some rich, entitled, fucking snob. He would drive a car that costs more than my parent's house, and wear yuppy clothes. He's none of that."

I huffed at the thought and fluffed the uncomfortable pillow behind my head.

The longer Mac remained silent, the more I recognized she was telling me the truth, then the night of Franklin's charity event at the Riverside Place came rushing back. I'd realized that night Hendrix was rich, and he admitted he came from money, but this was an entirely different level.

"Our first date," I said softly. "When we went to the event with Franklin, and I wore the blue dress you helped me shop for...Hendrix and I got into an argument."

"About?" Mac asked, pulling her knees to her chest.

"The longer we were there, I realized how comfortable Hendrix was with everyone. The women were dripping in diamonds and beautiful jewelry, and all the men wore high-end tuxes and watches. I freaked and needed to get some air. Once we were outside, I proceeded to accuse him of lying to me about who he was. It was then I realized he came from money and had never told me. A part of me was so embarrassed. You remember what I used to wear, Mac. My tennis shoes nearly had holes in them, and my awful oversized clothes were threadbare. You've stayed at my house. It was always clean, but I don't come from much."

"Gemma, none of that matters to us."

"I know that now, but I was angry with him for not being honest with me. Once he explained that he never knew if someone wanted to be with him because he sang or for his and Franklin's money, I got it. But I don't care about any of that. I just needed him to be honest with me. What fucked me up even more though, was that night, I had realized I'd already fallen in love with him—" Tears choked off my last words.

"We're not losing him," Mac said and squeezed my hand. "You'll see. Hendrix is a fighter, and I've never seen him happier than when he's with you, Gemma. You have to know that his love for you runs so deep that it *will* bring him out of this. He'll come back to you."

"To us," I whispered, wiping my tears away.

"Girls," Franklin rushed in. I'd forgotten how much Hendrix and Franklin looked alike. Same eyes, same gorgeous smile, but Franklin's dark hair was short.

Mac jumped out of her chair and ran to him. He wrapped his arms around her and kissed the top of her head.

"Are you okay?" He held her at arm's length, scanning her for injuries and fussing over her.

I closed my eyes, my chest tightening. At one time, I had what Mac had with Franklin. It hurt to now know it was all a lie. The man sitting in jail was never my father. He was a monster who would do anything to keep his vile secrets from being exposed…including killing my mother.

"Gemma," Franklin sat on the side of the bed and smoothed my hair. "You're not my daughter, but I know how much my son loves you, so in my mind you're already my daughter-in-law. You're family. I know you think you don't have anyone else, but that's not true. You have us regardless..." His eyes misted slightly. "Regardless of the future, you'll always have Mac and me."

Tears slipped down his cheeks, and I sat up to hug him. He wrapped his arms around me and held me as if I were his own child while I broke down again.

"I don't know what will happen, but my son's a fighter. He's going to be okay."

I sat back and dabbed my eyes.

"We've been here for a few hours, surely they know something by now," Mac said, her brows knitting together in concern.

"I'm going to go ask. I wanted to let you girls know I was here and to check on you first. I'll be back as soon as I have some information."

We nodded. I attempted to get comfortable again, and Mac sank back into her chair. Although I was in pain, I was restless and needed to know that Hendrix was okay. An ache spread through my chest. We should be snuggled up together in bed, not in separate rooms of the hospital.

"I know nothing has changed, but it helps that

Franklin is here," Mac said, twirling a strand of hair around her finger.

"I didn't realize you two were close."

Mac gave a half-shrug. "It's only been over the last few months, honestly. The more he and Hendrix grew closer, he brought me back into the herd so to speak. He has a lot of guilt about not being there for us," she said. "He can't change the past, but I think he's really trying to have a better future."

"That's good Mac." I cleared my throat. It wasn't like this was a good time to ask but waiting for news on Hendrix wasn't helping my patience. I stared at my best friend, who began to chew on a hangnail. "You've never told me about your biological Dad," I said, quietly. "Is the topic off the table?"

Mac peeked at me and dropped her hand into her lap. "Not much to tell. I don't know him. Mom got knocked up with me, then he took off."

"That's shit," I muttered, feeling protective of her.

"So Franklin's it."

"I'm glad you have him."

"Me too, actually. He was an ass to Mom for a long time, and he treated Hendrix like shit when he was younger. Plus the entire Kendra situation. It was bad for years. It's like he's a different person now that he's not drinking. I figure if he wants to get to know me, then I'll give him a chance ya know? It's more than my bio Dad ever did."

I nodded, wishing there was an opportunity for a second chance with my parents. But that door had closed. Hard.

Mac stood quickly when Franklin entered the room again.

"Shit," I muttered. His expression tightened when he looked at me, our eyes locking. "Is he alive?" I asked, my body trembling.

CHAPTER 8

My heart pounded against my sore ribs as I held my breath, waiting for Franklin to update us about Hendrix. He had to be okay. Franklin's expression must have meant something else.

"Yes. He's alive." He looked down at his black dress shoes and shoved his hands in his pockets.

I released the breath I was holding. Mac sat down, her leg bouncing. She was as terrified as I was.

"But?" she asked. "I know that look on your face."

"But he's in a coma."

A cry escaped me, and my hands flew up to my mouth in an attempt to contain my outburst.

"What?" Mac jumped out of her chair again, sending it skidding backward. The clatter cut through all the noise and activity in the hospital room. Patients and their loved ones shot us curious looks.

"Well when is he going to come out of it?" she asked, visibly shaking.

"They don't know. Hendrix has a head injury, and the doctors have induced the coma in an effort to reduce the swelling in his brain."

"I need to be with him." I held onto my ribs and sat up, wincing with the pain in my side and the throbbing in my head.

"Gemma, I know you need to see him, but slow down. They actually encourage the family to be with him, so we can go in. I've arranged for a larger room for Hendrix, and you'll have a bed, Gemma. You're in no condition to return to normal activity yet."

My shoulders slumped. He was totally using a dad voice on me, and even though I didn't know him very well yet, I understood not to argue.

"It will be about thirty minutes before they're ready for us, so settle back in. Since the doctors aren't sure when Hendrix will wake up, there's a good possibility it's going to be a long stay."

"I'm sorry," I said, finally looking up at him

and seeing the grief in his eyes. This was his son. He might be my boyfriend, but it wasn't right to have to see your child in this condition. I prayed to whoever might be out there to spare us all the heartache.

"I'm starving," Mac said. She slapped her hands over her face and groaned.

"It hasn't changed, huh?" Franklin said, gently.

"No," she replied.

"What's the matter?" I asked, confused.

"When I get super-duper crazy fucking stressed, I eat. Like, a lot."

"Language, Mac," Franklin said, arching a brow at her.

"Really? Like right now you're going to get onto me about my language?" She paced back and forth in the small space she had. "Ugh," she groaned, "This should not be happening."

"Since we're not leaving any time soon, why don't I send Charles out to grab some food?" Franklin suggested, attempting to ease the tension.

"Nothing is open," Mac sighed. "It's too early or too late."

"Taco Bell," I suggested.

"Really? I could do Taco Hell."

"Yeah, and typically one other fast food place

like McDonald's or something. A few are open for twenty-four hours. Since the tornado didn't touch down here, I'm sure he can find something."

"All right, I'll send Charles out to get us some food then," Franklin said.

"I'm not hungry," I replied.

"You need to eat, Gemma," he said firmly, ending the discussion. He seemed to have this father thing down pretty well.

"Who is Charles?" I asked Mac after Franklin left the room.

"Probably his driver. He always has one."

"Oh," I said, my mouth forming a big, round O. I rubbed my face, my thoughts drifting to Hendrix. My skin hummed with anxiety, and I was beginning to feel uncomfortable from all the dirt covering my body and clothes. They needed to hurry. I needed to see him. Maybe if he could hear my voice, it would help him recover faster.

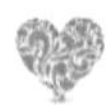

I'D NEVER SEEN anyone in a coma before. If I hadn't known better, he just looked like he was asleep. But I did know better. My heart wrenched at the sight of Hendrix lying there motionless. The gash on his head had been cleaned and stitched up, but his hair was a tangled mess. Multiple machines were connected to him, all beeping with a different tone. The energy in his private room was calm and serene compared to the noisy room where I'd been.

I rushed over to him, Mac and Franklin right behind me.

"Baby." I leaned down and kissed his warm, soft lips. "I'm here," I said, pulling a chair up to the bed and taking his hand. This time he didn't squeeze it in return, though.

Relief washed over me as it dawned on me that he might be unconscious, but he was alive. Hot tears streamed down my cheeks while Franklin and Mac pulled up seats on the other side of Hendrix's bed.

"I wonder if it's really true, that coma patients can hear you," Mac said, softly. "You should sing to him, Gemma."

"What? Like now?"

"Yeah, your song. He loved singing with you." She gave me an encouraging smile.

My cheeks flamed red. For some reason, I could perform in front of ten thousand people, but the idea of Franklin listening embarrassed me. Maybe it was because I knew how personal the song was to Hendrix and me.

I glanced at Franklin, took a deep breath, and began to softly sing "Couldn't Love You More." My voice cracked with emotion as I finished.

"I can see why my son fell in love with you," Franklin said kindly. "That was a beautiful song."

I nodded. "We wrote it together. He took me to the studio and played what he already had, then we spent hours working on it. It was during that time I finally let him in and past my walls, but Mac helped a lot with that, too. Since she knew him so well, it helped."

Franklin's hands steepled, his eyes studying me. I squirmed in my seat, feeling emotionally exposed. I shouldn't have sung in front of him, but it was too late now. He had a glimpse into my world with his son.

The alarm on my phone cut through the silence, and I pulled it out of my pocket.

"I need to call Ada Lynn and update her," I said, grateful for the excuse to move out from beneath Franklin's studious gaze. On the other hand, there was nothing about the upcoming conversation I looked forward to.

"Yeah, I gotta make a call, too," Mac said.

I knew Mac was going to call Jeremiah, but I

didn't mention anything in front of Franklin. It wasn't my place. We both stood, and my attention traveled to Hendrix. I leaned over and kissed his cheek.

"I'll be right back," I said quietly against his ear.

"Franklin, do you need any coffee or anything?" I asked.

"No thanks. I'll stay here with him while you two make your calls. Gemma, be careful walking around, and stay close to Mac."

"All right, thanks," I replied.

Mac and I walked into the hall and followed the exit signs.

"What are you going to tell Ada Lynn?" Mac asked me.

"The truth," I said, my stomach clenching. "I'll see if the nurse can stay a little longer. I'm not sure what to do concerning the long term, though. I mean, I won't go home until Hendrix is better..."

"Talk to Franklin. I'm sure he would be okay with hiring a nurse for a while. Honestly, I don't want Ada Lynn to be alone, either. I'll help you talk to Franklin about it."

"You think he'll go for it?" I asked skeptically. "He's not her family, and I don't have the income to pay him back, Mac."

"No, but she's your family, and Franklin already sees you and Hendrix together long term. And now that the shit with Andrea is over...so do I," she said, glancing at me.

"I hope so, Mac. I hope there's a future with him."

"Well if nothing else, Franklin will make sure Ada Lynn is taken care of just to keep Hendrix happy when he wakes up. Believe it or not, Hendrix has a temper, and Franklin isn't interested in being on the other side of it."

We stepped through the doors and outside into the fresh morning air. I sucked in a deep breath, trying to clear the hospital smell from my nose. The sun was a magnificent orange as it peeked over the hills.

"I've never been in the Baton Rouge hospital before, so I guess we can search for a private place to make the calls," I muttered, searching for some outdoor seating.

I led us around the corner of the building and spotted a few benches and tables.

"Well, here it goes," I said, my pulse two-timing. I was worried that the news might upset Ada Lynn enough to cause another heart attack, but I couldn't not tell her, either.

Mac walked across to the opposite side of the patio and paced back and forth while she called Jeremiah.

I tapped Ada Lynn's number on my screen.

"Hello?"

Ada Lynn sounded groggy.

"It's Gemma," I said, quietly.

"Gemma? Why are you calling so early? What's wrong?"

"Is the nurse still with you?" I asked.

"Until ten this morning. What's the..." Her voice trailed off. "Oh, dear Jesus," she gasped. I could hear her TV in the background.

"Turn off the TV, please. We're okay, but I need to tell you myself rather than you seeing it on the news. And are you sitting down? Do you have your heart medication next to you? Where's Kim?" I plied her with a million questions.

"Gemma, I'm fine, now focus. Are you okay?"

"Yeah, I have a concussion and some stitches in my forehead," I said, sinking into one of the outdoor seats.

"Mac?" Ada Lynn, asked, her voice trembling.

"She's with me and okay. She didn't get hurt. I smushed her in the corner and kept her as safe as I could, but I took a hit to the head."

A moment of silence filled the line.

"Hendrix?"

I could hear her fear through the phone.

"He's alive," I said, fear and dread catching in my throat. "He's in a coma." My words came rushing out while I told her about the tornado, the stage, and how we dug Hendrix out from under the rubble. The sound of her crying reached my ears, and I pulled my knees to my chest.

"I don't know when I'll be home, but..." I wiped my cheeks. "But I'll call and give you updates. Mac suggested I talk to Franklin about hiring a nurse to stay with you until we all come home."

"I'm fine, Gemma. There's no need to fuss over me while Hendrix is fighting for his life."

"I love you, Ada Lynn, but this isn't up for discussion," I said firmly, taking a page from Franklin's book. I'd never pulled rank on her before, but the only way I could focus on Hendrix was to make sure she was okay.

Sniffling, she chuckled through her tears. "My blue-eyed girl is growing up."

I peeked over at Mac who was still pacing.

"How's Kim. Do you like her?"

Ada Lynn cleared her throat, and I waited as she blew her nose.

"Ya know, she's really sweet. We played cards and enjoyed a few shows on television. She was very attentive, and it was actually nice to have someone around."

I released a big sigh.

"I'm happy to hear it. Maybe she can come back. I just...I don't know when I'll be home. If I walk into our house, without Hendrix—" Sobs choked off my words.

"I know you're scared, and so am I. He's family, and he's strong, Gemma. You do what you need to and bring him back to us. Do you understand?"

"Yeah." I wiped my nose on my shirt sleeve and swallowed the crazy ball of emotions inside me. My thoughts were laced with fear and doubt, but I couldn't let Hendrix sense it. What he needed from me was love and support.

"I need to get back to Hendrix, but I'll update you the second I know anything."

"I'll be waiting for the good news. I love you, Gemma."

My heart ached with her words. I wish I'd understood how fragile life was and had told the people in my life I loved them more than I had.

"I love you too, Ada Lynn."

Tapping the end call button, I looked over at

Mac. She was a mess. Her face was streaked with dirt and grime from the tornado, and her shirt tail was torn. Maybe Franklin could get us fresh clothes and some toiletries. At least we could shower and change while we waited for Hendrix to wake up.

Mac lowered her phone, wiped her forehead, and proceeded toward me.

"How's Ada Lynn?" she asked.

"She's a mess like we all are, but the nurse, Kim, is still with her, so that's good. What about Jeremiah?"

"It shook him up pretty hard. He offered to come to stay with me, but I told him only family was allowed in Hendrix's room. Besides, I don't want to deal with introducing him to Franklin, right now."

I stood, and we began walking back to the ICU. It was too soon to hope that Hendrix was already awake, but I couldn't stop myself from thinking about it. I wanted to be there when those beautiful blue eyes opened.

CHAPTER 9

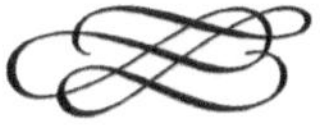

Two weeks passed with no improvements from Hendrix. Hour after hour, day after day, we sat in our chairs and stared at him, willing him to wake up.

Nurses and doctors continually monitored him, and we tried to keep our conversations upbeat, but our hearts grew heavier and heavier with each passing day. Fear played with me, and at times I wondered if I'd lost him forever. I Googled *coma* and read a ton of articles. I'd hoped it would shed a sliver of light on his situation, but it didn't. All I learned was that every coma case was different. There was no predicting when the person would regain consciousness, if they would retain their memories, or if they would wake up at all.

Franklin had hired Kim to stay full-time with Ada Lynn for as long as she needed. Although I talked with her daily, it was a comfort to know she wasn't alone.

Apparently Charles's job also included shopping. The second day we were there, he arrived with toiletries and clothes for Mac and me. Since Franklin had been on a business trip in Dallas, he already had clothes with him. We'd taken turns using the shower in Hendrix's room. I felt like I'd shed twenty pounds just by washing off the dirt from the night of the tornado. The dried blood in my hair had been more of a challenge to remove. If Hendrix had been awake, he would have insisted he wash my hair and brush it for me. It amazed me how strong he could be when necessary, but he also had a gentle side and knew when to bring it out. I'd landed the perfect mix of badass and good guy.

Mac and I were playing a game of solitaire when Franklin's phone chimed. He pulled it out of his jeans pocket, his forehead creasing for a split second while he peered at the screen.

"I have to take this, girls. I'll be right back."

My eyes followed him as he strolled out of the

room. When he'd arrived at the hospital, he was in a full suit, but that had changed quickly during our stay. Like the rest of us, he'd chosen jeans and comfortable shirts.

The second he was gone, Mac leaned forward, and caught my attention.

"I have no idea who that was, but something's up. Hendrix told me when Franklin is in court he's a shark, and his expression never gives anything away. But at home—he has a few tics I've pinpointed over time. I don't know if his poker face is out of practice, or if he's trying to be more transparent with us, but I can smell the shit coming from a mile away."

"You don't think it was a doctor about Hendrix, do you?" Panic clutched my heart. "Maybe they wanted to tell him the bad news first," I whispered.

"Nah, the doctor would have come in and gotten him. I don't think it has anything to do with Hendrix." She peered at him, sadness flickering across her expression. "I miss him so fucking much," she said quietly.

I grabbed her hand and Hendrix's too. At times, all I could do to keep my shit together was feel the warmth of his fingers in mine. At least he was still alive, but every day my heart broke a little more. Hope was more and more difficult to hold onto.

"Gemma," Franklin said, motioning to me from the doorway. "We need to talk."

"What's wrong?" I asked, scrambling from my chair toward him. I glanced at Mac over my shoulder as Franklin led me into the hallway.

"Gemma," Franklin began quietly. "That was Marcus. There's been a turn of events."

My eyes widened.

"What is it? What's wrong?" I stammered.

"Your father was released on a technicality. He's not going to prison."

I staggered backward with the news.

"No! How? Who in their right mind wouldn't see he was guilty?" I asked, my voice stepping up a notch. If I wasn't careful, hysterics would be next. This was more than I could handle.

"Unfortunately, it happens," Franklin said, a soothing tone in his response.

A sudden urge to scream shot through me, and my body trembled while my mind processed what was happening. Franklin pulled me in for a hug, and I allowed myself to clutch onto him tightly.

"Gemma," he said gently against my ear. "I can't imagine how you feel right now, but I need you to hang in there with me. We're in the middle of the ICU, so take a moment. Then, I'm going to tell you exactly what to do."

I nodded against his chest, grateful for the support. I could see where Hendrix got his level head and calm-during-a-crisis personality.

"Other than the legal issues, I would normally have this conversation with my son, but since he's in a coma, I have to discuss all of this with you." He paused and then, "I'm sorry, but you're no longer safe here, and neither is Ada Lynn. I'm in the process of planning for us all to go back to Spokane. I can't keep you safe here, and Hendrix would be super pissed at me if I didn't take every measure to take care of you."

I pulled away, horror spearing me. Kyle lived next door to Ada Lynn. Would he go after her? She'd pulled a gun on him. Spokane? No. This wasn't happening. It was a sick joke. But I knew better. There was no way Franklin would ever mess around about something like this.

"I can't leave Hendrix. He is in a coma, Franklin. How would you even move him? I'm not leaving them here." I folded my arms across my chest. No way in hell was I going anywhere with a fucking monster on the loose.

"Gemma, families move coma patients all the

time. I'll have a doctor on the flight with us. Hendrix will be safe. As for Ada Lynn, she's coming, too."

"Where is Ada Lynn going?" Mac asked, approaching us in the hall.

"You're going home, Mac. We all are," Franklin said in a matter of fact tone.

"What? To Spokane?" She stepped backward, her forehead creasing. "No, I'm not leaving."

Franklin frowned at her.

My head was spinning. "Where are we going to stay?"

"For now, everyone will stay at my house. I have plenty of space," Franklin replied.

"I'm getting married," Mac blurted out in a rush. "I'm not leaving Jeremiah."

A crushing silence lingered in the space between us. Franklin rubbed his chin while his eyes narrowed at her. "Mac, you've only been here a few months. Is this boy from here?"

"Yeah, I met him at school."

Franklin cleared his throat, and my focus bounced between the two of them, the tension growing thicker by the second.

"You're coming home," he stated clearly.

"No!" Mac yelled.

"We'll discuss this in a few minutes when we

have some privacy. Right now, my main concern is keeping your best friend and Ada Lynn safe."

"What? Why are we going back to Spokane?" Mac demanded.

"Kyle was released on a technicality. He's being processed and released from custody as you and I speak. Gemma and Ada Lynn are in serious danger. Do you understand?"

Mac's brows shot up in shock, her face a mixture of fear and anger.

"Gemma, Charles is waiting for you out front. He'll take you to your house to pack. Please pack for Hendrix, too. Charles will help Ada Lynn get some essential items together. Then he'll drive you all to meet us at the airport. Here's information concerning the plane and airport, just in case."

Franklin handed me a business card with the flight details scrawled in tight handwriting on the back.

"Mac?" My head was a mess, with a million thoughts bombarding me at once. I wasn't sure how to untangle them. I would have to trust Franklin and do what he said. At least Ada Lynn and Hendrix would go with us.

"Go, Gemma." She pulled me in for a big hug. "I'll see you soon."

I frowned. "You're not coming? Not even for a little bit?" I asked breathlessly. I understood how love could drive your decisions, but Hendrix was her family. Wouldn't she want to be with him, even for a little while longer? Surely Jeremiah would understand.

"Gemma, Mac will be on the plane. You need to go, *now*," Franklin said.

I nodded then hurried down the hallway. As I rounded the corner, I glanced over my shoulder at Mac and Franklin in an intense discussion.

Charles was waiting for me near the hospital entrance. Even though this was the first time I laid eyes on the man—not being family, he wasn't allowed in the ICU—I instinctively knew the big guy wearing a sharp black suit and sunglasses, standing next to Franklin's Mercedes was none other.

"Hi," I said, looking him over. I'm not sure what I was expecting, but this wasn't it. Charles was huge. Like weightlifter huge. His dark hair was in a buzz cut, and his face was deeply tanned.

Instead of greeting me, he nodded and opened the passenger door. I took my cue and climbed in. When he rounded the front of the car and slid into the driver's seat, I stole a glance at him. His presence filled the entire car. I stared as he adjusted his earpiece. Holy shit. Charles wasn't just a driver who ran the occasional errand, he was more. He was a bodyguard. Chills traveled through me. Why would Franklin need someone like Charles?

He pushed his sunglasses up on his nose and pulled out of the parking lot.

"My orders are to take you to your house. I'll be across the street with Ada Lynn. You have ten minutes to gather what you need. No more. Franklin will have all your other belongings packed and shipped back to Spokane. We're on borrowed time already, so you need to do exactly as I tell you," he said, his voice low and gravelly.

I nodded, my mouth gaping open. Orders? Not *instructions* or *Franklin said*, but orders. Charles wasn't anything close to what I'd imagined him to be. For some reason, I had him pegged as a tall scrawny driver who shopped and ran errands when asked to. And why did Franklin need protection? From what?

"Do you understand? Ten minutes, no more."

"Yeah," I croaked out.

"There's a chance Kyle will already be processed and released by the time we make it back to your house. You need to keep in mind that time is of the essence. He might arrive while we're there."

Nausea swirled inside my gut. There was no doubt in my mind if Kyle saw me, he would kill me. I'd testified against him in court and tried to put him away for life.

"I need to call Ada Lynn," I muttered, fumbling for my phone in my back pocket. "She won't open the door for you if she doesn't know what's going on."

Charles remained silent, his eyes on the road as I pulled up her number in my favorites.

"Hello?"

"Ada Lynn, it's Gemma. I'm on my way to you with Charles. Start packing, we're going to Spokane."

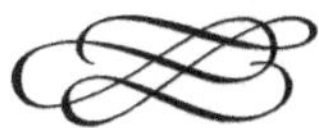

"What? Spokane? Gemma, slow down, you're not making any sense," Ada Lynn sputtered.

"Is your front door locked?" I asked, attempting to keep my tone level.

"Yes, Kim left a few minutes ago to run errands, and I bolted and chained it behind her."

My pulse raced, and I chewed anxiously on my bottom lip.

"Call her and tell her not to come back. Ada Lynn, the trial is over. Kyle was let go on a technicality."

"What in the hell?" Ada Lynn gasped.

"Start packing your most important belongings. Charles is going to drop me off at Hendrix's place, and I'm going to pack our essentials. You and Charles will meet me there, then we're off to the airport."

"What about Hendrix?" Ada Lynn asked, fear evident in her tone.

"Franklin will have a doctor on the plane. Hendrix is still in a coma, but he's going home with us."

It was funny how I'd lived my entire life in Louisiana but referred to Spokane as home.

"We're about thirty minutes away," I said. "Do you want me to stay on the phone with you, or are you okay to pack on your own?"

"I—I..."

"Listen, I know you're scared. I am too, but put your phone on speaker and carry it with you. I'll stay on with you until we pull up across the street. Charles will help when he gets there."

I stayed on the line with Ada Lynn, helping her choose what to pack. I wasn't sure how in the hell I could remain so calm and help her when everything around me was turning to shit.

"Hey, we just pulled up to Hendrix's house. Charles will be over in a minute. He's wearing a black suit, and his dark hair is in a buzz cut. Plus he looks mean." I peeked over at Charles, but he didn't even flinch. "I have a feeling he's more than capable of keeping us safe," I said softly. "Do not under any circumstances look out your window. Kyle could drive up any minute, and I wouldn't put it past him to run into the house, come back out, and open fire. I love you, and I'll see you in a few minutes."

"I love you, too. You hurry, now. I'll let Charles in when he knocks and I'll call Kim," Ada Lynn said.

"Bye." I tapped my screen, ending the call.

Charles turned toward me, the car still idling.

"Ten minutes," he reminded me and set the alarm on his watch. "Essentials only."

I looked across the street, but my old house remained dark with the curtains closed. There wasn't any movement that I could see, but it didn't mean he wasn't inside. Or maybe he was on his way home. I had no idea how long it took to be released from jail. Plus, he didn't have any transportation. Maybe it would play out in Ada Lynn's and my favor.

I hurried out of the car with Charles right behind me.

"What are you doing?" I frowned at him.

"I'm making a sweep of the house first."

"Charles, I'll be fine. You're right across the street. The best way you can help me is to protect

Ada Lynn. She had a heart attack a few months ago, and under the circumstances, I'm worried about her...go. I'm fine."

He paused, staring at me and cleared his throat. "I don't like it, but we're really short on time. I'll watch you go in," he replied.

Fumbling for the house key I'd put in my pocket, I took two porch steps at a time, then slid the key in and opened the front door. I glanced over my shoulder at Charles before I stepped inside.

Hendrix's woodsy cologne lingered in the air, and I pressed myself against the front door, inhaling deeply. A soft cry escaped me, and my mind whirled in a million different directions.

But I refused to succumb to this new round of *fucked up* that Fate had thrown at us. A tornado. A coma. And now my rat bastard of a father was being released on a technicality. I wanted to scream at the top of my lungs until I couldn't scream anymore. The unfairness of it all blew my mind. And now we were being forced to flee our home!

Since I only had ten minutes to gather our most important items, I quickly made my way into the living room and toward the bedroom.

"You're just as beautiful now as when you

were fourteen." The man's voice was deep and smooth, yet his words were laced with poison.

My head snapped up, and a scream ripped through the air. Shit. Was Kyle here? Had he broken into my house? I stood frozen, rooted in place.

"I highly recommend you not scream again," he warned, as he pushed the loaded clip into his pistol.

"Who the hell are you?" I demanded, eyeing his gun. My pulse pounded in my ears. It wasn't Kyle. I had no idea who he was, but I knew he didn't belong here.

"You don't remember me? I'm hurt." His laugh echoed through the room, causing goosebumps on my skin.

"Am I supposed to remember you?" I asked, forcing my voice to remain steady. If this guy was mental, he wouldn't even think twice about shooting me. My attention swept over him, trying to recall who he was.

He ran a hand over his spiky dark hair and gave me an evil smile. Chills shot down my spine.

"I'm a close friend of your father's. You wouldn't remember my face, though. I was wearing a hood the night I had my way with you."

Oh. My. God. My eyes widened in shock as

the pieces clicked into place. No way was this ass-hole going to hurt me again. I'd kill him before I let him touch me.

"I know you," I feigned casual. "You were in and out of my house when I was younger."

"Ah, now you have it. I set my sights on you the first time I saw you. You've grown up to be an intelligent young woman," he crooned, his lust-filled gaze traveling up and down my body.

"My mother *cooked* for you. She welcomed you into our home." Anger swirled deep inside me. "Did she know what you were? That you liked to rape little girls? That you raped her daughter, Carl Roberts?" I spat the last words at him. "What the hell are you doing here?"

"Well, I was waiting for your father, but when I learned you were living right across the street, I couldn't resist popping in to say hello." He stroked his salt and pepper colored beard, his leer never leaving me. "Your father mentioned you typically stayed close to the area, so I assumed you would be back home soon, and here you are." His gray eyes narrowed in thought. "The word is out that good ol' Kyle rolled over on some of the society members. Now the police are looking for us, too. It wasn't very smart on his part if you ask me."

His cold eyes bored holes in me as he aimed his gun at my chest.

"You can have him. He means nothing to me. Just walk out the front door, and I'll never tell anyone I even saw you." Pleading with my dad hadn't worked, but Carl appeared sober. Maybe there was a bit of reasoning or logic left inside him.

"You wish it could be that easy." He leaned forward in the chair and stood slowly, adjusting himself in his jeans.

A sour taste filled my mouth while he approached, and I swallowed the bile down.

"This is going to be so much fun," he growled.

He lowered the gun, and in one swift move, he pulled me to him, and his mouth crashed down on mine. I screamed, but it only allowed his tongue in my mouth. Before I really thought about it, I bit down. Hard.

"You stupid bitch!" He reached up to his mouth and stared at the blood on his fingers. The hand that held the gun flew up and smacked me against the temple. I dropped to the floor, my vision blurring. Black dots danced before me, and I struggled to regain my composure.

His gruff fingers gripped my neck, and he pushed me backward, pinning me to the hardwood floor. My feet scrambled for traction as I gasped for air.

His gun clattered to the ground while he un-buttoned my jeans and gave them a hard tug.

"Blue lace panties, how pretty," he said, licking his lips.

His hand loosened around my neck and quickly covered my mouth. Cold air brushed across my bare legs as he wrestled my jeans over my hips. My eyes fluttered closed. I had to breathe. I had to think.

I crossed my legs. If nothing else it would piss him off, and he'd have to work harder to get my clothes off. At least this time I wasn't wearing a dress.

He released my mouth in order to focus on my jeans, and I screamed again. He slapped me and continued to wrestle with my pants. I kicked against him, fighting with all of my strength.

My hand fisted into a ball, and I managed a punch to his throat.

"Fuck!" he yelled, grabbing his neck, his weight shifting off me.

This was my chance. I blinked hard and tried to clear the tears from my vision. Squinting, my focus landed on the lamp on the corner table. I fumbled for the cord and jerked it down next to me, wrapping my fingers around the base of it.

"Not again, motherfucker," I yelled and swung the lamp against the side of his head as hard as I could.

He fell off me and doubled over, covering himself with his hands. I scrambled to my feet, taking the opportunity to whack him again as he tried to stand up.

"Guess. Who's. Grown. The. Fuck. Up." I said, hitting him repeatedly in the head with the metal end of the lamp. I landed a kick to his side, and he crumpled on the floor the same moment my front door burst open.

"Gemma!" Charles said, hurrying to me. "Are you alright?"

I nodded and gawked as Charles trained his gun on Carl, then I quickly zipped and buttoned my jeans. Rubbing my temples, I forced myself to concentrate. Although I was still physically shaking, I was void of any emotion. I would count it as a blessing. I could lose my shit later.

"The cops want him," I said, breathlessly. "That's the motherfucker who raped me when I was fourteen."

In a rare show of emotion, anger flickered

across Charles's stony expression. "It looks like you did a pretty good job on your own."

"I tried." I wiped the sweat off my forehead and inhaled sharply. "I'm going to call the police if you'd be so kind as to watch him."

A small smile pulled at the corners of his mouth.

"I see why Franklin likes you. You're a fighter."

"Life has left me with no other choice." I nodded at him and then walked to the bedroom.

I tapped out 911 on my phone and listened while it connected. My brain had officially kicked into autopilot, and I provided the information to the police. Grabbing my suitcase from the closet, I tossed as many clothes and toiletries into it as I could. Kyle would most likely be home any minute, but at least the cops would be here. I didn't suspect he would try anything with them around, but I wouldn't put it past him to wait for them to leave. He was a sneaky son of a bitch.

Butterflies fluttered in my stomach as I realized we weren't safe yet. Maybe I'd taken one asshole down, but there was another on the way. The only thing that made me feel better was that Charles was with us. Now that I knew he was packing heat maybe he and Ada Lynn could trade tips.

I wheeled the suitcase into the living room where I found Carl's hands and legs duct taped behind him. A slab of tape also covered his mouth.

I turned away from him and focused on Charles.

"Where's Ada Lynn?" I asked.

"She's at her house. I was loading her suitcase in the car when Franklin called me. The second I hung up the phone, I heard you scream. Obviously I let myself in."

Sirens wailed in the air, and I shuddered.

"I want to see her, but I know I should wait for you. Hang on. What did Franklin need?"

"Excuse me, Gemma Thompson?" an officer asked from the front door.

I frowned. I needed to know if there was an update on Hendrix.

"Let's take care of this, first," Charles said quietly and slipped his gun into its holster.

I spoke to the police and gave them my account of the attack. Charles had stepped into the kitchen to make a phone call, but he stayed in the doorway the entire time. His eyes never left me.

Half an hour later, the police left with a furious Carl in handcuffs.

"Do you have everything you need?" Charles asked me, picking up my suitcase.

"Yeah, I need to lock up," I said. Until tonight, this house had been my safety net. Now it was tarnished, just like the rest of the area.

I pulled the door closed behind me and double checked the locks. Glancing both directions, I darted past Charles, across the street, and up Ada Lynn's steps. I wrapped my knuckles on the door.

"It's Gemma," I called. I scanned Kyle's house, but I still didn't see any movement.

Ada Lynn's door opened, and she grabbed my arm, pulling me inside. I nudged the door closed with my hip.

"Are you hurt?" she asked, hugging me hard.

"How did you know?"

"Oh honey, my phone blew up with calls from Charles and Franklin while you were talking to the police."

"Oh, I'm glad they called you. And yeah, I'm fine for now. I just want to get out of here before Kyle comes home. Carl was bad enough, but Kyle has had some time to sober up and plan his revenge while he sat in jail. I'm not interested in finding out exactly what he might have in mind for me."

"They're both rat bastards. Carl had some

crazy nerve showing up in your home like that," Ada Lynn spat.

"Well it won't happen again. Not only did I beat the hell out of him with Hendrix's lamp, but the police arrested him, too. I guess Kyle gave up a few names."

Ada Lynn nodded and patted my cheek, her eyes filling with tears. Our gazes locked. As far as I knew, this would be the last time we were in this house. There was no way she would be able to come back as long as Kyle was next door. His choices had affected her, and now she had to leave her home. An agonizing ache spread through my chest.

"Let's go to Spokane," I said, my pulse racing. Thanks to Carl, we were running behind, and I was terrified Kyle would show up before we were able to leave.

Ada Lynn nodded in response, snatched up her purse, and pulled the door closed behind us. Scanning Kyle's house for any activity, I ushered Ada Lynn down the stairs and to the safety of the car. Charles waited by the back door and opened it for her.

After she was settled, I jumped into the front seat and buckled up. Charles shifted into gear and started to pull away from the house, then stopped abruptly. I shot forward against my seatbelt and watched in horror as a silver car pulled up to Kyle's house.

I fisted my hands together, and fear clenched my heart as Kyle stepped out of the car.

"Shit. Go, go, go! Get down Ada Lynn!" I scrunched down into my seat and held my breath.

Charles pressed the accelerator and whipped around the other car.

Had he seen us? He had to have suspected something since the Mercedes had been parked in front of Ada Lynn's house, but it was an unfamiliar car, too. Maybe he thought Ada Lynn had company.

I peered in the side mirror and eyed him while he walked through the gate and toward his house. Thank God he hadn't gotten back in the car and followed us.

Laying low, I turned around to peek at Ada Lynn, who was stretched out in the back seat.

"Are you okay?" I asked, my eyes wide with fear.

"Yeah. Did he see us?"

"I don't think he knew we were in the car."

"The silver car has pulled away in the opposite direction. Kyle went into his house. Stay down for a few more minutes until I'm confident we're clear, ladies," Charles ordered.

A shudder traveled through me. We'd barely gotten away in time.

The sound of the turn signal broke my thoughts, and I forced myself to remember the day Hendrix had turned this same corner, and then driven right back into my arms.

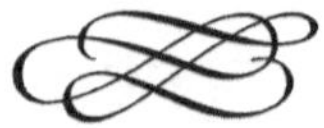

CHAPTER 11

If I were totally honest with myself, I was terrified of sitting up in the car again. Kyle apparently had connections everywhere, and the driver of the silver car could have been one of them. For all I knew, we were being tailed.

I reached back and held Ada Lynn's hand, my head pounding like crazy.

"Are you two doing alright?" Charles asked without looking in our direction.

"I think so. Do you see anyone following us?"

He hesitated. I figured he was discreetly checking if anyone seemed suspicious, but he still had his sunglasses on, and I couldn't see his eye movement.

"No. It appears the coast is clear."

"Can we sit up?" I asked, my neck and head throbbing from all the commotion.

He nodded, and I sat up in my seat, my gaze darting around nervously. After I glanced in all the mirrors and over my shoulder, I agreed. There wasn't a silver car anywhere around us.

"You can sit up, Ada Lynn."

She patted her chest and took a deep breath.

"That was way too close," she said.

"No kidding." I turned toward Charles. "Thank you. For all of your help."

"I'm just doing my job," he replied.

"Regardless if it's your job or whatever, you saved my life, and Ada Lynn's, too. So thank you."

His chin tilted slightly, ending the conversation.

Suddenly, I remembered Charles had mentioned something about Franklin.

"Wait, Franklin called you in the middle of the shitstorm, and I wasn't able to ask you if it was about Hendrix."

"We're almost to the hospital. You can speak with Franklin when we arrive. I'm under orders not to discuss anything."

"What?" I screeched louder than I'd intended. "I thought we were on the way to the airport. Charles, if something is wrong and I've lost Hendrix..." I hiccupped up through the tears that had started.

"He's alive." His tone remained even and calm.

I sank back into my seat, covering my hands with my face. There was no way Charles would say anything else, but at least he'd given me a nugget to hold on to. The only time his voice had any inflection, or I'd seen his facial expression change, was when I told him Carl had raped me. Otherwise, nothing. I wondered if they taught that in bodyguard school.

Ada Lynn's hand slipped over my seat and squeezed my shoulder. I patted hers in return. It had been one fucked up day, but at least we were together and safe for now.

Five minutes later, Charles pulled up to the entrance of the hospital. I darted out of the car before he'd even brought it to a complete stop. The entrance doors whooshed open and I hauled ass down the hallway toward Hendrix.

My shoes squeaked against the tile floor as I turned a sharp corner. Breathless, I ran into Hendrix's room and stopped cold.

"What the hell?" I asked, my focus bouncing between Hendrix and Franklin. He gently squeezed Hendrix's arm and stood, blocking my view.

Glaring, I sidestepped him, and the most beautiful piercing blue eyes met mine. I gasped.

"Hendrix?" I asked, moving toward him.

Franklin stepped toward me, attempting to stop me from reaching him. What was he doing?

Ducking Franklin's extended arms, I reached Hendrix's bed.

"Baby?" I grabbed his hand. "You're awake." My tears choked off my words.

Hendrix searched my face, worry lines creasing his forehead.

"Do we know each other?" He asked, his voice hoarse from lack of use.

I dropped his hand quicker than if I'd touched a hot stove. My mouth gaped open, and I nodded.

"I'm your girlfriend," I stammered.

"I'm sorry, I don't...I don't remember anything or anyone," he muttered and lay back against his pillow. Fear flickered through his eyes, and my heart dropped into my stomach.

Turning away from him quickly, I shot Franklin a horrified look.

"What's happening?" I mouthed.

Franklin took my arm and hauled me out of the room and into the hall.

"First of all, you have no right to stop me from seeing him." I started in on Franklin the moment we were out of earshot from Hendrix. My words were sharp with anger. "Second, you should have told me before I got here. What in God's name, Franklin? How is this happening?" I covered my face, attempting to hold my spiraling emotions in check. I'd kept my calm with Carl, but this was it. It was humanly impossible to manage anything else.

"Gemma, I'm so sorry. I knew you were safe with Charles, and I'd planned on waiting for you outside in the hallway. I didn't want you to have to find out this way. You just beat me here."

I shook my head and placed my hands on my hips.

"Are you hurt? Charles updated me on the attack from Carl. It never occurred to me he would show up. I was worried about Kyle and never saw Carl coming. I'm sorry I let you down. I should have had Charles go inside with you. It was my fault."

I peered up at Franklin. Pain and regret filled his eyes. Shit had happened so fast, I'd forgotten that everyone was hurting and scared. Not just me.

Sobs shook my shoulders, and I flung myself into Franklin's arms. Maybe Hendrix was alive, but we'd still lost him.

"How long? How long will the amnesia last, Franklin?" I pulled away, drying my cheeks.

"The doctors don't know when he will regain his memories. Maybe tomorrow. Maybe never."

My breath hitched in my throat.

"Never?" I asked, horrified.

"The doctor's said this might happen, but I didn't want to alarm you or Mac. There was no way they could be sure until he woke up. With a head injury, it's always a possibility."

All the articles I'd read about coma patients and unpredictable outcomes filled my mind. It never once occurred to me that something like that would happen to Hendrix. That he might wake up and not remember anything or anyone.

My body trembled, and I leaned against the wall, attempting to steady myself.

"What now?" I looked at him for guidance.

"We go home. Let's get the hell out of here and go home."

I DIDN'T HAVE the strength to go back into Hendrix's room. I would lose my shit for real, and they'd admit me for a mental evaluation. Honestly, I wasn't sure how I was walking around with a brain in my noggin right now.

Charles stood next to Ada Lynn in the waiting room. Since they weren't family, they weren't allowed to come into Hendrix's room.

Worry spread across Ada Lynn's expression when she saw me.

"Gemma?"

I sucked in a breath, gathering the courage to tell her.

"He's awake...but he has amnesia."

Ada Lynn gawked as I sank into the chair next to her, defeated.

Words were beyond my ability at the moment, so I took her hand in mine and sat still.

We remained quiet for a few minutes. She knew if I had any other information, I would have told her. At least he was awake, but everything he'd worked so hard for...his career, his relationship with his Dad and Mac. Me. It was all gone.

"Gemma, Ada Lynn," Charles said, turning toward us. "It's time to go. Franklin and Hendrix are in his rental car, and we'll follow them to the airport. Mac left, so if she's going back to Spokane, she'll meet us at the plane."

Standing, I helped Ada Lynn up, and we

silently followed Charles to the Mercedes. I scanned the other cars around ours and spotted Hendrix in the passenger's seat of a Lexus. He stared at me while I walked toward the car. A lump stuck in my throat as I held his gaze. Would he leave me and fall in love with someone else? Were we over, or was there a shred of hope again?

Charles opened the doors for us, and this time I let Ada Lynn sit up front. After I made sure she was comfortable, I jumped in the back seat and buckled up.

Charles settled in, and the car engine purred to life.

"How far to the airport?" I asked.

"Twenty minutes."

I sank into my seat. Soon I'd be in the same space as Hendrix, except this time I wouldn't hold his hand or kiss him. How was my heart supposed to handle being near him without being able to touch him?

Exhausted, I closed my eyes.

"GEMMA, HON." I woke to Ada Lynn gently shaking my shoulder. "You dozed off. We're at the airport." She stood outside the car, holding open my door for me.

"Huh?" I asked, wiping my mouth with the back of my hand. "What time is it?"

"A little after seven p.m."

It would explain why it was almost dark out.

"Where are we?" I sat up, peering around.

"Behind the FBO or wherever it is they load and unload the private planes."

"Yeah, makes sense." I got out of the vehicle and stretched, my body rebelling after the fight with Carl.

Even though it wasn't cold, I shivered, and it dawned on me we were in for a bit of an adjustment since the temperatures would be cooler in Washington. From what I'd Googled, Spokane was in the lower sixties for the high temps. We'd been in the eighties here. It would be good snuggle weather with...I caught myself before my thought finished with Hendrix.

"Get a jacket out of your suitcase. You'll need it when we land in Washington," I suggested to Ada Lynn. "Charles, can we get into our luggage before it's loaded, please?"

He popped the trunk for us, and we located what we needed. When we were finished, he grabbed the suitcases and locked the car.

"This way," he said.

Ada Lynn and I gave each other a look. Mac had mentioned Franklin's private plane, but I had no clue what to expect.

"I've never flown before," Ada Lynn whispered.

"I've only flown once, but from what Mac told me, this is a far cry from a commercial plane."

My shoulders slumped forward as my thoughts drifted to Mac. She'd made it clear to Franklin that she wouldn't be on the plane even though he'd insisted she would be. I wasn't a fan of a parent pulling rank on an adult kid, but this time, I hoped like hell Franklin won. Even if she didn't stay long, Hendrix would need her. Shit, I needed her.

A soft breeze blew across the tarmac while we walked toward the plane. Charles stopped at the foot of the stairs that led inside, lowered the handles on our luggage, and picked them up.

"Follow me," he said, proceeding up the stairs.

"You first." I motioned for Ada Lynn to go ahead of me. She held onto the handrails, and slowly made her way up the steps. I wanted to stay behind her in case she lost her balance. She might not have said so, but I knew all of this was weighing heavily on her. I was only nineteen and it had worn me out.

We entered the plane, and my eyes widened.

"Holy shit," I mumbled under my breath.

"My sentiments exactly," Ada Lynn replied softly.

Franklin stood when he saw us.

"Take a seat wherever you like. All of the chairs recline if you need some sleep." He motioned to several plush, cream-colored leather seats behind him and Hendrix. I searched the plane, eyeing the dark brown, thick carpet, the couch with a chaise, television, tables, and a fully stocked, built-in bar.

"I'm going to save the bedroom for Hendrix if he needs it."

My brow rose, and I nodded, stunned. A bedroom on a plane?

"Thank you," I mumbled and peeked at Hendrix.

"After you're settled, I need to talk to you, Gemma," Franklin said in a hushed tone.

I nodded. "I'll be in the back where I can stretch out. I'm exhausted."

"I'll find you after we take off and get in the air."

Ada Lynn had already sat in one of the chairs

in the back. Before I moved to join her, I reached out and touched Franklin's arm.

"Any word from Mac?" I wanted to know if she'd changed her mind, but I was afraid to hear the answer.

"We'll see," he answered, sadness flickering across his expression.

"Oh." I blinked back my tears.

It was then I realized Hendrix's gaze was on me. My entire body warmed. I knew Franklin wanted to talk to me about the situation before I approached Hendrix, but he was right in front of me, awake. We'd barely spoken two sentences to each other.

Glancing at Franklin, I moved to stand beside Hendrix's seat.

"I realize you don't have your memories, but I love you, and I'm so damned relieved you're alive and with us." With that, I walked away, a multitude of thoughts scrambled and collided inside my jumbled brain. I chanced a look over my shoulder at Hendrix. He'd turned to watch me walk down the aisle. Maybe that was a good thing. At this point, I'd take anything I could to help me hang on.

Collapsing in a chair across from Ada Lynn, I literally sank into the seat.

"Whoa," I muttered to her. "I've never sat in anything so nice before."

"You don't have to tell me that," she replied, chuckling. "When you mentioned Hendrix had money, I had no idea *this* is what you meant."

"That makes two of us. Mac filled me in on what money really means to Franklin the night of the tornado."

Pulling my phone out of my pocket, I glanced at the time. It was almost eight. Where was Mac? Dammit, I'd hop off this plane, find her, and drag her on it if I had to. I knew she loved Jeremiah, and I didn't expect her to stay in Spokane long, but a quick trip would be good for everyone.

I poked my head into the aisle and spotted Charles near the front, standing guard. Another gentleman had boarded, and I assumed it was the doctor. I was grateful we had one on the flight just in case.

Franklin paced back and forth, checking his watch every five seconds. Finally, he disappeared into what I suspected was the cockpit. When he returned a few moments later, his hands were shoved in his jeans pockets, and he was scowling.

"We have to go, Gemma."

"Are you sure? Mac's not coming?" My tone climbed in pitch with each question.

He nodded, exhaustion lining his face. "I've done what I could."

"I understand. We need to get Hendrix home, anyway."

"After we're in the air, you and I can step into the conference room and talk about his condition. I'll share with you what the doctors said."

"Thank you," I said. "For everything."

He nodded and returned to his seat.

The pilot's voice rang through the speakers while we prepared for takeoff. A young blonde stewardess entered the plane and smiled warmly at everyone. Her attention landed on Hendrix, and she winked at him. It took all the strength inside me not to shove her backward out of the plane. He might not remember me, but he was mine, and she needed to step back. When the stewardess suddenly tripped over her own feet, I wondered if Karma was on my side for once. I squelched my laughter, then I burst into tears.

CHAPTER 12

Just when I'd given up hope, a grumpy Mac appeared beside the blonde. She waltzed up the aisle like she owned the plane, her backpack hanging off one shoulder.

"Mac!" I jumped up and ran to her, pulling her into a bear hug. She clung to me for dear life, and we stood in the aisle, crying together.

"I didn't think you were going to make it," I kept my voice low as I grabbed her hand. She grimaced, her focus traveling to the floor. I'd experienced firsthand how hard it was to leave the person you loved, but she would return to him.

"I'm here for now," she said and shot Franklin

a look full of anger. She stepped toward Hendrix, a sad smile easing across her lips.

"I'm your sister, Mackenzie. Mac for short." Her hand covered her mouth, and she paused. "We're closer than best friends, and I miss you like crazy. I'm glad you're awake, but let's get something straight."

Hendrix frowned. "What's that?" he asked.

"Don't you ever fucking scare me like that again. And one more thing, I will bug the shit out of you until your memories come back, so get ready."

For the first time since he'd been awake, a small smile pulled at the corner of Hendrix's mouth. My heart thundered against my chest. Leave it to Mac to bring him around even for a fleeting second.

"I'll be in the back if you get bored." She flipped her hair over her shoulder and walked toward Ada Lynn.

"We're all here, now," I announced to Franklin. "I'm ready to go home."

My focus drifted to Hendrix. His eyes were trained on me again, and the familiar flush crept up my neck and cheeks. Resisting the urge to kiss him, I smiled and walked away.

I sank into my chair and turned to stare at

Mac, who was in the process of chatting Ada Lynn's ears off.

"What in the world happened? You're a wreck," I said.

"A fucking shit show," she replied. "I'll fill you in after we take off."

Apparently I would be busy with conversation most of the flight, and sleep would once again elude me.

We buckled up, and within minutes Louisiana was disappearing beneath us. Ada Lynn had reclined with a pillow and blanket, and her eyes were closed. She seemed to be holding up well, but I was still worried about her.

"Come on," Mac said and stood.

I unfastened my seatbelt and followed her. My mouth gaped once again when we entered the conference room. Mac closed the door behind us.

"Take a seat, girlfriend."

Another full bar and television lined the side wall. Eight leather chairs surrounded the oval mahogany table. Mac wandered over to the fridge and grabbed us both a Coke Zero.

She handed mine to me and plopped down into a chair, propping her feet up on the table like it was hers and not used for business.

My brows arched. Mac had never once acted like a spoiled rich kid. Something was up.

"Spill," I said, sitting down across from her, eyeing her feet on the table.

"Fine." She rolled her eyes and sat up, removing her shoes from the beautiful surface.

She blew out a huge breath and pulled her legs into her chest. Propping her chin on her knees, a tear slipped down her cheek.

"Mac," I whispered. "I know all of this has been hard on you. So much has happened so fast, but at least Hendrix is awake. I have faith he'll continue to come back to us." I had just lied to my best friend. Even the mere idea of God and faith had faded from my life years ago.

"Jeremiah broke up with me," she wailed.

"What?" I jumped up from the chair and wrapped my arms around her. What an asshole. Like she didn't have enough going on right now. What was his damned problem? While I plotted which shin I would kick him in first, relief washed over me that she wasn't jumping into marriage. I would never share that with her, though. Mac cried on my shoulder, and anger stirred inside me as I continued to mentally torment Jeremiah for hurting my best friend. I'd never felt this protective of anyone other than

Ada Lynn and my parents. At least not until I met Mac and Hendrix. I would go to great lengths for both of them. A pang of sadness nudged me with that thought. I knew no matter what happened, Mac would remain in my life. But Hendrix? I had no idea what might happen. Right now, I needed to support Mac in any way I could.

She pulled away and wiped her cheeks off with the back of her hands. I sat in the chair and waited for her to tell me about the breakup.

"Franklin wants me home, you heard that part, and he fucking shit his pants when I told him about Jeremiah. And I know he's trying hard to be a dad to me, but it also pissed me off." She paused, sniffling. "Franklin said Hendrix needs me, and I get it. I was coming back, but only for a weekend. It wasn't just about Jeremiah, I'm still in school. Well, for now..." She rubbed her forehead with the heels of her hands. "What I haven't told you is that Franklin isn't just paying my college tuition and for my car, but my allowance and basically everything right now. He wasn't around when I was growing up, and in his mind, he was and still is my dad." She gave a half shrug. "Now he's trying to help me by covering all my expenses while I get my degree. And he was so amazing when Hendrix and I told him I needed to get down here to you in Louisiana. Well," her voice trailed off. "We're not in Louisiana now since we're flying. Anyway, God, I can't stay on track for shit."

"It's alright. Take your time."

"Franklin told me if I didn't come back to stay, he would pull my college funding, take the car, the whole kit and kaboodle. I'd totally be up shit creek. No college for Mac. And ya know, Gemma, I work my fucking ass off. School is tough for me. Jeremiah helped me study, gave me techniques to try so I could stay focused, and..." Her shoulders slumped forward. "When I told him I was going back for a few days he was fine with it. He likes Hendrix, and he understands family, ya know. Then I lost my shit about Franklin manipulating me, and how I wasn't going to allow him to control me with his money." She stared up at the ceiling and swallowed visibly.

"What happened?" I asked gently.

"He went off. Like, smooth off. I've never seen him like that, but apparently money is a problem for him, and he had no fucking idea Franklin was richer than God. Everything changed. He told me I should go be with my family, enjoy Franklin's money, fly in the private plane, and not come back. He couldn't support corrupt morals."

I frowned. "What? Just because someone is rich doesn't mean they're corrupt. Why would he think that?"

"I have no idea. So really, we couldn't have worked anyway. I can't change who my family is. I know Franklin isn't my dad, but he is. And I would like to choke him right now for pulling rank on me but...I know I need to be there for Hendrix for as long as he needs me, Gemma. If it was me with amnesia, he wouldn't leave my side."

"I'm so sorry, Mac. I know you love Jeremiah."

"Fuuuuccckkk," Mac growled, dragging her hands down her face. "He was good to me in so many ways, and you know me, money isn't what runs my life. I mean, when you showed up in Spokane, you looked like Little Orphan Annie, but I still loved you. I didn't care what you wore or anything else. It's all about a person's heart to me. But if he can't accept Franklin and Hendrix because they have money...Houston, we have a huge ass problem."

I cracked a small grin.

"If I'm really honest with you—my heart broke even more thinking I was going back to Spokane without you. Mac, you're not only my bestie, but I've never had a friend like you. And...well, I love ya a shit ton."

Mac flung her arms around me and squeezed me tight. For being a petite person, she was strong as hell.

"I love you too, bestie! And slumber parties galore while we're all at Franklin's. Girl, remember the house we went to and played pool with Jeremiah and Alexander? Puh, ain't nothin' compared to Franklin's." She fanned herself almost as well as if she'd grown up in the South. "Ten," she paused holding up her fingers. "Ten bedrooms, twelve bathrooms, a game room, an indoor swimming pool, a kitchen you'll never want to leave, and the theatre room has a full-sized movie screen. Oh. My. God. I don't know why Hendrix ever left. Well I do, because he wanted to stand on his own two feet and he totally will again. And after he's better, he already has a house. Holy hell, Gemma." She stopped and clapped her hands together. "We're going to be roomies again!" She screeched. "Ohmigosh, should I be happy about that? Is that wrong? I mean Jeremiah broke my heart, Hendrix can't remember a damn thing, and I'm goofy excited over having you for a roomie again." Her expression fell as reality crashed down on us again.

"No, it's definitely the highlight, and we need something positive to hold onto."

She nodded.

"Mac, I'm here for you, and I hope you know that. But I need to tell you something."

Her shoulders sagged, worry lines creasing her forehead.

"What is it, bestie?"

"When I arrived at Hendrix's to pack our stuff. Carl Roberts, the guy who raped me, was waiting for me inside."

Mac gasped, her hands flying over her mouth.

"Oh my God! Gemma, what the hell? How could you not have told me that and let me go on and on about Jeremiah? Obviously you're alive, but are you okay?"

Over the next several minutes, I updated Mac about how Carl pretty much ambushed me and how Charles had helped. She pulled me in for a hug, swearing she would find some way to break into the prison and kill the sorry son of a bitch.

The conference room door opened, and I turned to see Franklin poking his head around the door.

"Hey, Mac, I need to talk with Gemma."

My shoulders tensed. I already knew this conversation would be about Hendrix, but I wasn't sure I was ready to deal with any additional bad news.

"Fine." She stood and sulked her way into the hall.

"Is she alright?" he asked, closing the door and pulling out one of the chairs.

I cleared my throat. "No, but none of us are right now."

He nodded and rubbed his chin, his brow creasing.

"I wanted to talk to you about Hendrix, and assure you that whether his memories come back or not, Gemma, you and Ada Lynn are welcome to stay in my home as long as you need to. Mac, too. I know she's pissed at me right now, and we'll work it through, but I just wanted to make that clear."

"Thank you. You guys are all I have left. Even if Hendrix never remembers me...maybe we can at least be friends." My stomach tightened as that last word tumbled from my mouth. How could I ever be just friends with the only guy I'd given my heart and body too?

"The other reason I want you all to stay with me is because the doctor said to surround Hendrix with people and things from his past, before the accident. Hopefully it will help to bring back his memory. We do need to be somewhat careful and not feed him memories, which is going to be hard. Especially for you, because of your relationship with him. You're the only girl he's ever allowed me to meet, Gemma. The only girl he's fallen in love with. And I have to think that it's deep and strong enough inside him that it will help him come back to us." His eyes moistened, and he rubbed them quickly. "I think you're the key. So yes, you living with us is also incredibly selfish on my part." He hung his head down, his shoulders shaking as he finally released his grief.

I stood and grabbed the box of tissues I'd spotted on the bar.

"I'll do the best I can. I promise," I said, my voice cracking with fear. "I just hope I'm enough."

I sat down and waited for Franklin to gather his composure.

Eventually, he straightened up and took a Kleenex. "I don't mean to put that kind of pressure on you. It's not what I meant."

"I know," I assured him. "We all want the same for Hendrix."

"The most important thing is he's alive, and we can create new memories with him."

"I told myself that too, but you and Mac are family. I'm his girlfriend, and he might not love me anymore." I stared at my feet, willing the tears away.

Franklin chuckled, and my head snapped up. He and Hendrix sounded almost identical when they laughed.

"What's so funny?" I asked, thoroughly confused.

"He's already been checking you out."

My cheeks flamed instantly. I cheered on the inside, but it was seriously embarrassing to have your boyfriend's dad notice and deliver that information.

"I didn't mean to embarrass you."

I covered my face with my hands and groaned.

"It's fine. I would rather you tell me." I paused. "But how do you know?" I asked, shyly.

"When we left the hospital, and it was just he and I in the car, he asked a few questions." Franklin smiled. "He wanted to know how he landed such a beautiful girlfriend."

"Oh," I said, the flush creeping higher. "What did you say?"

"I told him he would need to talk to you and see what he remembered. As hard as it will be for you, Gemma, you can't give him details. Just let him spend time with you and see what happens."

"Nothing? I can't tell him anything?" I croaked.

"It won't be easy. All I ask is that you do your best and refrain from telling him too much. We all have to do the same, so you're not alone in this."

"I'll keep it in mind. Thanks."

Franklin stood. "Would you like to spend some time with him?"

"Can I?" My pulse two timed at the thought. What would I even say?

"Yeah. I should spend some time with Mac, anyway. I need to see what she's willing to share with me and if we can talk things through. I take it something happened with Jeremiah."

"Good luck with that," I said, my lips pursing together. I strode across the room, but turned, my hand on the doorknob. "I won't get in the middle of your business, Franklin, but Mac loves you. Regardless of how she's feeling right now, she wants you in her life."

His eyes widened, and relief eased across his handsome face.

"Thank you," he said. "I know I'm not her biological dad, but in my opinion, it doesn't matter. She's my daughter. And sometimes a parent just needs to know their kid loves them."

"I get it. If Mom were alive, I would call her

the moment we landed and tell her I loved her." With that, I left the room.

Walking down the aisle, I tapped Mac on the shoulder and nodded toward the conference room. She grimaced and made her way back to Franklin. Ada Lynn was snoring softly in her chair, and I covered her with the blanket before I continued on to where Hendrix sat, my pulse pounding in my ears.

He looked up as I approached. My heart split in two. I wanted to pull him in for a kiss and tell him how happy I was that he was alive.

"Hi," I said softly, holding his gaze.

"Hey." He reached up and ran his hand through his hair.

I smiled. He did that a lot when we first met. Now I wondered if it was a nervous habit, but I doubted it. He already had my heart, why in the world would he be nervous?

"Can I?" I asked, motioning toward the seat across from him.

"Sure." His attention followed me. "Gemma, right?"

"Yeah, Gemma Thompson."

He rubbed his chin, just like his father, and peered at me.

"I'm sorry I don't remember. Dad said no one

can tell me much either, but I'm going to ask, anyway."

"It's fine. I would ask, too. I'll do my best, but my goal is to help you remember on your own."

"It fucking sucks," he mumbled. "I woke up, saw this dude in my room, and didn't have one damned clue about who he was. He *said* he was my dad, but nothing about him was familiar to me. Then the doctors rushed in, took my vitals and a bunch of other stuff. And while they poked and prodded on me, I wracked my brain for anything familiar. Where I lived, college, family...all I could come up with was a big fat blank nothing. I don't know if I've ever had one before, but I had a major panic attack." He paused, shaking his head. "Franklin sat down with me and I calmed down a bit. I don't remember him, but something felt right, so I rolled with it."

Longing swept through me, and I struggled not to pull him in for a hug. All I wanted to do was hold him, and tell him how much I loved him. I'd nearly died on the inside while he'd lain in a coma.

"It's lonely," he said, dropping his focus to the floor and back to me.

"It's lonely without you," I replied softly.

His facial expression didn't change with my

confession, but he pinned me with his stare. I fidgeted in my seat.

"Where did we meet?"

I hesitated, weighing the consequences of telling him.

"We met in Spokane at college. I'd just moved up from Louisiana."

His forehead creased. "So, since I woke up in Louisiana, I assume I was there with you."

"Yeah. My mom died a few months ago, and I had to go back for a while." Relief washed over me as I realized he wouldn't remember Kyle or Carl. He couldn't remember any of my past, and maybe it was best to start fresh. I'd changed since he'd come into my life. I wasn't the terrified young woman who had shown up on campus and been a target for Brandon. Hell, I'd even beat the shit out of my rapist earlier that day. But a nagging feeling continued inside me. What if this new Hendrix didn't love me? What if we had nothing in common?

I turned to stare out the window, reminding myself to find the positive in the situation. He was awake.

"Where did you live?" he asked, his fingers steepled together, staring at me.

Flashing him a small smile, I again considered what to say.

"We lived together," I replied.

He leaned forward in his chair, his blue eyes intense as he studied me. "Then it was more than just dating, we were serious."

I gulped and nodded.

"I'm so sorry. I can't imagine what you're going through," he said, compassion in his features.

Since he couldn't remember all the shit with Kyle and Andrea, he really didn't have a clue.

"You're awake. It's more than I had a few days ago. If you want to, we can spend some time together and see where things go," I suggested, twirling a strand of my red hair nervously around my finger. What if he said no? How would I deal with his presence around me each day, living in the same house?

"I would like that."

Tension eased from my neck with his response.

"Plus, it sounds like we're still going to live together," he said, his expression remaining serious.

"Yeah, just different beds," I blurted.

He flashed me the same beautiful smile that made me fall in love with him.

"Do I want to know what you're thinking?" I dared to ask, wondering if he was mentally undressing me like I was him.

He shifted in his seat enough to let me know his body had definitely responded to my comment. At least the attraction was still there between us. Time would only tell what else developed.

Suddenly, an idea crossed my mind.

CHAPTER 13

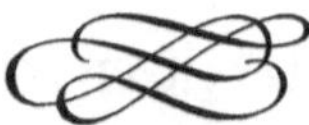

"I'll be right back." The moment I stood, the plane hit a pocket of turbulence. My arms flailed around, unable to grab onto anything substantial enough to keep me upright. The second dip of the plane sent me straight into Hendrix's lap. His arms instantly tightened around me as I yelped. Without thinking, I wrapped an arm around his neck, lay my head on his shoulder, and placed my hand on his chest. His heart beat wildly beneath my palm.

Reality hammered at my brain, reminding me of our situation, but I couldn't force myself to get up. Not yet.

His hand ran up my back, and I soaked up every second of being in his arms. His biceps and chest muscles flexed while he held me. The plane lurched again, causing me to shift my hips into him, and a small moan slipped from my lips. He was hard, and I was failing miserably at containing my emotions and desire for him.

The plane finally settled down, and I reluctantly let him go. As much as I wanted to look at him, I knew if I did, I would kiss him. This was already bad enough. I couldn't throw myself at him like a lovesick teenager. We couldn't force his memories to return. I had to accept that somewhere deep inside himself, Hendrix loved me. If … no, *when* his memory came back, his feelings for me would, too.

"Sorry," I whispered and stood.

"Are you okay?" he asked, a bit breathless.

I titled my head and studied him briefly. I'd always loved his protectiveness. He wasn't overbearing, but always wanted to make sure I was alright. He'd just done it again. Maybe my Hendrix was still in there somewhere.

I nodded. "If I can stand on my own two feet, I'll be right back." I rolled my eyes, attempting a little humor.

Holding onto the back of the seats, I made my way to my chair. Ada Lynn remained asleep as I rifled around in my jacket pocket for my headphones. With a quick glance toward the conference room, I noticed the door was still closed. Hopefully Mac and Franklin were doing okay.

"I'm back," I said. "This will be easier if we sit next to each other. How do you feel about using the couch?"

He looked over at it and stood. "It seems more comfortable, anyway. My legs are a bit stiff."

I turned away, attempting to hide my grin. He'd been stiff alright. Regaining my composure, I focused my attention on him again.

"Franklin said the seats recline, in case you didn't know."

"The couch is good," he assured me.

We sat down next to each other, and I busied myself with the Spotify app on my phone. I slipped an earbud in and handed him the other one. Hendrix scooted closer, but the cord still pulled taught between us. I tapped the screen and watched him closely as "Couldn't Love You More" spilled from the earbuds, our voices blending together perfectly.

"Do you like it?" I asked, hope swirling inside me.

He held up his finger and continued to listen. I wondered what he heard, since technically this was the first time he listened to our song. Would he recognize it was us, or could amnesia affect the kind of music he liked or if he liked it at all anymore? Anxiety hummed beneath my skin as I impatiently waited for his response.

"The harmony is crazy good. Whoever the female is...man her tone is breathtaking, and her pitch is spot on," he said, slowly removing his earbud. "The lyrics are strong, but I think I would manipulate the hook a little bit."

"Yeah?" I asked, grinning at him. Apparently his brain had stored information about music, and he was able to access it. Most people wouldn't know where a hook was in a song. This was a good sign. "What would you change about it?"

"Right where it goes..." He paused, then sang the notes but not the lyrics.

I held my breath, wondering if he would realize he'd been the one singing in the song.

"One more time?" I asked, sweetly. Honestly, I just wanted to listen to him sing. I didn't care if he sang "Row, Row, Row Your Boat." Yesterday, I wasn't sure I would ever hear him speak again.

His eyebrow arched. "Again?"

"Yeah, please," I said, encouraging him to continue.

His flawless tone sent shivers down my spine, and then he stopped abruptly.

"Wait," he said, confused. "Is that me on the song?" He frowned as he processed. "Sing for me, please."

I sang a few lines of SHY Martin's "Lose You Too."

"Shit," he said, staring at me. "It's not just me, it's us."

I nodded. "We've only written this song together, but we were about to write more."

"The lyrics are intimate as hell."

I blushed. I didn't want to say anything else. He would need some time to let it sink in.

"Do you want to listen to some other music?" I wasn't ready to leave his side yet.

His blue eyes softened. "Yeah, I would like that."

For the next hour, we listened to anything on my playlist I thought he might like or would jog his memory. Eventually, we relaxed into the couch and propped our feet up on the footrest. I'd been so intent on watching his face light up while we explored different songs together, I hadn't noticed Mac had joined us again.

Removing the one earbud I'd been using, I tilted my head at her.

"Are you okay?" I mouthed.

She scrunched up her nose, which told me no. Motioning for her to sit with us, I handed Hendrix the headphones and scooted over. She wiggled right in the middle of us. It wasn't exactly what I had in mind, but she needed to reconnect with her brother.

I stood, stretched, and handed Hendrix my phone. "You can continue to listen if you want to. I'm going to go to the bathroom and check on Ada Lynn. Mac is going to keep you company for a bit."

"Thanks for the music," he said, taking my phone.

"Anytime." Exhausted, I walked away and let Mac talk to him. If he got nosey, he'd find a bunch of pictures of us on my phone. I didn't care. Anything that helped him remember, he could have.

I strolled past a sleeping Ada Lynn and poked my head in the conference room.

"Hey, how much longer until we're in Spokane?" I asked.

Franklin glimpsed at his watch.

"About an hour and a half. Are you hungry? I have some food in the fridge," he said, pointing behind him at the bar.

"Not really. I've not had much of an appetite lately."

"How'd it go with Hendrix?" he asked.

I leaned against the door frame and folded my arms over my chest.

"As good as to be expected I guess. When we first met in Spokane, and he tried to get to know me, I pushed him away. Nothing he tried worked, actually." I laughed at the memory of him sitting at my table. "Until...until he was writing a song one day in the library."

"The library?" Franklin asked, surprised. "He's never stepped foot in one as far as I've known."

"He said as much. Anyway, it was our shared love of music that broke the ice. It worked for us then, so I hoped it would work this time, too. I wasn't sure he would even like it anymore, but it seems it hasn't changed. Who knows if he will write or sing again, but he enjoyed listening today at least. It's a start."

Franklin nodded. Dark circles had developed beneath his blue eyes over the last few weeks. Since he was an attorney, I knew he had a strong personality, but seeing the more fragile side of him was intense.

"How about you? How are you holding up?" I asked.

He put his feet on the table and locked his hands together behind his head. I nearly smiled when I realized that's where Mac had gotten the idea she could prop her feet on the beautiful furniture.

"Being a parent is the most difficult job I've ever had. Sometimes I wonder if I'll ever be okay." Sadness laced his words.

"I can't imagine. My life would be significantly different if I'd kept Jordan." My son had looked happy and well cared for, but I still knew I'd made the right decision to give him up for adoption.

He nodded. "I'm sorry you went through that, but I'm glad Carl was arrested. You never deserved any of it."

I glanced up at the ceiling, attempting to hold the tears at bay. With everything that had happened, I'd not had much of a chance to process the encounter with Carl or the fact Kyle wouldn't serve any jail time.

"How'd your chat with Mac go?" I asked.

"She's pissed at me, but she'll be okay. She finally opened up about Jeremiah, so now my girl's dealing with her heart being broken. I get it's a part of life, but it still hurts to see your kids go through a breakup."

"I'll be there for her. She's really excited about us all living together at least."

"Speaking of that, you and Ada Lynn will have your own rooms."

"Oh, it's okay. I don't want to…"

Franklin held up his hand, cutting me off. "You'll need your space, Gemma. I have more than enough rooms, so not another word."

"Thanks." The plane bounced with some more turbulence, and I clung to the door frame. "I'm exhausted, I think I'm going to see if I can rest a little bit before we land."

"Let me know if you need anything. I mean it."

I smiled and made my way back to my seat. I grabbed a blanket and pillow from the table next to me, sank into the chair, and settled in. Exhausted, I dozed off in record time.

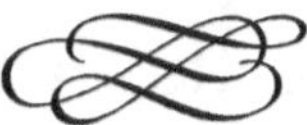

CHAPTER 14

Nights in Spokane were still chilly in late March. I pulled my jacket tighter around me as we all hurried toward Franklin's limo.

"Welcome to Spokane," I said, smiling at Ada Lynn as we climbed in and chose our seats. Charles closed our doors and slipped into the front seat next to the driver.

"Never in my lifetime did I think I would get to see Washington, fly in a private plane, or ride in a limo. I always wanted to see Idaho and Oregon, too. Maybe even Montana," she said, excitement in her features.

"I know we can get you to Idaho. And who knows, maybe the girls will take a road trip, and we'll take you to Oregon and Montana," I suggested.

"Just the girls?" Hendrix asked, closing the door behind him.

"Son, it means the guys stay home and watch football on TV while the ladies have some time alone without us," Franklin explained.

"Oh," Hendrix said, his shoulders slumping. "Well, guess we'll have to plan two trips then, because if I've seen those places before, I don't remember shit." His voice trailed off, fear flickering through his eyes.

"We'll take you, Hendrix," I promised. "Maybe after we all settle in, I can even take you to the college campus."

His face lit up. "That would be great. I don't want to stay in the house all the time. I need to see as much as I can, places I went to every day, routes I drove, and hope like hell it will spark my brain into working again."

"Babe, your brain is working, it's just overwhelmed. You'll remember, try not to stress too much." It took me a second to realize I'd called him babe. I cringed. "Sorry, I meant Hendrix."

I had no idea if I'd upset him when I called him babe. Other than the short time we'd listened to music together on the flight home, he'd only had two facial expressions. Serious or grim. I missed his laugh, but every time my thoughts went down a dark road, I reined them back in with the fact that he was alive and awake. Maybe it would help if I counted the positive things.

"I'll try to look at it that way. Thanks." Hendrix slumped into his seat and stared out the tinted window. Since it was late, the city lights broke through the darkness. I peered out the window myself, secretly grateful I was back in Spokane, but this time, I had everyone I loved with me.

The limo pulled off US 2 East and onto Interstate 90 East.

"I'm in new territory," I said to Franklin. "Where are we?"

"I live off of 5-Mile Road. My property is a little over fifteen acres."

"Oh, you weren't kidding about space," I said. "It'll be nice to take some walks."

"There's still snow there right now."

"Snow?" Ada Lynn said, stunned. "I've never seen snow."

I gasped. "What? You've never told me this. Have you not ever left Louisiana?"

Ada Lynn shook her head. "Not until today."

"Holy crap," Mac said. "Well Miss Ada, do we have a new world to show you."

"I'm actually excited," she said. "Thank you again, Franklin, for helping Gemma, and I stay safe. Not to mention giving us a place to live."

"The house gets lonely sometimes, so I'm looking forward to having people with me again."

Ten minutes later, after making our way down the longest driveway I'd ever seen, we pulled up in front of a mansion that literally left me breathless. At least what I could see of it in the dark. Spotlights illuminated the circular drive and enormous double front doors. My mouth gaped open like an idiot, then I peeked in Hendrix's direction. He was seeing it for the first time, too.

"Do you clean that?" Hendrix asked Franklin, his eyes growing large.

I couldn't help but laugh.

"No, son, that's why I have a staff. I don't cook, either. But it's well after midnight, so they're gone until tomorrow."

"Oh dear," Ada Lynn said, while Mac opened the door. "I might miss that. Maybe I can twist your arm to let me cook sometimes."

"Ohmigosh, her crawdads are delicious," Mac said, rubbing her tummy.

Franklin smiled. "I'm sure Ruby wouldn't

mind. I'll work something out for you," he assured Ada Lynn as she beamed at him.

I couldn't take my eyes off the house. Mac hadn't been joking. It was huge.

Charles exited the limo and entered the house first while we waited in the warm car for him to return.

"What's he doing?" Hendrix asked Mac.

Mac's face fell. Each time he asked a question he should know the answer to, it was a horrible reminder of the situation.

"When Franklin's gone for longer than a day or two, Charles inspects the house for any signs of intruders. I mean, no one needs to worry, nothing has ever happened, but I think it's just what he does."

My forehead creased with concern. The longer I was around Franklin, the more I realized his life was more complicated than I initially believed.

"Alright, come on in. The driver will bring in your luggage." Franklin opened the door and motioned us inside. "I'll take your jackets."

Ada Lynn and I slipped them off and handed them to him. He opened an enormous coat closet and hung them up.

I stood stupidly in the foyer, unable to

move. Taking Ada Lynn's hand, we both stared at the white and black swirled marble that not only graced the entrance but expanded down the hallway for as far as I could see. Large decorative pillars marked the opening of a formal dining room to the left, and a more casual living area was to our right.

"Let's get everyone some food. Ruby made a lasagna, so I'll heat it up."

Dazed, I followed everyone down the long hallway, past the winding staircase that led upstairs, and into the kitchen. I wasn't sure how Hendrix or Ada Lynn were feeling, but I was afraid to touch anything. Pristine didn't even cover it.

"Whoa," Hendrix said, strolling into the kitchen.

"Look at the stove," I whispered to Ada Lynn. "You can cook on five burners!"

Dark brownstone covered the wall and accented the stove and oven, and the dark cabinets complimented the tan marble countertops. The large stainless-steel refrigerator took up most of the wall. I could have fit three standard sized fridges inside it.

"Mac, I'm going to get some dinner ready for

everyone, why don't you show them to their rooms upstairs?"

"Franklin, I don't think Ada Lynn can take the stairs. Do you have anything on the main floor?" I asked, concerned.

"Of course. Please forgive me, I'm a bit tired and wasn't thinking." He gave us a warm smile. "My room and another large guest room are on this floor. I'd meant for Ada Lynn to have that one. Mac knows where it is."

For the first time I'd ever seen it, Ada Lynn blushed.

"I don't want to be a bother," she said softly.

"Don't even think like that. You and Gemma are family," Franklin said quickly.

"Yup, and not another word," Mac said, slipping her arm through Ada Lynn's. "Let's take you to yours first." She turned to Hendrix, who stood quietly next to Franklin. "Come on bro," she waved at him.

He nodded, and we walked out of the kitchen, through the formal dining room, and to the other side of the enormous house.

"Here ya go Miss Ada Lynn," Mac said, waving her hand in front of the light. "It detects motion, so all you need to do is walk in."

"Holy cow," I muttered. "Is the fireplace real?"

The same stone that was in the kitchen surrounded the fireplace in here, providing a comfy
and rustic look.

"Yeah," Mac said, walking over and flipping a
switch. "It's gas. No fuss. No mess." She grinned.
"The bathroom is there," she said, pointing.

My gaze swept the room that was almost as
large as Ada Lynn's house back in Louisiana, and
my feet sank into the plush beige carpet as I followed Mac. A king-sized four-poster bed was positioned in the middle of the room and a
matching dresser on the right. Multiple full-
length windows with blackout shades lined the
far wall. It was by far the most beautiful home I'd
ever been in. A full-sized couch sat in the corner
along with a reading table. I was pretty sure,
other than a refrigerator, Ada Lynn would have
everything she needed right here.

"Oh, and here's a phone next to the bed so you
can call us upstairs." Mac flashed a grin at her.

"I need to get her a cell phone, now. At least
she can talk to text if needed. I don't want you to
feel too far away," I said, squeezing her arm.

Tears welled up in Ada Lynn's eyes. "This is
too much. I don't know how to repay Franklin,"
she said, patting her chest.

"Um, not sure you need to repay him. I think

he's doing alright in the money department," Hendrix responded. I'd been so focused on the room and Ada Lynn, I almost forgot he was behind us in the doorway.

I smiled at him.

"Ada Lynn, I have your suitcase," Charles said from behind Hendrix.

Hendrix jumped, his face draining of color.

"Charles, you can't sneak up on the good guys," I said, rushing over to Hendrix. I rubbed his arm and took Ada Lynn's luggage. My focus traveled over Charles. He'd removed his sunglasses, and for the first time, I was able to see his deep brown eyes. His gaze fell on me, and for a split second, I felt as if something inside us connected. He averted his attention quickly, apologized to Hendrix for startling him, and left.

Although Charles sneaking up on anyone was enough to give them heart failure, I'd never seen anything or anyone shake Hendrix. A pang of fear traveled through me. How were we supposed to help him remember how strong and powerful he was when we weren't allowed to give him details of his life before the accident?

I placed the suitcase on the bed.

"Are you okay to get settled in while we go upstairs? If not, you can call me if you need anything." I nodded at the phone. "Apparently Charles lurks around, too, and I'm pretty sure he'll help if you need him."

"Ruby and Emilia will be back tomorrow," Mac chimed in. "Emilia is the housekeeper, and she's super awesome. You'll have plenty of help when you need it."

"Thank you. I'll be fine. I'm eager to get settled in and get some food."

"I'll be back down in a little bit," I said, kissing her cheek.

Mac led Hendrix and I out of the room and up the grand staircase. I ran my fingers along the mahogany, allowing myself to feel the luxury. The same plush carpet covered each stair and the long hallway.

Mac stopped and waved her hand in one of the rooms that was closest to the stairway.

"Game room," she said.

Hendrix and I glanced at each other and poked our heads in.

Three black, oversized leather couches took up most of the room, along with an entire wall of bookshelves filled with games and movies. A pool table was to the right and a foosball table near it. I gulped, the memories of the night with Alexander rushing back. Maybe Hendrix would teach me to play pool … if he remembered how.

"I think I could spend some time in here," he said, his tone full of awe.

"Oh, we will," Mac assured. "I used to kick your ass in Grand Theft Auto."

Hendrix arched his brow.

"It's a PS4 game. I'll teach you, no worries." Sadness flickered across her expression, then she continued down the hall.

"Here's a bathroom, but each bedroom has a full bath and a huge walk-in closet."

We nodded and followed. She stopped at a room on the left side of the hall.

"Gemma, this is yours." As she stepped inside, the light flickered to life.

Once again, I found myself speechless while I tried to wrap my mind around my new living space. A king-sized bed with a plush cream-colored bedspread and a half dozen pillows propped against the cherry wood headboard. The dresser and TV stand all matched the bed. Three windows provided a view I suspected would be breathtaking during the daylight. The closet was as large as my childhood bedroom, and the bathroom included a vanity area, a whirlpool tub, a massive walk-in shower, and dual sinks. I wondered if I owned enough products to even cover a quarter of the counter space.

"This bed is soooo comfy and definitely big enough for like five people," she said, giggling and bouncing up and down on it. "Not that I recommend that you share your bed with anyone other than myself and Hendrix of course. I mean, I don't think you would because you're not into one nighters, but they do happen, and..." Mac's rambling slowed, and my attention landed on Hendrix.

Usually, he'd just tell her to hush, but he stood awkwardly near the bed and shoved his hands in his pockets.

"You don't like to have casual...sex?" he asked, clearing his throat and looking at me.

The possibilities that might be running through his mind right now were endless. I'd totally be up for a night with him in my bed, but it wouldn't mean anything if his heart wasn't in it. I wanted all of him, and not for one night.

"I don't," I confirmed.

"Nope, she's only been with you, bro."

I cringed. "Mac," I whisper-yelled at her. "Not now."

"Sorry," she said, glancing at the both of us. "Well, Hendrix, you'll have your old room. I don't think it's changed much since you moved out after Kendra … died." The last word was a whisper.

I frowned, and my heart skidded to a halt. Hendrix didn't need to know anything about Kendra at this point.

His brows knitted together.

"Kendra? Was she a girlfriend or something? I mean, obviously before you," he motioned toward me.

Mac opened her mouth to reply, and in one swift movement, I stepped in front of her, cutting off her response.

"Yeah, it was a while ago, though," I said.

"Off we go," Mac piped in from behind me. She grabbed Hendrix's wrist and led us down the hallway. She peered over her shoulder at me and mouthed thank you. I nodded. I suspected we would have to cover a lot for each other.

Stepping into Hendrix's childhood bedroom gave me a significant glimpse into who he was before we'd ever met. It was almost nostalgic. His room was painted a dark beige, with a navy-blue accent wall. A keyboard and a few different types of guitars were situated in the corner. A large oak desk sat next to it. He also had a king size bed with a matching dresser, and a large TV was mounted on the wall.

He strolled cautiously to the keyboard and placed a hand on the keys. Mac and I stood silently, waiting for what he would do next. Hendrix flipped the power button on and played the middle C. Since he had his back to us, I couldn't see his facial expression, only the tension in his shoulders. He positioned both hands on the keyboard and slowly began to play. I shot a look at Mac, and she crossed her fingers.

Hendrix's voice was so soft I almost couldn't hear him. I stepped closer, holding my breath as he grew louder. My hand flew to my mouth while he continued to sing "Church with No Ceiling" by Lostboycrow.

Mac tapped my arm, unwilling to interrupt him. I knew she had questions, but I needed to hear him sing. Tears pricked the back of my eyes, and I remained rooted in place until he was finished. He ran a hand over his hair and turned back toward us.

"How would I know that?" he asked, puzzled.

"It was...it was the first song you ever shared with me."

"Oh shit, that's amazing!" Mac screeched.

Hendrix cringed at her volume, and I broke

into giggles. I wondered if the look on my face had been similar the first time I met her.

Mac dashed across the room and threw her arms around him. A startled Hendrix stared at me helplessly.

I grinned. "Hug her back," I mouthed.

He did as I suggested, and then he closed his eyes and held onto his sister. My heart soared right out of my chest. This was good. The music and his hug with Mac were all a good sign. But did I dare hope he was coming back to us?

Mac let go and flashed us a grin.

"My turn!" she said, clapping her hands together. She bolted out of the room and turned right.

Hendrix and I hung back a few steps, our gazes locking.

"Welcome home," I said.

He smiled gently, then made his way in the direction of Mac's voice. I laughed when we arrived in her room. She was full on jumping on her bed. Her braided pigtails flew up in the air as she giggled.

"Ohmigosh. I totally forgot how fun this room was. Hendrix, you and I used to jump on my bed together when we were younger."

A grin eased across his face while he watched her.

"I'd tell you to come jump with me, but we weigh a little more than we did back then, and I'm pretty sure Franklin would not be happy if the first night we were back home, I broke the bed. And no offense, but I can so think of a better way to break a bed," she said breathlessly, continuing to jump.

It was evident that Mac had been a lot younger when she'd lived here. Her walls were pale pink with white furniture. A large pile of stuffed animals filled the corner of the room. A TV was mounted over a white matching desk. Blackout shades covered the windows, and light wispy curtains flowed from the ceiling to the floor. It was a dream bedroom for a little girl.

She landed on her butt and bounced on the bed for a second.

"So, as you can see, we have the top floor just for us. Which means games, movies, late nights in each other's bedroom. It's an ongoing slumber party." She bounced off the bed and landed on her feet. She flung her arms up, proud of her dismount.

I couldn't help but laugh. It was so good to see her happy and for us all to be together.

"I'm starved! I'll meet you downstairs."

With that, she bolted out of the bedroom, leaving Hendrix and me alone in her room.

"Can I ask you something?" Hendrix asked.

"Sure." I knew there would be a ton of questions, but with each one, I found myself holding my breath. Would it be good or bad?

"Mac, she talks a lot."

I grinned at him.

"Yeah, she has ADHD, which stands for Attention Deficit Hyperactivity Disorder. She blurts shit out without thinking, she has more energy than the sun, and she can dance on my last nerve." I paused. "But she is the most loyal person I've met other than you. She has a big heart and loves you more than her own life. You, of all people, know how to help her manage her ADHD, too."

"Me?" he asked, incredulous. "Not sure how I pulled that one off. She's a handful."

"Yeah, but I wouldn't have it any other way."

"How did you two meet?"

"She was my roomie at college."

"Oh, shit."

I barked out a laugh. "That's pretty much how I felt at first, but then she became my best friend."

"Got it. Is she how we met?"

A thick ball of sadness swirled inside me.

"No. I didn't even realize you and she were step brother and sister."

His shoulders slumped forward. "You can't tell me, can you?"

Suddenly, the urge to close the gap between us and kiss him was so strong, I wasn't sure if I could stop myself. Being alone with him wasn't a good idea. I willed myself to take a step backward.

"Hopefully you'll remember soon. But for now, why don't we get some food?"

He nodded, and we made our way back downstairs.

CHAPTER 15

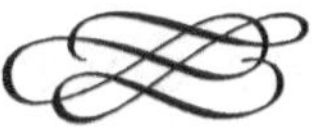

Ruby's lasagna was amazing. Each bite had literally melted in my mouth. After we had all eaten dinner, I walked Ada Lynn to her bedroom and told her goodnight. It was after two in the morning, which meant it was after five a.m. in Louisiana. Hopefully we would all sleep-in tomorrow morning.

I wasn't sure where Mac and Hendrix were, but I slowly made my way up the stairs toward my new room. With each step, the exhaustion grew heavier and heavier. Reaching the top of the stairs, I practically dragged myself to Mac's room. Her door was partly open, and I knocked lightly.

"Yeah?" she asked.

I opened the door and gave her a tired smile.

"I wanted to say goodnight," I said, stifling a yawn.

"Night bestie. I think Hendrix made some progress earlier," she said quietly.

"I hope so." I folded my arms across my chest and leaned against the doorframe. "I guess we'll see what happens tomorrow."

"Yeah. Get some sleep."

"You too," I said, and closed her door behind me.

My shoes didn't make a sound as I padded down the hallway, pausing for a second outside Hendrix's door. My chest tightened, and unshed tears stung my eyes. I wanted to go into his room and crawl into bed with him. I inhaled sharply and continued to my room. Before I rounded the corner, I waved my hand inside it, so the light would turn on. Frowning, I turned back toward Mac's. I needed to know how to turn the sensor off so it wouldn't turn on every time I rolled over in bed. The light would definitely wake me.

I halted when my attention landed on Hendrix. He stood outside his doorway, watching me. His deep blue eyes stared holes straight into my soul. My attention traveled from his bare, muscular chest to his ripped abs that disappeared beneath the sweatpants that hung seriously low on his hips. Heat shot through me, my core throbbing with need. Without a word, he slipped inside his room. I clutched the wall, trying to calm myself from a hormone overload. He looked dangerously sexy, and I wanted him. Bad.

I hurried down the hall in the direction of Mac's bedroom. She would be the only thing that kept me from barging into Hendrix's room and jumping him.

"Mac," I said, knocking on her door.

"Open," she hollered.

I hurried in and closed the door behind me.

"You okay?" she asked, sitting up on her bed.

"Yeah," I said breathlessly. "Hendrix...he," I choked on my words, "wasn't wearing much," I said wide-eyed.

Mac laughed and patted the bed next to her.

"Girl, it sucks ass when you need some and you can't get any."

I grimaced and sat next to her.

"First, how do I turn off the bedroom light so it doesn't come on all night?"

"Easy, there's another switch to turn it off. It's on the wall plate. Second?" she asked.

"I don't know how to deal with being this close to him and unable to touch him," I said, my pitch climbing along with my anxiety.

"Not sure how to help there. Maybe get a vibrator."

I could literally feel myself blush. "What? No. No way, it's Hendrix or nothing."

"Seriously? Like, you won't stroke the kitty while you wait for him?"

My hands covered my face, and I flung myself backward. Oh. My. God. I'd never talked about my sex life, and here she was suggesting I get myself off.

"Mac, some stuff is private," I said, peeking at her through my fingers.

"Fuck. I've never seen your cheeks so damned red before. I really didn't mean to embarrass you, but if you decide you need some artificial relief, I'll take you shopping. We have an Adam and Eve store in town. Besides, you could get a few fun things for you and Hendrix for when he 'comes' around." She laughed hysterically at her own joke while I stared at her absolutely mortified.

I stood up and walked over to her window.

"Never in my wildest dreams did I think we would be here," I said, scanning the darkness outside. My eyes landed on a long structure, its floor to ceiling windows illuminated with soft outdoor lighting. "A pool?"

"Indoor," she replied. "Franklin's a big swimmer."

My attention traveled across the property as a light flickered to life.

"Is that another house?" I asked, squinting to see better.

"It's where Charles lives."

I spun around and crawled back on her bed. Apparently I was too full of questions to sleep right now.

"Who is he? Holy hell, Mac. He's not just a driver. You have to know that, right?"

Mac shrugged. "Yeah, and he's been with Franklin since last fall. Charles goes everywhere Franklin does."

"But why would Franklin need a bodyguard?"

"Gemma, all the seriously rich guys have them. People are fucking crazy. They'll kidnap your kids or whatever else they think of to get access to your money."

"So Franklin isn't doing anything illegal? I mean, how did he get so rich?" I blushed at my boldness. "I'm sorry, I didn't mean to imply he was doing something wrong."

"No, it's fine. I get it. I would be wondering the same damn thing. As far as I know, he's on the up and up. Remember when I told you that while he was a total lush, he still had his money working for him? Well, he was already super comfy in the financial world, but then his investments made him some mad money. What investments or who he worked with? I don't know, other than..." Her words trailed off. "Other than with Asher's dad. I know they've had multiple business deals that have turned to gold for both of them."

"Yeah, I remember you talked about it when we lived in the dorm." I hesitated before I asked my next question. "You've not mentioned Asher since the day you showed up on my porch steps in Louisiana."

Mac closed her eyes. "I'll fill you in eventually, just not yet if that's okay. And as far as Jeremiah goes, I think you were right."

I frowned at her. "What do you mean?"

"I'm a very passionate person in case you haven't noticed."

I smiled at her. It was an understatement, but this wasn't the time to tease her about it.

"I can get so caught up in the moment, I can't see anything else, and I get pissed when the people in my life try and tell me I'm headed for trouble. It's like I can't wrap my brain around the possible consequences. You tried to tell me, and I refused to listen."

I sat up straight. "I never wanted to hurt you. Ever," I said gently.

"I know, and I won't give you a line of bullshit. My heart hurts, but I'm pissed at myself for rushing into the relationship with Jeremiah. Because..." She took a deep breath and let out a huff. "Because not one single day went by that I didn't think about Asher." She searched my face for my reaction.

"Mac, I wished you'd told me. I could have helped."

She shook her head and jumped off the bed, pacing back and forth across her large room.

"Bestie, don't take offense, but you couldn't help me with shit. Andrea had thrown a serious wrench into yours and Hendrix's relationship. Your mom had just died, your dad beat you and broke your ribs, and the second time he would have killed you if Hendrix and Ada Lynn hadn't gotten to you in time. Ada Lynn nearly died of a heart attack. And to top it all off, you found out your own father, the man who was supposed to protect you, arranged your rape. You. Were. A. Fucking. Mess."

"What?" Hendrix's voice came from Mac's bedroom door.

Mac halted, her eyes wide. I spun around on the bed and saw anguish and disbelief clouding his expression.

"How much did you hear?" I asked, my fingers digging into the comforter. I was afraid to hear his answer.

His eyes traveled from me to Mac and back to me. A cold shiver moved up and down my spine.

"All of it." He held up his hands, stepped back into the hall, then disappeared.

A cry escaped me, and Mac made a beeline out of the room after him.

CHAPTER 16

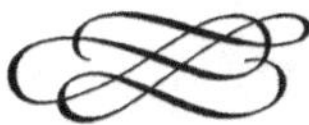

I sat on the edge of my new bed and attempted to hear Hendrix and Mac talking, but the walls in Franklin's house were too thick. Mac and I had been so deep in conversation, we'd not realized he'd been standing in the doorway. He may not have gotten the full picture, but what he'd heard gave him at least some insight into every horrible thing I'd lived through in the last several months. No way would he want to have anything to do with me now.

I closed the blackout shades, curled up in bed, and cried myself to sleep.

My eyes fluttered open, and I shot up in bed. Squinting into the darkness, the red glow of the alarm clock told me it was after 3 p.m.

"Holy hell," I muttered, flopping back into my bed. The blackout shades did a great job, but it was hard to tell whether it was day or night out in the real world. I willed myself to get up and flung the covers off me. Reaching toward the nightstand, I flipped the lamp on and rubbed my forehead. No matter how much I wanted to hide, Ada Lynn still needed me. I'd slept almost the entire day, and my muscles screamed with stiffness while I stood and stretched. I'd been so exhausted last night that I'd not unpacked. My suitcase was still next to the dresser where Charles had put it. He had no idea how much I appreciated him.

Thirty minutes later, I was showered and dressed. I stepped into the well-lit hallway, and my bare feet padded to Mac's room, but she wasn't there. Hendrix's door was also open, so I assumed he wasn't there, either. I sure as hell wasn't going to look for him after last night.

The growl in my stomach broke through the silence as I entered the kitchen. This is what I got for sleeping so long. Eyeing the fridge, I opened it and scanned the contents. Grapes. It would work for now. I grabbed a small bunch and shut the door.

I screamed as a short, robust, gray-haired woman stared at me.

"Who are you and what are you doing in my kitchen?" She glared at me while she placed her hands on her hips. Then, she broke into laughter. "What do you want to eat, Gemma?" she asked, grinning.

I stood rooted in place. She had scared the shit out of me.

"I can make you breakfast or a light snack instead. Dinner is at six, and I have a roast in the oven. I guess it depends on how hungry you are." She walked to the other side of the kitchen and peered into the stove.

My stomach growled as the aroma of the meat reached my nose. "I don't want you to have to cook for me. I can make some pancakes or something if you would be so kind as to point me in the right direction."

Her nose crinkled at me. "Sit down, you're not cooking anything. I can make you pancakes, or I'm happy to whip up some French toast and eggs."

"Ohh," I said, smiling. "That sounds phenomenal. I'm starved."

"You got it. I'll have it ready in about ten minutes. In the meantime, Mr. Franklin asked me to send you to his office when I saw you."

"Okay? Um, where is his office?" Dread tugged at me. It was almost like being called into the principal's office in grade school.

"Through the family room, then turn left down the hall," she replied, grabbing a skillet and bowl. "Tell him Ruby said you have ten minutes, or your food will be cold."

Sure, I would tell Franklin precisely what to do in his own house. Apparently Ruby was quite comfortable here.

"I'll be right back."

I followed Ruby's instructions and knocked on a door to what I hoped was Franklin's office. The door opened, and Franklin ushered me in as he finished his phone call.

"Yeah. Thanks. I appreciate the update."

He hung up the phone and sat down behind his desk.

"Have a seat."

Feeling a bit uncomfortable, I did as he asked.

"How'd you sleep?"

"Fine, the bedroom is great, thank you."

"Mac took Hendrix and Ada Lynn out for a while. It's a good opportunity for Ada Lynn to see

Spokane as well as to test the waters with Hendrix's memories."

I nodded. "That's good."

"Mac told me about last night, Gemma."

I slid down in my seat, Hendrix's expression when he overheard our conversation flashing through my mind.

"After speaking with Hendrix...I think it's best that you keep your distance for a few days and let him settle in as much as possible. It really messed him up last night."

I pinched the bridge of my nose, attempting to keep my emotions under control. How could this have happened?

"What? He doesn't want to talk to me?"

"I didn't say that. I'm telling you to give him a few days. He didn't ask for them, but he asked a lot of questions I couldn't answer. He needs some rest instead of trying to save the world. That part of him hasn't changed."

Chewing my lower lip, I tried to control the tears that appeared, anyway.

"Gemma, it's going to be alright. All I'm asking is for you to give him some space, and let's see how he does."

"Sure. I understand." But I didn't. How was me staying away from Hendrix going to help bring him back to us?

"Dinner is at six."

I frowned. "How am I supposed to give him space if we have to eat dinner at the same table?"

"You won't need to worry about it tonight. I'm taking the kids out. Ruby is cooking for you and Ada Lynn."

"Oh," I mumbled. All of a sudden, I saw exactly where I stood. No matter what Franklin had said, we weren't family. But now, at least I knew my place.

"Thanks," I said, standing. "I'll keep my distance."

Franklin nodded and returned his attention to the papers on his desk. I closed the door behind me and sulked on my way back to the kitchen. Ruby had my food waiting for me in the dining room, and I sat down alone at the table for ten. Picking at my food, I couldn't ignore the overwhelming feeling of loneliness.

DINNER TIME ARRIVED, and I meandered into the dining room again. I'd never been so happy to see Ada Lynn in my life.

"Hi," I said, smiling and sitting next to her while Ruby began serving us.

"Isn't it strange to have someone cook and bring our food to us?" Ada Lynn asked after Ruby left the room.

"Yeah, very. But tell me about your day. Did you have a good time? What did you see?"

I nibbled on my roast and vegetables as she described downtown Spokane and the Little Spokane River. It sounded like Charles drove them all over the city, and then they headed north toward Deer Park.

"It was beautiful," she said, taking another bite of her dinner. "Charles stopped the car and Mac, Hendrix, and I all stomped through the snow. Hendrix was as wide-eyed as I was. The snow was so cold and fluffy," she said laughing.

"I wish I could have gone. I'm just not feeling very well. I think after Hendrix's coma, Carl's attack, and Kyle walking free, I'm done. I'm exhausted, Ada Lynn."

Concern filled her face, and she patted my cheek.

"We're safe. Take some alone time to recharge, but I do expect to see you every day. If not, I'll send Mac up to get you."

"That's fair. I think I'm going to finish eating and maybe watch some TV in my new room."

"You and me both. I'll have to acclimate myself to the time so I don't miss my news."

"Yeah, the time change will take a bit to get used to, but you will."

Ada Lynn continued to tell me about her day as we both finished our meal. It seemed like it had been months since I'd had real food. I didn't count all the takeout we'd eaten while Hendrix was in the hospital. And even though Ruby had just fed me a couple hours ago, I was still ravenous.

I walked Ada Lynn to her room, kissed her on the cheek, then made my way back upstairs. The silence was nearly deafening.

Flipping on the light switch, I entered my bedroom and closed the door behind me. If Mac wanted to hang out later, I planned on acting like I was asleep. I wasn't in the mood for company tonight.

I didn't feel like I belonged, but I unpacked anyway. I grabbed my laptop and got situated at the desk. It hummed to life, and I opened Google, but it only greeted me with a 'this page can't be displayed' message.

Groaning, I texted Mac for the internet password. Regardless of where I was, I still had a college class to finish. Thank God the professor hadn't cared when the work was completed as long as it was all in by the end of the term.

My phone buzzed with the information I needed, and I logged in. First I searched Kyle Thompson, Louisiana. Article after article filled my screen. Not only had he made local news, but he'd also made national news.

Anger swirled deep inside me, and my chest ached. I hoped every one of the motherfuckers were caught and sentenced.

After a few hours of research and homework, I stood and glanced out my window. It was a little after ten pm, and I realized I'd not been outside once today. Suddenly, the air inside the house suffocated me. I located my winter coat, tossed on my tennis shoes, and opened my bedroom door. Quietly, I pulled it shut behind me and crept down the hallway.

"Where are you going?" Hendrix asked from behind me.

I turned slowly and held my finger up to my mouth. I hoped he would remember it meant to be quiet, but I wasn't sure. He sauntered in my direction, his attention traveling down my body and back to my face again.

"Where are you going?" he asked again, his voice barely above a whisper.

"Out. Don't wait up."

Hendrix frowned, but he let me go.

The front door chimed when I stepped outside. It hadn't dawned on me that Franklin had an alarm system. How was I going to get back in without raising suspicion?

"Shit," I said, a puff of cold air forming in the night air. I stepped back inside and made my way to Franklin's office. I suspected he would have work to catch up on after his evening out.

"Hi," I said, poking my head in. "I, uh, well. I need to get some air. I've not been outside since we arrived, but I don't know how to get back into the house without setting off the alarm and scaring everyone."

"Ah, right. Another thing I didn't think about. I'm not used to having visitors." He gave me a warm smile. "We don't need the added drama of the police responding. Plus Charles would have you pinned to the ground in seconds." He paused and scribbled something down on a piece of paper. "Here's the code to the door in the back of the kitchen. It also works for the pool house. When I can't sleep, I go for a swim. There's a full gym in there as well...weights, cardio equipment, punching bag, and more."

"Thanks," I said, shoving the paper into my front pocket. I didn't even own a swimsuit. I would have to talk to Mac about buying one later.

Franklin leaned back in his chair and surveyed me.

"Are you alright, Gemma? I didn't mean to hurt you when I asked if you would give Hendrix some space, but I'm afraid I did. It wasn't my intention at all. I'm just trying to keep us all together. Intact as one family unit. It's hard sometimes to know the right thing to do."

"A family unit?" I asked, my voice hitching.

"Yeah, I meant what I said. You're family. I'm sorry if I made you feel otherwise. Right now, and probably forever, I'll need time alone with Hendrix and Mac, but that doesn't mean you're not a part of us."

Relief flooded through me. Franklin shuffled some papers on his desk and sighed. "He asked about you tonight at dinner."

"Oh," I said, my heart dropping into the pit of my stomach. After what he'd overheard, this couldn't be good.

"He asked if you were okay since he hadn't seen you all day."

"He asked about me? Shouldn't he be concerned about himself?"

"That's just it, Gemma. It's why I asked you to give him a few days. Despite his amnesia, I don't think he can keep himself from caring about you."

Finally, I understood. Franklin wasn't being a cold-hearted asshole, he was doing the best he could in the middle of a shitstorm.

"I'll try to give him some space. I'll ask Mac if she wants to go shopping with me tomorrow, which will get me out of the house. I don't own a swimsuit or any workout clothes, so maybe we can have some girl time."

"I think she would love that. You two need to stick together. You're good for her. Hell, Gemma, you're good for all of us. You're our inspiration."

I stood there staring at him completely dumbfounded.

"How in the world could I be anyone's inspiration, Franklin?"

His brow furrowed. "Gemma, you walked through hell and back, and you're still standing. You're not just inspirational, you're a hero. Do you realize you single-handedly took down your attacker and sent him to jail? There's no telling how many young women's futures you saved."

Shit. It had never dawned on me.

"I hadn't thought about it like that," I said, Chaos and memories slammed into me, and I clung to Franklin's encouraging words.

"You've not had any real time to process yet, but as you do, I'm here for you."

"Thanks for the door code," I said, overwhelmed with our conversation and suddenly needing some space. "I'm going to get some fresh air and explore a little bit."

"I have motion lights all around the house but stay nearby and in the well-lit areas. Coyotes and cougars are common up here."

I yelped. "Cougars?"

"I've never seen one, but I've seen the tracks, so just be aware."

"Got it."

Backing out of his office, I pondered how badly I needed some fresh air. After weighing his words, I decided to go anyway.

Now that Franklin knew I was heading outside, there was no need for me to tiptoe around. But if Mac heard me, she would want to come, too. I needed some time alone, so I made my way quietly to the kitchen.

Slipping out of the kitchen door, I tested the code and opened it again. The last thing I needed was to lock myself out and have to call Mac or

Franklin to let me back in the house, but at least I had options in case of an emergency.

The crisp air filled my lungs as I tilted my head up to the crystal-clear night sky and gazed in wonder at the blanket of brilliant stars. I scanned the area, noting the large patio, the outdoor furniture obviously still stored away. Clumps of snow were piled up on the edge of the concrete and along a walkway. The motion lights turned on, allowing me to see better. I inhaled deeply and shoved my hands into my coat pockets. My heart pounded with every step I took.

I meandered past the pool house, the garages, and down the hill. I'd stepped away from the floodlights, and only small decorative solar lights lined my path. Suddenly, Franklin's warning about cougars roaming the property seemed like a genuine possibility. Without further thought, I took off in a full run. My eyes had adjusted to the darkness, but the light from the small house at the bottom of the hill helped me see. Hopefully I wouldn't trip and face plant before I arrived.

Chills shot through me as I reached my destination. I glanced over my shoulder at Franklin's house, but I didn't think anyone had seen me.

What in the hell was I about to do? I held my breath and knocked on the door.

CHAPTER 17

Alert, brown eyes stared at me.

"You shouldn't be here," Charles said.

"No shit. Nice to see you, too," I shot back defensively. "But it's dark, and I'm freezing. Please, can I come in?"

He hesitated for a minute, looked me up and down, and then opened the door.

"Why are you here?"

Apparently manners weren't his strong suit. I shed my coat and held onto it. Honestly, I was surprised he'd even let me in the door. But there'd been a connection between us. He might deny it, but it was there. I was sure of it.

"Because..." I swallowed. "I need your help,

Charles. Please. You have no idea how hard it was to show up here tonight."

He tilted his head and walked away. This was the first time I'd seen him in jeans and a sweater. The dude was huge, not to mention hot. He easily cleared six three, and if I'd not seen it myself, I would take bets his shoulders wouldn't fit through a door frame.

He sauntered into the kitchen and pulled out a leather bar stool for me. I hung my coat on the back and crawled into the seat.

"Coffee? Tea? Hot chocolate?"

I grinned, and my anxiety calmed down a bit. A few months ago, I would have never even considered knocking on a guy's door I barely knew.

"Hot chocolate sounds great."

He raised an eyebrow at me. "Figured."

"What? That I'm a hot chocolate kind of person?"

I wasn't sure, but I could have sworn I saw him crack a small grin.

He made my drink and leaned against the black granite counter on the other side of his kitchen. If I had been in any other guy's place, I would have expected it to be messy, but not with Charles. His place was spotless. The only thing on the counter was a stainless-steel coffee maker. I almost wanted to spill something to make it look lived in. Did this guy have a life other than working for Franklin?

"Damn, this is good," I said, sipping it.

"You shouldn't be here. If Franklin catches wind of it, I could lose my job. How old are you, anyway?"

I choked on my cocoa. "I'm legal Charles, it's okay. I'll be twenty in a few months."

He nodded and folded his arms across his massive chest, pinning me with his brown eyes.

"How old are you?" I asked, fumbling for something to say before I got to the real reason I was here.

"Twenty-six."

"Oh geez, I thought you were in your thirties. It must be the consistent stoic expression you wear." Shit, I was nervous and rambling. Maybe Mac had finally worn off on me.

"You have ten seconds to tell me why you're here, or I'm walking you back to the main house."

I stared at him, my rehearsed words disappearing from my mind. This guy was all business.

"Ten, nine, eight, seven," he started counting.

Shit.

"Six, five."

This dude was for real.

"Four, three, two."

"I need you to teach me some self-defense techniques," I finally blurted out. I rubbed my face and straightened my shoulders. "Charles, you were there when Carl nearly raped me again. It was pure luck I'd been able to grab Hendrix's lamp. I...I don't know how to protect myself, and I'm scared all the time. I was about to ask Hendrix to teach me, but then he got hurt. I don't know who else to ask. Plus I have no idea if Kyle will show up, and there's this rapist on the college campus...I...dammit, please. Help me," I pleaded.

Charles moved across the kitchen in four steps. He placed his hands on the countertop and leaned toward me. His face a mere inch from mine. I stopped breathing, my entire body tight with tension.

"What rapist?" he growled.

"Brandon Montgomery," I whispered, leaning back a little. "I got away from him, but he also raped one of Mac's friends. I'm scared to go back to school because of him." My body trembled with my words. I had just bared my soul to an almost stranger. But Charles had seen me in action when he burst in as I was taking down Carl. He told me he knew I was a fighter. He was also the only person I could turn to with this request and know I would be in safe hands.

A flicker of anger flashed across his expression.

Even though my insides had turned to mush when I shared my secret, I held his gaze. I wouldn't apologize for showing up on his doorstep and asking for help.

He straightened and ran his hand over his short hair.

"I have my concerns," he began. "First, this needs to be kept quiet. I don't want to lose my job. Second, if I train you...there will be contact. I'll be close to you and vice versa."

My heart stuttered.

"What do you mean?" I asked, my tone climbing in pitch.

"Some techniques I can teach you without physical contact, but others I'll need to touch you."

I hadn't thought about that. Shit. But if Franklin trusted Charles, so did I. Plus I'd seen Charles in motion in Louisiana. There was something about sharing a shitty experience that resulted in a sort of weird bond.

"Show me what you mean by contact then I can really understand. If it's too much for me, I'll walk out of here, and we'll act like we never had this conversation."

"No, I'll walk you back. You're not going alone." He sighed. "Come here."

I hopped off the barstool, approached him, and stopped a few feet away.

"Charles, my gut says I can trust you, but I need to hear it from your lips. You know the worst of my past and what I've faced. Am I safe with you?" My voice trembled.

His attention traveled over me.

"As long as Franklin tells me to, I'll protect your life with mine. You have my word."

"Thank you." I glanced away. Feeling strong and safe had been a rarity in my life. Now I needed to find my inner strength and use it without hesitation.

"Come here," he said softly.

I stepped forward, relieved he was going to help me.

Faster than I could blink, he'd grabbed my shoulders, spun me around, placed his strong hand over my mouth, and pulled me against him. With one arm he'd silenced me, and I couldn't move.

"It's alright," he said, easing his hand from my

mouth, but he continued to pin me against him. I couldn't move my upper body at all.

"This is part of the training," he said, his breath tickling my ear. "I can feel your heart racing inside your chest. You reek of fear. Any predator can smell it a mile away. They look for people like you. Beautiful, petite, shy. I'm not going to let you go yet, but are you alright?"

I nodded, feeling his entire body against mine. It had paralyzed me with fear.

"I'm going to talk you through breaking free from me, now. Focus on my voice."

I listened to his instructions, and in three moves, I'd slipped out of Charles's hold. My legs wobbled, and I stumbled backward, busting my ass on the tile floor.

"This won't work," he said, staring at me.

"What?" I glared at him as I picked myself up. He reached out to give me a hand, but I angrily waved him off. "You know what, Charles? You're right, this was a mistake. I mean how dare I ask the one person who shared the moment when I kicked my rapist's ass for help. What was I thinking?" My words were clipped with white-hot anger. "Fine! Thanks for nothing!" I yelled. Before I realized it, I charged at him, my hands landing on his chest, and shoving as hard as I could. He didn't even wobble. "Fuck you! Fuck you for saving me! Fuck you for not letting me die! And fuck you for not helping me learn to protect myself!"

He quickly snatched my hands off him and held my wrists together with one hand.

"That's the Gemma I need," he said quietly. "You have to deal with the anger in order to tap into your power. We'll start training tomorrow night."

A sob escaped me while he let my hands go.

"Bathroom?" I hiccupped, a full-blown meltdown on its way.

"Second door on the right," he said, pointing to the hall off the kitchen.

I rushed out of the room before my emotions ripped me in two.

AFTER MY CRY FEST, Charles reheated my hot chocolate and made me drink it. An hour later, I slipped my coat on, and we slowly walked back to the house.

"I'm sorry I scared you tonight," he said.

My lips pursed together. "It was shitty of you, but I get it. I don't want to be a target anymore.

How did you end up working for Franklin by the way?" I asked, walking up the large hill.

"It's a long story, but my father used to work for him until he retired."

"Oh, being a badass runs in the family?" I asked, cracking a grin.

"Dad was definitely that."

"Do you have any brothers or sisters?"

"No."

"Ya know, I think we need to slow down this budding relationship between us. I mean, you're so forthcoming with your answers, and a bit pushy."

I stopped in my tracks when Charles actually laughed.

"You're a smartass," he said, smiling.

"And you're human?" I asked, gasping. "I had no idea." I wondered if Charles and I had more in common than I realized. We both hid our real selves from the world.

"My life has been filled with loneliness. After I was raped at fourteen, I refused to leave the house unless my parents forced me to. I'd go to Ada Lynn's next door almost every day, though. She was my best friend until I met Mac. I don't really know you, but I'm taking a wild guess your life gets pretty lonely sometimes, too. Just because you're going to teach me to protect myself doesn't mean we can't be friends."

"We'll see how it goes. I suspect you might hate me before it's all over."

"Hmm, I'll keep that in mind."

"Be ready to have sore muscles and more than a few bruises. At least the weather is still cool enough you can keep them covered and not raise questions."

I nodded, enjoying the cold, fresh air now that I wasn't scared a cougar or coyote would attack me. I might not be able to see it, but I knew he carried a gun.

"What are we going to say if Franklin finds out?" I asked.

"I'll tell him you forced me against my will," he said, his expression serious.

I laughed. There was no way I could force him to do anything. Who knew Charles had a sense of humor.

"We'll tell him the truth, together," I said, looking at him.

"Okay. But unless that happens, you need to know I guard secrets as well as I do people."

"Me, too. Well, the secrets part anyway."

We reached the patio, and Charles stopped.

"I'll watch you go inside."

I turned to face him. "Where and when to-morrow night?"

"Ten thirty in the gym. We can use the bag and mats. It's pretty soundproof, so we won't alert anyone we're there. For now, we'll train twice a week to allow your body to heal and grow stronger. We don't need you to start off with an injury right out of the gate. You'll need to practice every day as well. I recommend the punching bag, swimming, and lifting weights to gain some strength."

"Alright, well, this is it then. Thanks." I turned on my heels and headed for the kitchen door. Pulling the piece of paper out of my pocket, I then punched in the code and let myself inside.

CHAPTER 18

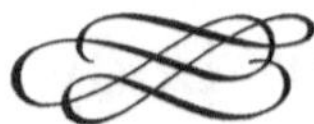

I would have to practice my stealth mode if I was going to slip in and out of the house a few nights a week. It was slightly weird to interact with Charles as a regular person rather than a bodyguard, but it was also comforting.

My stomach growled, and I realized that even though I'd eaten dinner with Ada Lynn, I hadn't been eating on a regular schedule. I opened the fridge and grabbed a handful of grapes. Quietly, I got a bowl to put them in and made my way to Ada Lynn's door. It was closed, and I couldn't see any light from beneath it. So far, she'd seemed to do okay with the move, but we'd only been here for a few days.

Popping a grape in my mouth, I climbed the stairs. Both Hendrix and Mac's doors were closed. I opened mine and flipped the switch on. I jumped, my grapes bobbling out of the bowl and onto the floor.

"Holy hell," I whisper-yelled. "Please don't do that again, Hendrix," I said, bending down to pick up my food.

"Sorry, I didn't mean to scare you, but I didn't want Dad to know I was in your room either." Hendrix turned in the chair that was at my desk, his expression grim.

Had he seen Charles and I walk up the path tonight? It hadn't occurred to me that Mac's and my windows faced his place. If she found out, I would bribe her, but Hendrix was another story.

"It's fine, but you should have at least texted me or called."

I closed my door and rinsed the grapes off in the bathroom sink.

"I guess I have your phone number, huh?" he asked, pulling his iPhone out of his back pocket.

"Yeah. I'm in your favorites," I said, popping another grape in my mouth. "Want one?" I held out the bowl. Trying to act all nonchalant had me rattled. Hopefully I wasn't overdoing it. I just didn't want to come on too strong and scare him off. The other night hadn't been the direction I'd hoped we'd move in. He should have never overheard what Mac had said about my past. But I'd kept my word to Franklin. Hendrix had invited himself into my bedroom. I hadn't initiated it.

"How are you doing?" I asked, sinking down onto the end of my bed.

He shrugged.

"Was it nice to see Spokane? Ada Lynn said she loved it. She said you two stomped around in the snow together, too." I couldn't help but smile with the mental picture of them. I was sorry I'd missed it.

His face lit up. "Yeah, she's pretty awesome. I don't know who had more fun seeing it for the first time, her or me."

My mood grew serious. It wasn't his first time, but I wasn't going to mention it.

"I found my Spotify app," he said, watching me eat my grapes.

"Yeah?"

"I listened to the playlist titled Gemma."

I coughed. "You have a playlist for me?"

"Apparently so."

I had no idea, but now I was super curious.

"I...I wondered if you wanted to listen to it with me."

"Hendrix," I said, standing. I put the now empty bowl on my nightstand and faced him. "I don't know what to do right now." My hands grew clammy, and I wiped them on my jeans. I approached him in the chair, then sank to my knees, peering up at him.

"I don't know what you need," I said. "I don't want to force you into loving me again." My gaze fell to my lap and traveled back up to his beautiful face. "Franklin asked me to give you some space. But between us...I don't want to. I just want you back."

Pain etched across Hendrix's face, and his jaw tightened.

"I'm here because I can't *not* be near you." He reached his hand tentatively toward me and touched my cheek. "You're so beautiful," he whispered. "I don't know what it is about you, but something keeps drawing me back."

My breath hitched. Did he still love me even though he couldn't remember our days together? His thumb traced my cheek, and I closed my eyes, leaning into his touch.

"I miss this. Us." I said, looking at him again.

"If this is really you, how do I know? I mean, you've listened to the playlist, everyone has told you we're together, but you have to come back to me on your own, Hendrix. Otherwise it'll rip both of us in two when you change your mind."

He dropped his hand, fear flickering in his features. "I don't want to hurt you. You've been through enough."

I rubbed my forehead. "I'm so sorry you heard all of that. Mac and I were talking about her break up with Jeremiah, and the rest of the shit that happened while we were all in Louisiana. I had no idea you were listening."

"Gemma?" he asked, searching my face with his piercing blue eyes. "Did we save each other?"

Nerves clenched my stomach. "Yeah, Hendrix. I think we did."

We sat silently, not touching each other. Finally, he cleared his throat. "I have a doctor's appointment tomorrow, but I was hoping you would take me to the campus the next day. I mean, if you want to?"

My heart leaped. I'd do anything to spend time with him.

"I'd be happy to take you anywhere you want to go," I said. "It's where we met, so maybe it would be a good place to start."

"Will you show me where exactly? Take me to the places where we spent time together?"

"Yeah. I think that will be fine."

"And tonight," he paused. "Tonight, can I stay with you and can we listen to music? Some nights it's too much, being alone and stuck inside my head."

It took all my strength not to crawl into his lap and comfort him.

"If that's what you really want, then yeah."

He stood, extending his hand to me. I grabbed it, electricity sparking between us. I stood, only inches between us. His eyes darkened and my core throbbed with desire. One touch. One kiss. But we wouldn't stop, and it was too soon.

Stepping back, I glanced over at the bed.

"Here are the rules for now." I mentally kicked myself. There was only one thing I really wanted right now. Him. Naked. Inside me. "We can lie on top of the bed, fully clothed, and listen to music. If you need to sleep in here, okay, but sleeping only. If there's any chance you still love me, Hendrix, I don't want to fuck this up and lose you for good. We need to take it slow."

"Understood," he said.

I turned on the lamp and flipped off the overhead light. We slipped off our shoes and crawled onto the bed next to each other. A few inches remained between our bodies as he handed me an earbud and then tapped his phone screen. Citizen Shade's "Forfeit Tomorrow" began to play. My eyes fluttered closed, memories of hearing Hendrix performing for the first time flooding my mind. "10,000" by Elliot Root played next. I turned my head, peeking at him. His expression softened while he held my gaze. There wasn't anything else we needed to say. The music spoke for us when we couldn't.

Exhaustion seeped from deep inside me, and my eyes fluttered closed. The back of Hendrix's hand touched mine, and I sighed, content to be next to him again.

THE SUN PEERED through the curtains and directly into my bedroom. I rubbed my face, my hand tangling up in the headphones. Sitting up quickly, I focused on Hendrix.

"Good morning," he said, smiling.

I flopped back onto my pillow and smiled at him in return.

"Hi," I said. "Did you get some sleep?"

"Yeah, the best night's sleep I've had since waking up in the hospital."

I turned on my side, facing him.

"I'm glad. It was nice to have you here," I said, biting my lip in order not to start gushing about how much I loved him.

"I watched you sleep," he admitted.

"Ugh, did I drool? I've been exhausted lately."

He chuckled, and every inch of my body woke up.

"No, you didn't," he assured me.

I took a few minutes to wake up, reveling in the fact that the love of my life was in the same bed with me again. Maybe we weren't where we were before the tornado, but I hoped like hell it was a new beginning for us together.

"What time is your doctor's appointment today?"

"One, I think. Dad's taking me, then we're going to grab a late lunch."

"That's good. I'm going to see if Mac will go shopping with me. I need a swimming suit. I don't even own one."

"I'll go with you," he said, bolting upright and grinning.

I couldn't help but giggle. "Sorry, but you're

not going to watch me try on a bunch of swimsuits."

"Can you at least get a bikini? Maybe even two?"

"Hendrix," I groaned, embarrassed. "I've never owned a bathing suit, so we'll see how it goes." I gave his arm a gentle squeeze.

"Never?"

"No," I said softly.

"Can you swim?" he asked. I was pretty sure I could see the wheels turn in his head.

"No."

"Well I guess we'll have to figure it out to-gether then." A mischievous smile spread across his face.

"Guess so. But for now, you need to get out of here before anyone catches you. I don't need your dad breathing down our necks in case you decide you want to come back another night."

We crawled out of bed and walked to my door. I opened it slightly and peered into the hallway.

"The coast is clear."

"Thanks. And I'll definitely want to be back." He flashed his smile that turned me into a puddle and slipped out of my room.

I pressed my body against the door, my heart

pounding against my chest. Then, I did a major happy dance on my bed. For the first time, I had a flicker of hope he would make his way back to me. But sometimes hope could also be dangerous.

"Damn, if I were into girls, I'd definitely want you in that," Mac said. "Turn around and let me see your sweet little ass."

I covered my face, hiding my embarrassment as a mother with two daughters entered the dressing room, glaring at us.

"Girl," Mac ran up and slapped my butt cheek.

"Hey!" I screeched, "Hands-off in public."

Mac giggled. "Ohmigod. I so needed this. Thanks for talking me into going with you."

"Well, who else would I ask to go shopping with me? You've seen me nearly naked, anyway."

I laughed. We were totally being silly. It felt good.

"Well that teeny bikini is my choice. Hendrix will blow his wad the second he sees you."

"Mac," I hissed while the mother took a daughter in each hand and hauled them out of the dressing room, huffing loudly. "Shit," I mumbled, giggling into my arm. "That poor woman. She has no clue what we've just lived through."

"Yeah. No kidding. Anyway, get that one. Your boobs look great in it, too. If you want Hendrix back, you need to remind him of what he's missing." She winked at me, and I disappeared into the dressing room to change back into my boyfriend jeans and a long-sleeved T-shirt.

I opened the door and stepped into my tennis shoes.

"Have you heard from Jeremiah?" I asked, gathering the other bathing suits and draping them over the return rack. I'd only opted for one suit instead of two like Hendrix had asked. It wasn't worth the money when I couldn't even swim.

Mac rolled her eyes. "Asshole," she said quietly.

We made our way over to the workout gear, and I pondered what I'd need when I trained with Charles. "Who works out in a bra top?" I asked, my cheeks reddening.

"Buy it. Your boobs will thank you after a good run." Mac said.

I located a few pairs of yoga pants and some additional tops that covered my stomach. I would save the cute bra top for the times Hendrix was with me.

"You didn't really answer me about Jeremiah," I said, loading my arm up with my selections.

"I've texted him a few times, but he never responded." Mac's face fell with the confession. "Why do I want a guy who doesn't want me for who I am? I mean, I'm the same Mac with or without money. I didn't change. He was the one that freaked out."

"Maybe he just needs some time?" I asked, laying my items on the counter to check out.

"Time for what? I mean, he either wants me or he doesn't. It should be that easy, anyway. Apparently I can't get it through my noggin that he doesn't want me, though."

I flashed her a grin. "You said noggin."

"Well, shit. It's not like you can spend three months in the South and not pick up some of the slang and twang."

"I haven't lost any of my accent, either. Have I?" I shot her a look as I inserted my debit card into the machine.

"Nope, not one damned bit." She laughed.

"Thank you, have a nice day," the cashier said and handed me my bag.

Mac and I walked back through the mall and stopped for lunch at Red Robin.

"This reminds me of Jeremiah," she said, plopping down into the chair.

"I'm sorry. We can go somewhere else," I suggested.

"Nope, I love this place. I'll get over it."

Another hour passed while Mac and I chatted about college plans. She took some incompletes and had already enrolled for the next term here in Spokane. I knew I should do the same, but I wasn't sure if I was ready. I would have a better idea tomorrow after I took Hendrix to campus.

I glimpsed at my watch. It was almost three.

"I wonder how Hendrix's appointment went?" I stuffed a fry in my mouth. At least I would work off my lunch with Charles tonight.

"Text him," she suggested.

"You think that would be okay?"

"If you don't, I will," Mac said around a bite of hamburger.

I nodded, grabbed my phone out of my pocket, and set it down on the table. Franklin might find out I'd contacted him, and I'd agreed to leave Hendrix alone. But if Hendrix was the one who came to me, it wasn't my fault, was it?

Or should I have sent him away last night? Ugh, I was so confused.

"You should text him," I suggested.

"Fine," she said and tapped out a message. Her phone buzzed back quickly with a response.

"What did he say?" I asked, leaning across the table.

"He said the doc told him his brain looked great."

I frowned. "Nothing about the possibility of his memories returning?"

Her fingers flew across the screen then her phone buzzed again.

"Nope, but the doc is encouraged with his progress."

I sank back into my seat. "That's good then."

"Yeah. I know it's not what we'd hoped for, but at least it's not bad news, right?" She took a sip of her water.

Just as I took a nibble of my burger, my phone buzzed. Frowning, I picked it up and stared at the screen. A stupid grin spread across my face.

I can't wait to see you later.

My fingers tapped against the screen with my reply.

Me, too.

"Oh snap. He texted you, didn't he?" Mac asked, flashing me a major grin.

"Yeah."

"Well, bestie, don't keep me waiting. What the hell did he say?"

"Nothing really, just that he couldn't wait to see me."

"Yes!" She whisper-yelled. "He still loves you." Mac did a little dance in her seat, and I laughed.

"Let's not get ahead of ourselves, but it's a good sign."

CHAPTER 19

I thought I would never ditch Mac in time to meet Charles. At ten thirty, I showed up at the gym and stretched a little. My yoga pants and top felt a bit revealing, but I figured they'd be the easiest to work out in. I'd pulled my hair up into a ponytail, too.

"You're on time, that's good," Charles said, entering the workout room wearing basketball shorts and a T-shirt that stretched across his broad chest, showcasing how ripped he was. There wasn't an ounce of fat anywhere on him.

"Yeah, I think some nights might be tough to slip away, but I'll be here."

Charles tossed his keys and hand towel on a

workout bench and motioned for me to follow him.

"This will be the best place to land," he said and stepped on the mats, his eyes raking over me. With one quick step, he was behind me and had me by my ponytail. "Easy target," he said. He let go, and I spun around and faced him, highly irritated.

"Can you actually talk to me instead of attacking me?"

"No, because the person that comes after you won't ask your permission to pin you down or seize your hair, they'll just do it. You need to learn not to be caught off guard. Be aware of your surroundings at all times. Never let your guard down."

Although he'd already pissed me off by snatching my hair, he had a good point.

"Then what am I supposed to do? I have long hair regardless."

"Don't wear it up unless you're with Hendrix or Franklin. It's easier to slip out of it if someone grabs *some* of your hair than *all* of your hair."

"Alright. But when it's just us, I'm keeping it up, and you can show me what to do if someone does do that."

Excited, I hopped up and down on my toes and threw a few punches.

"Come on Charles, I'm ready." I narrowed my eyes while he moved in a circle. His right leg swiftly moved behind my heel, sending me on my back. Hard. My breath whooshed out of me as I stared up at him from the floor.

"You're a prick," I gasped, trying to catch my breath.

"I tried to warn you."

I pushed myself off the floor, seething with anger.

"You can't even offer a hand to help me up? I bet you're Mister Manners on a date."

He didn't bat an eye. "Are you ready to quit fucking around now? Or would you like to continue to bounce around like a little bunny rabbit and waste my time?"

My fists clenched and unclenched at my sides.

"Let's get something straight. I'm not here for you to waste my time, and I'm not here to become your new friend. I'm here to teach you to protect yourself. That's all," he said firmly.

My entire body went rigid. What had happened since last night when he walked me back to the house? We'd talked like two ordinary people.

If it's not what he wanted, fine. I wouldn't waste any energy or put in an effort to be nice.

I tilted my chin up in defiance. "Let's do this."

"Come here," he ordered, his voice gruff.

I walked to him but kept enough space between us that if he lunged at me, I might have enough time to escape. But instead, he took my hand and turned it upward.

"This," he said, tapping the heel of my palm. "If there is enough space between you and the attacker you can strike quickly, here." He guided my hand up, making contact with the underside of his nose. "When you punch," he said, folding my fingers into the proper form, "your power comes from here." He dropped my hand and grabbed my hips, turning them slightly. "Stand with your legs hip-width apart and sink into your stance a little bit. It will keep your balance centered."

I did as he instructed, incredibly aware of his hands on my body. My thoughts flashed to Hendrix immediately. His touch. His warmth. His mouth.

"And when you punch, your hips will snap forward. Don't ever punch with your arm only," Charles said, breaking me from my Hendrix euphoria.

"Let's try some punches, and I'll correct your form."

After several hits, I failed to even move the bag. My lips pursed, and I placed my hands on my waist. "What if I'm not strong enough?" I asked.

"Bullshit. You'll get there. Stop feeling sorry for yourself."

"I'm sorry, what?" I asked, my temper flaring. This guy certainly knew how to piss me off.

"Over here," he said, walking to the other side of the punching bag.

I gasped. "Are you for real?" I was staring at a full-sized image of Carl. Charles had blown up a picture and attached it to the bag as my target.

"Now use what I taught you and throw a punch."

I doubled my fist and snapped a throw at Carl's face.

"How did you feel at fourteen, Gemma?" Charles asked, stepping backward. "When he took your entire life away from you. No dates, no prom, just years of living in terror and constantly looking over your shoulder. What do you have to say to him now?"

I planted my feet, hip-width apart, and let my fist fly. The bag jerked with the impact, and I hit it again.

"Change arms," he said, watching me.

For the next hour, sheer hatred flew out of me with every punch and kick I delivered. My body burned like a motherfucker when we were done. I collapsed in a heap on the mats, panting.

Charles tossed me a hand towel, and I wiped the sweat from my forehead.

"I don't smell very good right now," I mumbled, screwing up my face.

"No. You don't."

I laughed. I couldn't help it.

"I don't think I can crawl up the stairs to my bedroom." I closed my eyes and allowed my heart rate to calm down.

"It's why I wanted to start with two days a week," he said, sitting down next to me.

I peered at him through one eye, wondering if I was about to talk to asshole Charles or human Charles.

"When is the next training session? I'll need to make sure I can sneak down here."

"Thursday night if you can make it work. The only reason I'm flexible with you is that if Franklin finds out, shit will hit the fan. I like my job."

I sat up slowly, groaning.

"I don't want you to lose your job, Charles, but you're the only person I know and trust who can teach me. You have no idea what this means to me."

He gave me a curt nod and grabbed my phone as he stood.

"Unlock it," he said, handing it to me.

"What do you want with it?" I punched in my code and handed it back.

He quickly tapped something on it before setting it on a workout bench.

"Text or call if you're ever in danger, Gemma. But also if the schedule changes. No chit chat, though. Only use this number if you have no other choice."

I gawked at him. This was human Charles, at least for the moment. My focus dropped to the screen where the name Quantico had been entered along with a phone number.

"Quantico? Isn't that?" My voice trailed off, and my mouth dropped open. "Were or are you FBI, Charles?" I hurried to my feet, staring at him. Shock rippled through my body.

"I never enter my real name. That word is specific to you and it's for a burner."

"Oh. My. God. Is your name even Charles?" I whispered, slowly approaching him.

"To you, yes." He held my gaze, his deep brown eyes sharp and dangerous.

I tossed my hands up in surrender. "I don't need to know. Whoever or whatever you are is beside the point. If you're on my team, it's all good, and I don't need to know shit about you."

The corner of his mouth twitched slightly.

"Shit, do Mac and Hendrix know?" The intense look Charles gave me was borderline chilling. "Sorry, sorry I asked," I held up my hands again and turned away from him. "Franklin would know, right?" I whirled around, my brain refusing to let this go.

"Gemma, all you need to understand is that you have access to me twenty-four hours, seven days a week. Don't question the protection right now."

I sauntered up to him. No matter what situation he was in, his posture never changed. He stood ramrod straight, legs slightly apart, and hands at his sides.

"Just because you're some super badass doesn't mean you can't have friends. You can be a dick when we're training, but that's it. Loosen up a little, try to be nice. If we're done for tonight, I would like to crawl into a hot shower and into my bed. I think I could actually get some sleep."

"We're done. Go home."

I rolled my eyes at him and gathered my belongings.

"Night, Charles. Thank you again for all your help."

AFTER THE RAPE, when I was fourteen, my pain was excruciating. But it went beyond the physical wounds which heal with time even though they may leave scars. Carl had ripped out my soul, and nothing inside me had ever fully healed.

The pain Charles inflicted on me the night before had been draining and exhilarating all at the same time. Releasing so much anger had left me limp. I'd not understood the impact of holding in my anger and grief for so long. Every moment I'd carried that anger inside me, it had suffocated me more and more, preventing me from moving forward. Until Hendrix. And now, Charles.

I crawled out of bed slowly and headed for another hot shower. For the first time since the tornado, I'd slept through the entire night. I was sore, but a new energy buzzed inside me.

And this afternoon, Hendrix and I would visit the campus.

An hour later, I descended the stairs dressed in the cutest skinny jeans I owned and an emerald green shirt. Even though I'd be with Hendrix, I left my hair down. If there were ever an altercation, I would rather lose a chunk of hair than allow someone to control me with a ponytail.

It was a little bit after nine, and I was starving. I wandered into the kitchen to find Ada Lynn and Ruby discussing recipes. I smiled and made my way to Ada Lynn, joining her at the bar. Leaning my head on her shoulder, I peered up at her. "Morning."

"Good morning. How are you?"

"Fine, but I need a full pot of coffee and a big breakfast."

"You have an appetite this morning?" Ruby asked, grinning widely. She hurried toward the fridge, her hips swishing with every step, and began whipping together who knew what for a meal. At this point, I didn't care as long it was edible.

"How's your room. Are you comfortable? Do you have everything you need?" I asked Ada Lynn quietly.

"It's wonderful. The bed is so comfortable, I literally sink into it." She flashed a smile. "It's been fun to see Spokane and stay in such a nice home," she whispered.

"Right?" My eyes widened in agreement, and I nodded.

Ruby brought us each a large cup of freshly brewed coffee, creamer, milk, and sugar.

"Aww, that's super sweet. Thank you, Ruby," I said, inhaling the strong aroma of my favorite beverage in the entire world. I'd hated the taste of coffee until Mac introduced me to the good stuff. And it was a necessary evil during all the late nights of studying.

"I'm a little lost not cooking and taking care of my own laundry," Ada Lynn admitted.

I took her hand.

"You deserve to be pampered. We can find some other things for you to do if you're bored."

"Franklin has already set up some doctor's appointments for me. Charles will drive, and I don't have to stress over getting lost in a big city. It's nice to have help while getting situated in a new state."

"Yeah. I know. I felt so lost when I arrived on campus, but Mac jumped in and helped. Now that you're here, maybe we can take you. You can see a lot of the buildings and area just by us driving around it. You can see where Mac and I lived, too."

"I'd love to," she replied.

"You two eat up. If you want more, I'll whip up another batch," Ruby said, placing a large plate of eggs, bacon, and pancakes in front of us.

"Yummy!" I rubbed my hands together like a little kid.

Ruby fluttered across the kitchen and brought us plates, silverware, and placed a pitcher of fresh squeezed orange juice on the bar. I wasn't sure who was more excited, Ada Lynn or me.

We ate slowly, savoring every bite, and chatting about places to sightsee. Neither of us brought up Kyle or much about Louisiana. A part of me wondered if Ada Lynn had been ready to leave a long time ago, but never had. Maybe she'd stayed for me. Maybe she just didn't have anywhere else to go. I wasn't sure, but I would do anything I could for her now. She was the last real link to my childhood, and she knew all of my good and all of my bad. Regardless, she still loved me unconditionally.

"Hey," Hendrix said from my bedroom doorway.

I turned and smiled.

"Hey," I said softly, missing the ability to run to him and jump into his arms. The shadows beneath his eyes had lessened, and he'd put on a bit of weight, but Ruby's cooking would do that to anyone. For the first time in weeks, he looked good. Damned good. Seriously fuckworthy.

Heat traveled across my cheeks when I realized I was staring. Clearing my throat, I turned away and searched for my phone and keys.

"Franklin said your new car is here. Do you want to take it? He asked me to drive, but he wouldn't need to know if we snuck off to an empty parking lot and let you take it for a spin," I said.

"I can see why we were together, you're a bit of a rule breaker, huh?" Hendrix asked.

My face fell. Not even close.

"No, I just thought it would be nice to see what you remember or if...or if someone needed to teach you to drive again."

"Yeah, makes sense." He shoved his hands in his pockets, and an awkward silence filled the space between us.

"Are you ready?" I asked.

"After you."

I stepped past him, his cologne penetrating

my senses. A moan nearly slipped through my lips. Not touching him was pure torture, and I wasn't sure how I was going to make it through the day with him this close to me.

THE EARLY APRIL afternoon was perfect to tour the campus. Rays of sun filtered through the oak and maple trees and the flowers were just beginning to bloom. My stomach tightened as I pulled his Lexus GS into a parking spot. I pushed the button, and the engine turned off. The new brown and black leather interior smell permeated the car. It was in pristine condition with only twenty-nine miles on it. Franklin went all out for him. It was a beautiful car, and I was secretly giddy about driving it.

"Where to first?" I asked, scanning the buildings.

"To the first place we met."

My nose scrunched up in thought.

"The first time you saw me, we didn't talk. But it might be a good place to start."

We exited the car, and I shoved my phone in my pocket along with the key.

A light breeze blew as we wandered up the

sidewalk toward the library. Memories flashed rapidly through my mind. Hendrix, Mac, Andrea, and Brandon. This wasn't just a test for Hendrix, it was one for me, too. After everything that had happened, and knowing Brandon was still on campus, could I come back?

I glanced at Hendrix, who walked next to me without speaking. If I'd been in his shoes, I would be wracking my brain for anything familiar. It was best if I allowed him to process and not bombard him with too much at once.

"The library?" he asked, stunned as we approached the front of the red brick building.

I laughed. "Sort of. Come on." I walked around the side of the structure and then to the back where I'd had a panic attack and collapsed on the ground my very first day. "Here," I said and stood back, allowing him to search the area. "I didn't see you, but apparently you were sitting over there writing a song." I pointed to the corner with the grassy area.

"Why did you come back here?" he asked.

I'd put a lot of thought into my answers when we'd made plans to come here. I wouldn't lie to him, but I didn't want to feed him information, either.

"Like you, I needed some privacy. It was my

first day and it was overwhelming to say the least."

He took his time and walked over to where he'd sat, leaned against the building, and searched my face.

"Something happened, didn't it?" he asked quietly.

I turned away from him. If he was remembering, the pain and fear in my expression couldn't give anything away. Sighing softly, I turned toward him again.

"As I said, I didn't know you were back here. Next, I went into the library. Come on."

He shoved off the wall and walked next to me as we climbed the steps and entered the library.

I led him to the fiction section and was glad to see our table was empty. Tears clouded my vision, remembering the first day I met him.

I pulled his chair out and sat across from him the exact same way we had the first time we spoke.

"We sat right here," I said. Nervous silence stretched between us, my mind scrambling to fill the gap.

"What did I say to you?" he asked, frowning.

"You asked if I was okay." I avoided his intense gaze and scanned the library. I missed this place. I missed the campus, and the way life had been with Hendrix and Mac.

"You look so sad right now," he said softly.

"I'm sorry. I know this can't be easy for you. We spent a lot of afternoons here," I explained.

He scanned the library, his focus resting on a group of gorgeous girls. The brunette eyed me and gave Hendrix a little wave and winked at him. My attention landed on Hendrix, and my heart skidded to a stop. This was the first time he'd been hit on by a hot girl that I was aware of. Eventually, he'd realize there were a lot of other women out there, and I would most likely lose him. A part of me wanted to deal with it now rather than later. But honestly, I didn't want to deal with it ever.

"Do you know those girls over there?" he asked, nodding in the brunette's direction.

"Nope."

"Isn't it rude to wink at a guy who's at a table with another girl?"

I shrugged. "Flirting and dating were never my things, so I don't really know what to tell you."

"Let's go," he said standing. "I might not have my memories, but I can smell entitlement and bitchiness from a mile away."

I dropped my head, my hair hiding my smile. It made me happy to know *my* Hendrix, the one I fell in love with, was still inside this different version of the man. As long as I'd known him, he'd never been interested in rude, snotty people. It gave me hope he would eventually come back to me.

He waited for me and placed his hand on my back while we walked past the table with the gorgeous girls. A chill shot through me with his touch. Pushing open the door, he held it for me.

"Can you point me in the direction of the bathroom?" he asked.

"Yeah, it's around the corner and to your left. I'll wait for you outside."

He nodded and took off in that direction.

I stepped outside, inhaling deeply. The circumstances sucked, but I was happy to be back. I descended the stairs and strolled to the large oak tree, the sunshine warming my back. Leaning against it, I watched the students walk by, and then stared up at the cloudless blue sky. My heart sang. I definitely wanted to return with Mac and hopefully Hendrix.

"Well look who's here."

CHAPTER 20

My head snapped toward the voice, fear zipping down my spine. I would recognize it anywhere. I straightened my shoulders and met his leering gaze.

"Go away, Brandon," I said, my tone strong. Images of my earlier training with Charles flickered through my mind. Realizing I'd cornered myself against the tree, I moved just in time. His long, quick strides narrowed the space between us. Four of his friends circled me, but I held my ground. *They can smell your fear,* Charles's words whispered in my mind.

"You need to leave," I said.

"But Gemma, it's been months since I've seen you." He stepped into me, taking a strand of my hair, and twirling it around his finger. His nose touched my neck and my ear. "You came back so I could bury my cock inside you, didn't you?" he asked. His focus dropped, landing on my chest.

My arm flew up, the palm of my hand connecting with the underneath of his nose. He yelped and stepped back. Blood trickled from his right nostril.

"I told you to leave me alone. I'm not playing with you, Brandon."

"Hey, what's going on?" Hendrix elbowed his way through the circle of guys.

"You need to keep your bitch on a leash. I told her, and I'll tell you, I'll fuck her senseless and leave her in a ditch where she belongs," Brandon said, sneering at us.

Hendrix was so fast, I nearly missed the punch that smashed into Brandon's face. Brandon stumbled backward, tumbling to the ground. Hendrix straddled him and landed another hit to his nose.

"Shit! Hendrix! No!" I screamed, running toward him. But Brandon's asshats were already on him, tugging him off. Hendrix struggled against them, but four on one was too much and he staggered backward.

"That's it," Brandon seethed. "You crossed the line, motherfucker." Brandon spit out a mouthful of blood while his friends helped him off the ground. Blood oozed from his nose, and a deep gash split his left eyebrow open.

"Let's go. Now!" I pulled on Hendrix, forcing him away from the fight before he lunged at Brandon again. My leg muscles screamed with every step I took, but we had to leave before the cops showed up. Brandon's father would twist the truth, and I didn't want Hendrix or I to get arrested.

Fumbling for the key fob, I unlocked the doors and urged Hendrix to get inside quickly. Then I pulled out of the parking lot as fast as I dared.

I gave Hendrix a look. His hair was a mess and anger twisted his features. There was only one other time I'd seen him like that—when my father had nearly beaten me to death.

My entire body trembled as I whipped the car in the direction of the first place that came to mind where we could have some privacy. I peeked over at Hendrix who remained quiet and stared out the window. Our plan to jog his memory and spend some time together had been ruined within a few minutes.

Silence filled the car as I finally pulled into the empty lot where we'd taken Mac to meet Asher.

Thank God it was behind an abandoned building. After parking the car, I got out and walked away. What in the hell would I even tell Hendrix?

"What the fuck was that?" he yelled from behind me.

Tears streamed down my face. I was completely shaken by my encounter with Brandon but worse than that, Hendrix's reaction was off the rails. He'd never raised his voice at me. Ever. Despite Franklin's orders not to feed information to him, I had to explain what had happened on campus. I couldn't hide something this big and hope his memory would return to make sense of it all.

"And no lies, no half-truths. Tell me what happened goddammit, and don't give me a bunch of sugar-coated bullshit."

I cringed, my pulse racing with his anger, and my mind scrambling for what to say.

"I want an answer," he said, grabbing my shoulders and whirling me around. I visibly shook in his hands, my eyes wide with fear.

His face fell, and he released me. His chest heaved as he ran his hands through his hair.

"Jesus, I didn't mean to scare you. I snapped when I thought he hurt you."

A cry escaped me, and I sank to my knees.

Brandon's attack and Hendrix's reaction were almost too much.

"You asked me if something happened outside the library...yes. It was the first day Brandon tormented me. I panicked and hid behind the library from him."

"Gemma, I'm sorry." He reached out to help me to my feet, but I pulled away from him. I didn't know this Hendrix. I'd never seen him act like this.

"I need a minute before we go home," I muttered. I heard his footsteps as he walked away from me.

Hendrix had been the one person that had kept me safe. But today, he'd shaken me to my core with his temper.

I inhaled sharply and remembered I had Charles's phone number if I ever needed him. Sometimes, just knowing I had a backup plan gave me strength. I stood and made my way back to the car.

Hendrix leaned against the passenger side, his head hanging down.

"Let's go," I said, my voice barely above a whisper. Without another word, we got in the car, and I drove in the direction of our house.

My eyes were irritated and swollen after my meltdown in the parking lot. I scrambled to make sense of Hendrix's reaction, but all I could think of was his amnesia. Although we hadn't seen a ton of personality changes, the doctors had told us it might happen, and I'd experienced it firsthand.

Parking the car in front of the garage, my focus darted down the hill. Regardless of how much I didn't want to tell Charles what had happened with Brandon, maybe I would the next time we trained.

"Gemma," Hendrix said, his words laced with guilt. "Please, can we talk? I know there's more you're not telling me."

"It's not a good idea to tell you right now," I said, getting out of the car.

His expression was gut-wrenching, and even though I knew how much I loved him, I was still shaken as well as worried that he might have gotten hurt from his fight with Brandon. I needed time to process, and I needed to talk to Franklin.

I hurried past him and into the house.

"Bestie!" Mac shouted, barreling down the stairs.

"I'll find you in a bit," I said, veering to the right and down the hall toward Franklin's office.

Clearing my throat, I knocked lightly on his partially open door.

"Come on in," he called.

"Hey," I said, closing it behind me.

"Hi there, how did the visit to campus go?" he asked, shuffling a stack of papers on his desk. The smile disappeared from his face when he glanced up. "What happened?" he asked, leaning back in his chair and folding his hands on top of the desk.

"Hendrix lost his shit and beat the hell out of Brandon," I croaked, sitting in the chair across from him.

"Dammit!" Franklin dragged his hands down his face. "Start from the beginning," he said, his blue eyes staring holes in me.

"Brandon saw me today, and he made some rude suggestions. I took care of it. Well, I tried to. Anyway, Hendrix stepped in. Brandon told him to keep his bitch on a leash and that he planned to fuck me and toss me in a ditch." I gulped, my cheeks flaring hot with embarrassment. "Hendrix went off, pounded him in his face, and Brandon's friends had to pull Hendrix off him. I grabbed him, and we ran before the cops could show up. I was so rattled I drove to a parking lot and pulled over.

The second I was out of the car, Hendrix started yelling at me and demanding to know what happened." Tears pricked the back of my eyes.

Franklin sighed. "If I can be brutally honest right now, Brandon is a sorry piece of shit. He needs to be dealt with, and I know it scared you, but I'm glad Hendrix beat the hell out of him. Let me make some calls and see what can be done. Since Hendrix could be charged with assault, I'm going to try and keep the police out of it. We'll see how it goes since Brandon's father loves to involve them. At least the ones on his payroll."

My brows furrowed. Payroll?

"I know how Brandon works first hand." I hesitated. "Hendrix hasn't ever yelled at me, Franklin. And I could have handled that, it was when he grabbed my shoulders and spun me around. It scared me. I don't think his intention was to hurt, but he's strong." My attention fell to the floor.

"Are you alright?" Franklin asked gently.

"Yeah, other than being rattled, I'm fine. He didn't hurt me, it was the raw anger in his eyes, and at the moment, it had been aimed at me."

"I'll call the doctor to let him know, but Gemma, unfortunately the anger is part of the situation. However I do think we can help him. He just needs to take out his frustration in an appropriate way."

"Boxing," I said.

Franklin nodded. "Yeah, but not in the ring, we can't risk a head injury."

The longer Franklin talked, the sound of his soothing voice continued to calm me. Hendrix had never laid a hand on me before, and the entire situation had been emotionally charged. Maybe he didn't know how to handle it but yelling at me wouldn't work.

I sighed, stared up at the ceiling, and rubbed my forehead.

"Hendrix said at one time that you and he were investigating who paid Andrea to lie. Since I can't talk to him about it, looks like you're stuck with me. I...do you have any new information?" I asked.

Franklin rubbed his chin, pausing.

"Some, but not enough to share with you yet. But I promise I'll keep you updated."

"I would appreciate it. The entire ordeal caused a lot of heartache. Andrea's lie could have ruined Hendrix's life."

"Yes, it certainly could have. I'll talk to Hendrix in a little bit, too. He probably needs some time to calm down."

"Thanks for listening."

"Anytime."

I left his office and made my way upstairs. The afternoon had left me exhausted, and all I wanted was to throw myself into my bed and sleep.

MY EYES FLUTTERED OPEN, the only light in my room the red glow of the clock numbers. It was after ten at night. I groaned, my head throbbing. I'd slept for several hours. Apparently I was more exhausted than I realized. I'd planned on finding Mac and Ada Lynn tonight, but Ada Lynn would be asleep by now.

I swung my feet off the side of the bed and flipped on the lamp. My toes grazed the plush carpet, and my heart ached with the thought of Hendrix's earlier outburst. I hoped it was something he could manage. Longing for the old Hendrix tugged at me. I'd give up everything to have him back.

Deciding a dip in the pool sounded good, I changed into my bikini and selected a towel from the bathroom cabinet. I looked to see if Mac was in her room, but she wasn't there. I would check the game room and kitchen on my way to see if she wanted to join me.

After searching the rest of the house, I couldn't find her. I quietly moved through the kitchen, out the side door, and into the pool house. The smell of chlorine assaulted my nose as soon as I walked in. The pool was huge. Walking over to the edge, I held onto the rail and stuck my foot in. Thank goodness it was heated. I was already freezing my ass off.

Voices from the gym caught my attention, so I tiptoed toward it. I hugged up against the wall and peered around the corner.

"Right, left, uppercut, and again," Charles instructed Hendrix. Relief washed over me. Franklin had done exactly as he had said he would. Grateful Charles was working with him, I was about to let them know I was there when Hendrix dropped his gloved hands to his sides. He grabbed a hand towel and wiped his face.

"Man, I fucked up, and I don't know what to do."

I frowned. What was he talking about? Mom had taught me it was rude to eavesdrop, but this time I was going to break her rule.

"I totally lost my shit. But this Brandon bastard..."

My pulse raced. Holy hell, he was talking to Charles about what had happened earlier.

"How could he talk about raping my girlfriend and throwing her in a ditch?"

Girlfriend? I covered my mouth with my hand in order not to squeal with joy. He still considered me his.

"How did Gemma react?" Charles asked.

"I don't know. She seemed like she was holding her own when I showed up, but I put the motherfucker on the ground."

"Next time don't get caught and don't terrify your girlfriend in the first place. She's strong, but she's been through a lot of shit, and you're one of the few people she's trusted with her life."

Oh. My. God. Human Charles had shown up tonight for Hendrix.

"What do I do? I have to make it right with her. I've been so damned pissed at not remembering shit, too. Between the loss of my memories and Brandon, I snapped. Amnesia's a bitch. And when I think things are going well between Gemma and me, I grab her shoulders and yell at her. I acted like a total douchebag. I might not remember shit, and I can't really explain it, but I can tell you that every fiber of my being loves her. I'll do anything to win her back."

"First you need to talk to her, and you and I will redirect your anger. Then we'll take the son of a bitch down. No one fucks with the Harringtons or anyone they love."

"Damn straight," Hendrix said and punched the bag again.

A mix of emotions flooded through me. Hendrix was genuinely sorry and was already trying to make sure he didn't lose his temper in front of me again. And Charles, he really did care about us, we weren't just a job to him. But the most important thing I'd heard...Hendrix still loved me. My heart galloped inside my chest, and I leaned my head against the wall, willing myself not to run in there and kiss him. Regardless of what he'd said, things could still change. Plus it needed to be a hundred percent his choice.

Passing up on a swim, I hurried back inside. I didn't want to eavesdrop anymore in case Hendrix needed to talk openly with Charles.

My foot hit the stair, and Franklin rounded the corner, nearly colliding with me.

"Gemma," his voice was hoarse. "We need to talk. You might want to sit down."

CHAPTER 21

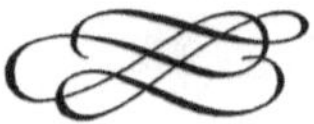

I'd seen Franklin worried, exhausted, and angry, but this mood was a new one. I sank onto the stair, holding my towel around me. He sat down and sighed heavily.

"I don't know whether to tell you I'm sorry or to congratulate you." He turned his head, staring directly into my eyes. "Marcus called tonight. Your father, Kyle, was found murdered," he said gently.

A truck couldn't have hit me harder.

"What?" I asked, my emotions thick in my throat. At nineteen, I'd officially lost both my parents. I clutched at the towel around me, my body trembling violently.

"He was shot outside his house. Gemma, he

turned on too many people, and unfortunately it was only a matter of time. I know he caused a lot of harm, especially to you, but he was still your father. Some days you're going to grieve the loss of him and other days you're going to hate his sorry guts. No matter what, allow yourself to feel whatever it is. And please know that you have our full support."

"I need to go." I ran up the stairs and fled to my room, slamming my door behind me. The towel dropped to the floor and I crawled into bed, my sobs shaking my shoulders. I didn't know whether to be relieved he'd never hurt anyone again, or shattered I'd lost my father. I knew I'd lost him years ago, but the news had affected me on an even deeper level than I could have imagined. How was I supposed to process the loss of both my parents and Hendrix, too?

Nausea swirled inside my stomach, and I curled into a ball, willing myself to calm down. I was safe. But even in a house full of people, a wave of crushing loneliness pushed against my chest. I gasped for air, images of my past mixed with the fear of losing Hendrix flashed in front of me.

At some point I fell asleep, because when I sat up and glanced at the clock, it was nearly two in the morning. My hand landed on my chest, and I forced myself to breathe. Flipping on the lamp, I immediately felt better. Safe. But the tears returned.

A soft knock sounded at my door. Shit, someone had heard me crying. I wiped my eyes and nose with the back of my hands.

"Yeah?"

The door opened quietly.

"Gem," Hendrix said gently.

My heart fluttered with the sound of his voice. I needed him so much right now. He closed the door behind him.

"I'm sorry, did I wake you?" I asked, sniffling.

He approached me slowly, his expression filling with love. "Gem."

My body shot to attention, and I stood.

"The first time I saw you, Brandon had harassed you, and you'd had a panic attack behind the library. When I went to check on you inside, you weren't happy to see me at all. I fell in love with you the night I walked you and Mac back to the dorm. We sang "I Can't Breathe" by Bea Miller together. Then, I sent the same song to you after Andrea had told you I'd raped her, and you were in Louisiana with Kyle after your Mom died in a car accident."

I gawked at him, my hands flying up and covering my mouth. I ran to him, flinging my arms around his neck. A heart-wrenching cry escaped me as I clung to him.

"We made love for the first time at my house," he whispered in my ear, clinging to me. "And then I met Jungle Gemma after you'd had too much to drink one night."

Sinking to my knees, I continued to sob against his chest while he held me and told me about every beautiful memory he had of us together.

"You totally fangirled over Billy Raffoul. So, did Mac," he chuckled in my ear. "Baby, I'm back. And I love you so fucking much," he said.

"I love you, too," I said through my tears. "I love you so damned much it's nearly ripped me in two." I peered up at him, his arms wrapped tight around me.

He smoothed the hair away from my face and bent down, brushing his lips against mine. At that moment, all of the other shit with Brandon and Kyle no longer mattered. Our mouths parted, and I moaned as his tongue caressed mine.

"Baby, I've missed you so bad," I said, still hanging onto him.

"The second I saw you in this bikini I thought

I was going to lose it. Has anyone else seen you in this?" He asked, his eyes darkening.

I laughed. "No, just Mac."

He helped me off the floor and pulled me against him, my hands resting against his chest. I'd been crying so hard I'd not noticed he'd shown up with only basketball shorts on. His chest muscles flexed beneath my touch.

"I'm so sorry I scared you after all the shit with Brandon. I've always had a temper, but I've had years of practice controlling it and directing it into boxing. And when that son of a bitch said that about you, I fucking snapped."

"I know," I said, peering up at him and recalling his conversation with Charles.

"I'll never grab you like that again, either. Not after..."

"Do you remember everything?" I asked, my heart racing. Some things would have been best if he hadn't.

"I drove you to Seattle and saw Jordan." His voice was gentle. "And I know Kyle arranged your rape. So yeah, I do remember. And something's changed since I've gotten my memories back, Gem. I loved you then, but I love you even more now." He kissed my forehead and held me.

"How? How did your memories come back?" I asked.

"It was the weirdest thing. I was asleep, and at first, I thought I was dreaming. Then it was like I watched myself slam into a wall of images that barreled at me a hundred miles an hour. I jerked myself awake and everything was crystal clear again. The moment my brain wrapped around what had happened, I came directly to you."

I pushed up on my tiptoes and kissed him. His hands encircled my waist and pulled me against him as he walked me backward. My knees hit the edge of the mattress, and I released him long enough to lie back on the bed.

His eyes slowly traveled up my body, his gaze resting on my face.

"I love you," he whispered and crawled onto the bed.

"I love you, too," I parted my legs, allowing him to relax his weight on top of me.

He shifted his hips, and I grabbed his ass while his mouth crashed down on mine. My hand drifted up his muscular back, and I threaded my fingers through his hair.

He trailed feather light kisses down my neck and across my collarbone. His fingers grazed my skin, pulling back the top of my bikini and exposing my breast.

"I missed these even when I had amnesia," he muttered, his tongue teasing my nipple.

I laughed softly and gasped when he nipped me gently.

"Oh my God. Hendrix," I fisted his hair as he freed my other breast, his mouth on one, his hand cupping the other.

I slipped my hand into the back of his shorts, the muscles in his ass tensing with my touch.

"I need you inside me," I said while he trailed soft kisses down my stomach.

"Not yet," he growled, tugging my bikini bottoms off and tossing them on the floor. His head dipped between my legs, his tongue swiping across my sensitive bud.

My back arched off the bed, and a loud moan escaped me. During the month he had amnesia, I'd tried not to think about his hot mouth on my sensitive skin, or how alive I felt when we made love. But my body was primed to explode the minute he'd kissed me.

He slipped a finger inside me, his mouth continuing to work his magic.

"Hendrix," I moaned.

He pinched my swollen clit, and my entire

world exploded in ecstasy. Black dots danced before my vision as I climaxed, but he didn't stop. He positioned his hands beneath my ass cheeks and continued. My core was so sensitive it almost hurt, and I attempted to scoot away from him, but he held me firmly. Then the familiar heat flooded my body again. Clutching the bedspread, I relaxed into his touch. His finger gently pumped in and out of me, his thumb massaging my swollen flesh.

"Did you miss me?" he asked, his voice low and gravelly.

"You have no idea," I said, breathlessly.

His tongue swirled around my bud before he pulled it gently between his teeth. My body tensed, and electricity shot through me while I shuddered against him and released again. He propped up on his knees and wiped his mouth.

"You taste so damned good. I can't get enough of you." He was panting, and his pupils were dilated.

"No arguments here."

"Are you still on the pill?" he asked.

"Yeah," I replied, eager to have him inside me.

He lowered himself on top of me, the tip of his cock at my entrance. His eyes never left mine as he slid deep inside me.

"Welcome home, baby," I whispered and wrapped my legs around his waist, tilting my hips upward.

He moaned and gently rocked back and forth, filling me with every magnificent inch of himself.

Kissing softly, we moved together, reveling in each other's touch. Hendrix was finally back where he belonged, and I'd never let him go again.

Rolling on top of him, I sat up, shifting my weight.

"I love seeing you like this. You're so beautiful," he said, his hand lightly traveling up my side to my breast. His fingers teased my nipple while I tilted back, feeling him deeper inside me.

He grabbed my waist, lifted me a bit, and then sat up. My legs circled around his waist as he touched his forehead against mine. I placed my arms around his neck and kissed him passionately. His fingers dug into my ass cheek, and he thrust upward.

"Gem," he whispered in my ear. "I love you so much. I love being with you. I love being inside you. I love your heart. I love every breathtakingly beautiful thing about you."

Tears streamed down my cheeks. I never

thought I would hear him say those words to me again.

"Oh babe," he said, kissing my grief away. "It's alright. I've got you now."

I fisted his hair, grinding against him. All I wanted to think about right now was him inside me.

He moved his hips in a circular motion, and I groaned against his mouth.

"Come for me," I encouraged.

"Gemma," he growled.

Our eyes held each other's as he gripped my waist, his pace quickening.

"That's it, Hendrix. Oh, God. You feel so good," I whimpered.

With one final thrust, his body shuddered, and he released inside me. He continued to move, my core tightening around him. He sucked and licked my nipple while I pushed against him, pure ecstasy swirling inside me. My fingernails dug into his back and my body tensed against his. A loud moan slipped from my lips, and his mouth crashed down on mine, silencing me as I came.

"Sorry," I whispered, breaking our kiss after I'd calmed down.

He chuckled. "I'm just not ready for Mac to

barge through your door with a million questions. I want you all to myself tonight."

"Me, too," I said, resting my head against his and regaining my breath. Neither one of us attempted to move.

Eventually, he lifted me off him, and we crawled under the covers. He wrapped his arm around me while I rested against his chest, the steady thrum of his heartbeat in my ear.

"I'm afraid for you to go to sleep. What if you wake up tomorrow and your memories are gone again?" I asked, attempting to shut down my panic. I looked up at him, and his blue eyes held mine.

"If I lose my memories again, Gem, then you hold onto tonight with everything you have inside of yourself, and know I'll *always* find my way back to you."

He kissed me gently, and I snuggled up against him.

CHAPTER 22

My eyes fluttered open, the sun spilling through my curtains. I'd forgotten to use the blackout shades again. Memories from last night came flooding back, and I bolted upright in bed.

"Morning, babe," Hendrix said, smiling. "You're beautiful when you sleep."

"You're okay? Do you still have your memories?" I asked, hope rising inside of me.

"Oh yeah. Every one of them," he said, propping up on his elbow. "And, this morning, when I make love to you, you need to be quiet so Mac doesn't come bursting in here," he said, laughing softly and pulling me down into the bed with him.

I bit my lip, muffling my giggle.

My fingers traced across his jawline and neatly trimmed beard.

"How did I get so lucky?" I asked, peering at him through my eyelashes.

He rolled over on top of me, his erection throbbing between my legs.

"You've got it all wrong, Gem. The day you waltzed into my life, you unlocked the chains around my heart and taught me how to love." He eased inside me and guided my arms over my head, our fingers intertwining while he kissed me.

"You're my forever," he whispered.

"And you're my always," I replied against his lips.

Hendrix moved slowly, and I savored every moment. Not only had my body missed him, but I'd missed our connection on this level. The last several months without him had left a gaping hole inside me. When he'd knocked on my bedroom door last night and called me Gem, my heart came back to life. I had my baby back.

Our kiss deepened, and his pace quickened. I squeezed his hands, trying not to moan too loudly. He covered my mouth with his as we released together, and then we lay in each other's arms.

Unfortunately, I couldn't avoid the next conversation any longer.

"Last night when you found me crying," I said, pausing. I sat up in bed so I could look at him.

His forehead wrinkled with concern. "Shit, I was so caught up in remembering you. Us. I...babe, I'm sorry. I should have asked."

"No, I needed you more than I needed to talk about this. I wasn't ready, anyway. I still don't even know how to..." I tucked a piece of hair behind my ear and gathered my courage to speak the words out loud. "Franklin told me Marcus called."

Hendrix bolted upright and rubbed my arm, his expression grim.

"Shit. I guess you were in a coma when Kyle walked away from prison time on a technicality. It's why we all came to Spokane. Ada Lynn wasn't safe living next door to him, and I sure as hell wasn't. Anyway, we barely missed him. In fact, he pulled up while we drove away from Ada Lynn's house. Charles whipped around the car as Kyle got out. So that's the quick and dirty version. But yesterday...he...Kyle was shot outside his house."

Hendrix's jaw tensed and he pulled me into

his lap. Tears spilled down my cheeks and onto his chest.

"I don't even know what to do with that. I fucking hate him for what he did to me, but the second the news reached my ears, it devastated me. I should be thrilled he'll never hurt another girl again, but somewhere inside me...he's still my father, and I hate myself for even feeling that way."

"It's okay," Hendrix said and kissed the top of my head. "There are no right or wrong feelings with this. You can't tell yourself how you should feel. Give yourself permission and just allow it." His arms tightened around me, and he rocked me gently while I cried. Mixed emotions traveled through me, and for the first time in my life, I accepted it for what it was. A healing process.

"You're surrounded by people who love you, and you're safe, babe. Neither he nor Carl can hurt anyone again."

I sniffled and wiped my nose.

"I want to stay here all day and hide from the rest of the world," I whispered, my heart aching with the news of Kyle and content with Hendrix at the same time.

"Me too. And we will, but I need to tell my family the good news."

I nodded. "Mac is going to talk your ear off, Ada Lynn is going to be tickled silly, and I suspect your dad is going to finally allow himself to break down. Get prepared for squeals, crying, and a lot of hugs."

He smiled and tilted my chin up. "Well, for right now, I'm going to be selfish for a few more minutes," he said softly, kissing me. "And we're going to use that amazing shower of yours together."

"I'm not going to argue with you."

"ARE YOU READY?" I asked him, taking his hand in mine. We'd enjoyed a long, hot and steamy shower together, and I sure as hell wasn't complaining, but I was sore. Hendrix would have to be gentle with me tonight.

"Yeah." He kissed my forehead, opened my bedroom door, and led me down the stairs and into the kitchen. It was only eight, so we hadn't missed breakfast. We'd woken up a little before six, which most days never happened, but I needed to know if Hendrix was okay and that his memories hadn't lapsed again.

The clink of silverware reached our ears before we entered the dining room. Ada Lynn and Franklin sat reading the paper, and Mac shoveled a spoonful of eggs into her mouth.

"Morning," Hendrix said.

Mac nearly spit her food out when she saw us holding hands. "Are you two back together?" she asked, bouncing in her chair.

Franklin and Ada Lynn laid their newspapers down in unison, everyone's attention on us.

"Yes, we are, but last night," he paused, glancing at me, "my memories came back. All of them."

Mac gasped, and Franklin stood slowly, staring at him. I released Hendrix's hand and walked over to Ada Lynn. I'd had my time with him, and he needed his family right now.

Franklin grabbed hold of Hendrix and hugged him. There wasn't a dry eye at the table as the reunion took place.

Franklin stepped back, and he searched Hendrix's face. "Be patient with me son, but I have questions," he said.

Hendrix flashed his smile, and my heart melted on the spot.

"Do you remember the accident?" Franklin asked, hope in his voice.

"Yeah. Mac, Gemma, and I were at the concert

in Louisiana. Gemma and I had just performed together when the tornado hit. I tried to get to her, but the stage had collapsed, and then everything went dark."

A cry escaped Mac, and I clenched my hands together, recalling how frantically we had searched for him.

"I remember that Gemma went back to Louisiana because her mom was killed in a car accident that was ultimately caused by Kyle…"

Ada Lynn grabbed my hand, holding on tightly.

"I remember you kicking my ass in Grand Theft Auto, Mac," he said turning toward her. "And I remember you're the best friend I've ever had."

Mac jumped out of her chair and nearly knocked him over with her hug. His chuckle filled the room, and he hung onto her.

"Don't fucking leave us again," she said and smiled sheepishly. She let go of Hendrix and shot a guilty look at Franklin. "I know, language."

Ada Lynn chuckled, and Franklin actually grinned at her.

"Sit down, son. Let's eat, and you can tell us anything you want to."

Ruby literally jumped up and down and hugged Hendrix when she received the news.

"What's your favorite breakfast, Hendrix?" she asked, her hand on her hip.

"Boston Cream Crepes," he said, his face lighting up.

"Yup, he's back," she laughed and flitted out of the dining room and into the kitchen.

"Crepes?" I asked.

"Oh my God. Wait until you taste them," he said, rubbing his stomach.

The next few hours we all spent time together at the table. Mac plied Hendrix with a million questions, and so did Franklin. For the first time in a month, laughter filled the house. For a while, it was enough to help me forget about Kyle, but not for long.

"We need to talk," I said, leaning over to Ada Lynn.

Her smile disappeared when she looked at me.

"Let's go to your room."

"We'll be back in a few," I said, standing and helping Ada Lynn. My focus bounced between Franklin and Hendrix, and the weight of the upcoming conversation grew heavier by the minute.

"I'm so happy for you two, Gemma," Ada Lynn said as we walked to her room.

"Me too. I'm never going to let him go again." I closed the door behind us, and she sat on the end of her bed, waiting.

"There's no easy way to say it, so I'm going for it. Kyle was murdered, and he was found outside of his house."

Ada Lynn gasped, her hand flying to her mouth.

"Franklin told me late last night, then Hendrix got his memory back, so this is the first chance I've had to talk to you about it." I joined her on the edge of the bed. "I don't know how to feel. Relieved. Angry. Heartbroken. Regardless if I hate him, he was still my father. I guess." I released a big sigh, my shoulders slumping forward. "Are you alright?" I asked.

"Oh honey, I'm not worried about me. I've been on this earth for eighty-three years, and I've seen a lot of people come and go. This one doesn't hurt my heart a bit. I'm relieved. Your safety was my number one concern, and with him gone it's one less thing to worry about."

"Ada Lynn," I paused, staring at the floor and back to her again. "I can't go back. There's nothing for me there. But if you said you wanted to go home, I would go with you." Inwardly, I cringed. I wasn't even sure I could step foot in the neighborhood again. But for her, I would try anything.

"I would never ask you to go back, Gemma."

"I know, but are you happy living in Spokane? I don't know what that will look like now that Hendrix has his memories back, but I assume we'll move into his house. There's room for you there. You can stay with us forever."

She pulled me into a hug and patted my back.

"I don't think there's a big hurry to decide, but...it would mean the world to me to stay with or near you, Hendrix, Mac, and Franklin."

A smile broke out over my face.

"Okay, we'll figure it out later, then. I suspect Franklin will want us to stay here for a while longer to keep an eye on Hendrix. If I were him, I would do the same."

"Franklin is a lonely man, Gemma. He needs us as much or more than we need him. He's lost a lot, too."

I nodded. "He's been really good to us and wants nothing in return."

"Oh, he does. He just doesn't realize it."

I frowned at her. "What do you mean?"

"He wants a family, and to be loved like we all do."

AFTER ADA LYNN and I chatted, I located Mac and Hendrix in the game room, talking serious trash to each other while they played a video game I'd never heard of.

"Who's kicking whose ass?" I asked, plopping down on the leather couch. Mac was standing, bobbing back and forth as if Hendrix was really shooting at her. Their fingers flew over the controls as they laughed and flung insults at each other.

"We're celebrating tonight," Mac said.

"We are?"

"Yup, we're going out for drinks. Charles will drive."

I blanched and shot Hendrix a look. A mischievous grin spread across his face. He knew what I was like when I drank.

"I'm in," I said, winking at Hendrix.

He coughed and dropped his controller on the floor.

"I have a doctor's appointment this afternoon, so we were talking about grabbing dinner and drinks around seven. What do you think?"

"It sounds good. I'm ready to have some fun." I

flicked my tongue across my bottom lip, my heated gaze traveling over him.

He rubbed his chin and turned around for a moment. I assumed he was trying to control the sudden bulge in his jeans.

"I'm kicking your ass, bro!" Mac yelled, utterly oblivious to mine and Hendrix's foreplay.

"I see Mac's competitive spirit hasn't changed," Franklin said, laughing from the doorway.

"Ugh," she cried and paused the game. "I just died."

Hendrix laughed and turned to Franklin. "I think that's an understatement."

"Gemma, I need you for a few minutes."

Shit. What now? Every time he needed me all hell broke loose.

"What's wrong?" Hendrix asked, protectively.

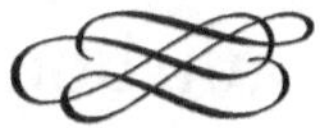

CHAPTER 23

"It's fine, babe. I'll be right back." I got up from the couch and followed Franklin down the stairs and into his office, my anxiety climbing with each step.

"He really does love you," Franklin said, taking a seat at his desk.

I sat in my usual place, my fingers tapping nervously on the arm of the chair.

"Gemma, it's okay. I need to discuss funeral plans and Kyle's will."

"Oh," I said, releasing the breath I'd not realized I'd been holding.

"Most everything was included in Kyle's will, and there's money to pay for the cremation and burial next to your mom." His voice trailed off.

He'd known that Kyle's abuse had caused Mom's death. And I seriously doubted she would want to be buried next to him. Not after what she'd learned about him.

Franklin continued to talk, and I tried to pay attention, but my brain bounced around like a ping pong ball. This was the second time I'd buried a parent in six months.

"I'm going to help you make the arrangements if that works?"

I nodded.

"There was a small insurance policy, and you now own the house you grew up in."

"What?" I asked, startled. "What in the world would I do with that house? He...I...Mom."

Franklin laid the papers down on his desk and waited for me to process.

"Gemma," he said kindly, "What do you want? Where do you want to live?"

"Here!" I said too loudly. "I mean, in Spokane with Hendrix, Ada Lynn, Mac, and you. I have nothing left in Louisiana." I sank into my seat. "I don't even know if I can look at that house again, Franklin."

"I wouldn't either, honestly. You've been through more than most people go through in a lifetime. It's fine, you don't have to deal with it right now, anyway. The insurance policy actually paid the house off, so you're not stuck trying to sell it or making payments. You have a hundred grand left from the policy, so it should help with college or anything else you decide you need it for. I would recommend, at least for now, you invest some of it, then decide what you want to do with the rest later. There's no hurry."

I nodded. The money would definitely help with school, but I could literally feel the color drain from my face at the mere idea of walking into that house again. Nausea stirred inside my stomach, and I swallowed hard.

"I've not talked to Hendrix yet, but I will this afternoon when I take him to see the doctor. I realize he's grown and has his own life, but I'm hoping he'll continue to stay for a while. I would like to keep an eye on him a little longer, plus...plus, Gemma, I like having you all here." A sad smile eased across his features. "I've screwed up a lot, but I would like to take care of the kids I have left."

A tear snuck down my cheek. "Thanks, it actually helps to know we don't have to make any decisions yet. I'll need some time to think about it. I do want to go back to school, but I don't know if Hendrix will want to tour again soon, or what our future looks like yet. I know I can attend online, too. I've done it before."

"You have plenty of options, but I'm happy to hear you want to finish college."

"Yeah. I do."

"Let's get some paperwork signed, and I need to get Hendrix to his appointment."

Thank God Franklin helped me with the insurance, death certificates, and all the other legal matters I would needed assistance with. Kyle had somehow managed to at least take care of that when Mom had died.

Lost in thought, I made my way back to the game room where Hendrix and Mac were sprawled out on the couches, talking.

"Hey," Hendrix said, sitting up. "What did Dad want?"

I sank into the seat next to him and stared at my hands.

"Just shit. Funeral arrangements, the will, insurance papers and crap."

"I'm sorry," Mac said, hopping off the couch and sitting on the other side of me. She wrapped her arms around me for a gentle hug.

"I'm not. At least right now I'm not. Hell would be too good for him."

Hendrix took my hand, and Mac took the other. We sat there silently. Together.

"I KNOW you've had a partly shitty day, Gemma, but I'm so excited Hendrix has his memories back, and we're going out!" Mac jumped on my bed, giggling. "I missed him so much."

Her giggle was infectious, and for tonight, all I wanted to do was focus on the positive.

"Where are we going anyway? And what should I wear?" I asked.

"Well, Hendrix and I wanted to surprise you. Ya know, since your Dad...Kyle and stuff."

"Yeah?"

"Charles will drive us to the airport, and we'll all fly over to Seattle and eat at the SkyCity Restaurant."

"Everyone? Ada Lynn, too?" I asked, excited.

"Yup. Franklin won't care if we drink, so no biggie there. And no dress code, it's nice and casual. We figured it'd be fun, especially since you can go up into the Space Needle and see the entire city. The restaurant actually has the world's first revolving glass floor!" She clapped her hands. "The floor is new, so we've not seen it yet. Let's get ready together like we used to."

"That would be great. Sometimes I miss when we shared a dorm room," I said, grinning at her.

My phone buzzed, and I pulled it out of my back pocket.

Doc says everything looked excellent and congratulated me on the return of my memories. I'm guessing Mac told you we're flying to Seattle tonight for dinner?

"Hendrix said the doctor's appointment went well," I said, grinning.

Yeah, we're about to get ready. Ya know, girl time. :)

I can't wait to get you back home tonight. The idea of you having a few drinks has given me a major boner all damned day.

I barked out a laugh, and Mac raised an eyebrow at me.

"Don't ask," I said.

I'll be happy to help you with that. :)

I think a midnight swim will be in your favor.

A slow grin eased across my face.

Skinny dipping?

I thought you'd never ask.

Heat swirled deep inside me at the idea of making love to him in the water.

Gotta go tell Ada Lynn the plan. I'll see you in a while. Love you.

Love you, too. You're my forever.

And you're my always.

I glanced up to find Mac full on staring at me.

"You two are planning sexcapades. I can tell by your expression."

"Mac!" I chided. "Has anyone told Ada Lynn we're going tonight?"

Mac half shrugged and laughed.

"Let's go," I said, motioning to her. "She'll need time to get ready, too."

Over the next few hours, Mac and I hung out, danced to our favorite music, and got ready for the trip to Seattle in my bedroom. I talked her into wearing her hair down, and she presented me with a low-cut blue top that apparently showed a bit of cleavage.

"I picked this up for you while I was out the other afternoon. So no arguing, just wear it. I actually picked it out before he got his memories back. Ya know, I was thinking along the lines of making him remember what he was missing. But now? He can play with them all he wants. But still, it's fun to work your guy up a little," she said, wiggling her eyebrows at me.

Embarrassed, I snatched the top away from

her and tried it on. I hurried to the full-length mirror in the bathroom.

"Mac!" I yelled. "My boobs are barely in my shirt!"

"No, it's not that bad...Whooa!" she said, stepping into the bathroom. "Can you stuff the girls in there at all?"

"In where? The only material available covers my nipples."

She burst into giggles, and I did, too. Maybe I would keep it for Hendrix, but no way in hell would I wear a shirt that allowed my breasts to be on full display.

"Thanks for trying," I said, hugging her before slipping out of it. I folded it and left it on the bathroom counter.

Mac rifled through my closet and picked out a more appropriate plum colored polo shirt. She straightened my hair, and I curled hers. We sang out of tune at the top of our lungs and giggled at our bad jokes. I'd never had so much fun with a friend in my entire life.

At four o'clock, we made our way downstairs to wait for the guys and met Ada Lynn in the family room. I'd not spent any real time in here, but it was decorated with white plush leather furniture, a marble tiled fireplace, television, and an oak coffee table. It was definitely more relaxed than the formal room across the entryway.

"Miss Ada," Mac said, hurrying toward her and flinging her arms around Ada Lynn's neck.

Ada Lynn chuckled and hugged Mac back.

"I'm so excited you're going with us. You're going to love it. And, ohmigosh the prime rib melts in your mouth. Oh wait, have I ever seen you eat meat? Do you have your own teeth? Shit, do you wear dentures? I've never thought to ask you. Crap, it's probably none of my business, anyway, but really the prime rib is like fuckin' butter on your tongue."

"Mac," Ada Lynn said, laughing. "I eat beef sometimes, I have my own teeth, and watch your language."

I snickered while Mac blushed furiously at her outburst.

The front door opened, and Hendrix and Franklin stepped inside. They were deep in a hushed conversation that stopped the second they spotted us.

My brow arched. What was going on?

"Hey babe," Hendrix said, pulling me off the couch and into his arms. He planted a quick kiss on my mouth and took my hand. "You look beautiful," he said softly.

"Thanks," I said, leaning my head against his shoulder and then grabbing my jacket off the couch.

"Is everyone ready?" Franklin asked, clapping his hands together. "Hendrix has a clean bill of health, his memories are back, and I have my entire family together under one roof. Let's go celebrate."

Mac helped Ada Lynn off the couch, and we all made our way to the limo out front.

Charles stood beside the door and opened it for us when we arrived. I peeked at him, but he stared straight ahead, sunglasses in place. We were supposed to train tomorrow night, but I wasn't sure how I was going to manage it now that Hendrix was back to normal. I chewed my lip, debating how to handle it as we settled into the car. Charles had been firm on not telling anyone, but I didn't feel right about training behind Hendrix's back either.

"Are you alright? You're thinking pretty hard about something," Hendrix said quietly as the car pulled out of the driveway.

"I'm good. I'm excited about seeing Seattle again. This time...this time it's under better circumstances, and we're together." I glanced up at him and smiled. It seemed like a lifetime ago when he'd taken me to Seattle to see Jordan, and I'd revealed my secrets.

"I know you've been through a lot. I'm just checking to see how you're doing." He smoothed my hair and kissed my forehead.

"Get a roooom," Mac said, giggling.

Hendrix gave her a playful kick while Franklin pointed out places and buildings to Ada Lynn. The last time we'd been at the airport, we'd flown in from Louisiana in the middle of the night.

The flight to Seattle was less than an hour, but I loved every minute of it. I could get used to traveling with Hendrix like this.

Franklin had another limo at the airport and Charles drove us to the Space Needle.

"Oh my," Ada Lynn said, patting her chest as she got out of the car. Her brows shot up, and she peeked over at me. "We're going all the way up?" she asked, stammering.

"Are you comfortable with that?" I asked, my head tilting upward. "I bet the view will be magnificent."

Hendrix stood between Ada Lynn and me, slipping an arm around each of us. I snuggled into him as Mac took Franklin's arm.

"Our table should be ready, let's go on up,"

Franklin said. "You'll be able to see the city lights, plus the sunset over the Puget Sound. It's an absolutely breathtaking view."

"If it makes you feel better, Ada Lynn, the Space Needle was built to sustain two-hundred-mile per hour winds and an earthquake up to a nine-point one magnitude," Hendrix said.

"Holy wow," I replied.

"We'll go through a security screening," Franklin said over his shoulder. "It's standard protocol so don't worry."

It was a good thing Charles wasn't going up with us. I knew for a fact he carried a concealed weapon.

After our security check, we made our way up to the top of the building. My gaze traveled across the restaurant that allowed for three hundred-and sixty-degree views of Seattle. Hendrix squeezed my hand and guided Ada Lynn and me to our table. The sun had begun its descent, lighting up the sky with a brilliant pink and orange display.

"We're five hundred feet in the air, and the observation deck is up a little higher. You can see the Cascade Mountains and Mt. Rainer from here," Hendrix said, pointing to them while we settled into our table.

"I've never seen anything so beautiful," Ada Lynn said, her eyes misting slightly.

"I know, right? Even I slow down a little bit when I'm up here. It's like all the beauty and the grandiosity of nature...well, it's calming," Mac said, tucking her hair behind her ear.

The waitress placed our waters in front of us, then Franklin ordered appetizers. Mac, Hendrix, and I ordered drinks. I opted for a vodka and cranberry.

"Feeling brave tonight?" Hendrix said against my ear, his hand sneaking beneath the table and between my thighs.

"You're not playing fair," I said, my lower lip jutting out in a pout.

"I'm not playing fair? I don't know how in the hell I'm going to make it until we get home."

I smiled, taking a sip of my water.

"The thought of you in that bikini has made it difficult to walk all damned day. I might have to sneak you into the restroom and lock the door behind us."

Nearly spewing my water out, I shot him a startled look. Sex in a public restaurant? Was he kidding?

"Behave," I said. But he didn't, and by the time our drinks were here I took several big gulps, attempting to calm my raging libido. Maybe the right amount would relax me instead of turning me into a sex fiend.

Hendrix chuckled and placed a quick kiss on my cheek.

"I love you so much," he said.

"I love you, too," I whispered, gazing into his blue eyes. The night he walked into my bedroom with his memories intact had been the happiest moment in my life. Over the last few months, he'd become the air I breathed and the beat of my heart. He'd given me back parts of my life I'd never realized were missing.

Mac was right, the prime rib was absolutely amazing. I wasn't sure about Ada Lynn, but I'd never eaten it before. We chatted, drank, and ate until I figured I would have to waddle my way out of the restaurant. I'd never seen Ada Lynn so happy, either, which made the evening even more special. She deserved some fun.

Three drinks later, I was ready to take Hendrix home, but I knew there was one more detail to the evening.

I kicked Mac under the table as the wait staff approached with a small birthday cake. The second they began to sing, everyone at our table joined in and sang Happy Birthday to Ada Lynn.

Her mouth gaped while they sat the cake on the table and finished the song. The entire restaurant clapped and cheered. Ada Lynn blushed slightly and grinned at me.

"You thought I forgot your birthday, didn't you?" I asked, standing up and walking over to her. I grabbed her in for a big hug and kissed her cheek. "I love you. Happy birthday."

"I did wonder a little bit, but you've had a lot to deal with. Plus you know I've never made a big fuss over it."

"Yeah, I know, but it doesn't mean we can't tonight," Mac chimed in. "You only turn eighty-four once. And no cake for me." She shot Ada Lynn a guilty look. "You can have my piece."

Ada Lynn chuckled, her eyes welling with tears as everyone took a turn with hugs and birthday wishes.

"This has been a wonderful evening," Ada Lynn said, dabbing her mouth after eating. "Thank you all so much."

"I'd already made reservations when Gemma told me it was your birthday. I figured this would be a perfect place to celebrate," Franklin said.

"One more thing." I reached into my jacket pocket that I'd only worn to hide her gift in. I placed a little white box in front of her.

"You didn't need to get me anything," Ada Lynn chided, lifting the lid off. Her mouth dropped open as she pulled a delicate gold necklace out of the box. The sapphire glinted against the lights in the room.

"I'll put it on for you," Mac said.

Ada Lynn turned, and Mac slipped the jewelry around her neck.

"I'm speechless," Ada Lynn said, peering down at the stone. "It's wonderful, thank you all so much. I don't know what to say."

"Gemma and Mac chose it for you." Franklin smiled at both of us.

Ada Lynn gushed over her gift a bit longer, then it was time to go home. I literally counted the minutes until Hendrix and I were alone.

THE SHARP SCENT of chlorine tickled my nose as we entered the pool house.

"Jesus, I've waited for you all night," Hendrix said, trailing hot kisses down my neck and flipping open the button on my jeans.

He eased his hand inside my G-string and made small circles against my clit. The alcohol had taken full effect, and all I cared about was being with him. We'd not even bothered to change into our swimsuits. Instead, he'd grabbed my hand after we'd told everyone goodnight and quietly made our way to the pool house. We'd nestled into the corner, making out like teenagers.

I pushed my hips against him while his finger teased my entrance. Pulling his hand away, he led me into the gym. He pulled my jeans down, and I stepped out of them. He then removed my shirt, his eyes traveling up and down my body. Tingles of anticipation shivered through me.

"Sit," he said, his voice low and gravelly as he pointed to the weight bench he used on a regular basis.

I sat as he kneeled then spread my legs apart, moving my G-string aside. His mouth was on my sensitive flesh before I could even get my balance. When he carefully draped my legs over his shoulders, I threaded my hands in his hair. His fingers dug into my waist as I moved with him. No way would I ever get enough of him. I moaned in protest when he backed away, wiping his mouth with his hand and giving me a sexy grin.

"Stand up and turn around," he ordered, unbuttoning and lowering his jeans. My attention landed on his erection before I turned, bent over, and leaned my hands on the bench.

The alcohol usually turned me into a fiend, but tonight he'd taken control, and I actually liked it. I trusted him implicitly.

I moaned while he eased inside me slowly, nearly bringing me to a climax on the spot.

"God, you're so tight, Gem," he panted, thrusting deep. "I've thought about being inside you all day."

I whimpered as he picked up the pace, our lovemaking turning into a full-on frenzy. Pushing my hips into him, my core tightened with anticipation.

"Harder," I said over my shoulder. "You feel so damned good."

He moved his hand between my legs, teasing my clit while he pounded into me. Our moans echoed through the gym, the smell of sex in the air.

"Gem," he gasped. "Come for me. I want to feel you tighten around my cock."

A swirl of heat shot through me with his words. His fingers gently pinched my throbbing bud, and my world exploded.

"Oh. My. God. Hendrix."

His body tensed, his fingers grabbing my ass

cheek as he came deep inside me. He thrust one more time before pulling out. I stood and turned around. He was still hard.

I dropped to my knees and ran my tongue along his shaft, sucking the tip into my mouth as I looked up. His eyes were on me, watching as I slid him in and out.

"Oh shit." He grabbed a handful of my hair and moved his hips with the rhythm of my mouth. He moaned while I continued to stroke him.

Cupping his balls in my hand, I continued to suck. My tongue swirled around him, his body tensing as he released.

His hands loosened in my hair while he relaxed. I stood slowly, wiping the corners of my mouth.

"I don't want this night to end," he said, looking at me.

"Me either." I kissed the tip of his nose.

"Hang on," he said, walking away bare ass naked. My eyes scanned his muscular body as he walked into the bathroom and returned a moment later with two full sized white towels.

"Hold your hands up," he said, bundling me up in the soft fabric.

He wrapped the other towel around his waist

and took my hand, gathering our discarded articles of clothing along the way. I followed him out to the pool and stared into the water. Glancing around, he dropped our clothes in a pile, released his towel, and hopped in the water.

"Come on," he motioned to me.

"I can't swim," I said, embarrassed.

"You don't have to."

I dropped my towel, grabbed the rail, and walked down the steps. The warm water felt amazing as it glided over my bare skin. Hendrix took my hand and pulled me against him.

"Wrap your legs around me," he said.

The water made me feel weightless as I brought my legs up and around his hips.

"Just hang on." He brought my arms around his neck and stepped into the deeper water.

"I can't believe I'm skinny dipping in your dad's pool," I giggled quietly.

Hendrix sank down into the water up to my chin.

"Are you doing alright?" he asked, his hand trailing up my back.

"Yeah, this is nice," I said, smiling. "I've never been in a pool before. We never went swimming when I was growing up, so I haven't been around water much.

He kissed me gently.

"I love the water. Maybe you'll learn to like it, too."

"I like this for sure," I said, kissing him. Our mouths parted, his tongue caressing mine while we held onto each other.

A cough echoed through the room, startling us out of our kiss.

CHAPTER 24

"Shit," Hendrix said while Charles walked in, eyeing us. "Don't move." He shifted me down slightly in order to make sure I was covered as much as possible. His hands grabbed my ass, shielding me from Charles's view.

"Hey," Hendrix said, nodding.

Charles stared at him, his expression unchanging.

"I'm going to use the gym," he said, his voice low.

Mortified, I buried my face against Hendrix's shoulder.

"Have a good workout, man," Hendrix replied.

Charles's footsteps faded from the room, and my head popped up.

"Oh. My. God. That just happened didn't it?"

Hendrix chuckled and kissed me.

"Yeah, but we were taking a risk the moment our clothes came off."

"How are we going to get out of here?" I asked, searching for our towels.

The clanging of weights told us he was at least in the gym and not near us.

"I'll get out and get my towel. I had rather him see me naked than you."

My palm smacked my forehead. "I would fucking die."

"Oh, yeah. You and him both," he said, an edge to his words.

"What?" I asked, frowning.

"Once a guy sees a hot girl naked, it's over, the image is imprinted on our brains forever. No way in hell do I want him to look at you like that. You're mine," he growled against my ear.

"Yes, I am." Worry swirled inside me. How would he react if he knew Charles was training me? Was he being this protective because we were naked? Or was it in general? I had to figure it out and fast. I couldn't have them butting heads. Franklin would fire Charles, and it would be my fault.

Hendrix walked along the bottom of the pool

until I could touch. Placing my feet down, I sank into the water while he walked to the side and hoisted himself out of the pool in one strong, swift move. Grabbing his towel, he wrapped it around his waist and carried mine over to the steps at the shallow end.

"Over here." He held the towel open, ready to wrap me up.

The closer I got to the steps, the shallower the water became. Slowly I emerged, Hendrix standing directly in front of me. His mouth opened and closed before he found the right words.

"You're so fucking beautiful." His eyes slowly drifted to mine, meeting my gaze.

Another clank from the weight room broke him from his hormone-induced haze. He walked down the steps, into the water, and draped the oversized towel around me.

"Thanks," I said, relieved.

Hendrix took my hand and led me out of the pool room and back into the main house. We scurried up the stairs, giggling like two little kids. I'd never imagined my life would turn out this way, or that I could honestly be happy. Carl and Kyle had stolen everything from me, but it had led me to Hendrix.

Flipping on my bedroom light, we closed the door quietly behind us. Our towels dropped to the floor as Hendrix picked me up. I wrapped my legs around him, his erection pressing into my ass cheek.

"Shower," he muttered before he kissed me again.

He held me with one arm and turned the shower on with his other hand. I nipped at his neck while we waited for the water to warm up.

"I'm not sure who is more insatiable tonight. You or me," he teased, stepping into the spray. The hot water traveled over us as his mouth crashed down on mine and he backed me up against the cool tile wall. I unwrapped my legs from his waist and slowly lowered my feet to the floor, Hendrix's strong arms supporting me.

"Turn around," he whispered against my lips, then guided me to face the wall.

I leaned my head back against his shoulder and moaned as he brought his arms around me, cupping my breasts in his hands and pulling on my taut nipples. Another moan escaped me, this time to complain when he pulled away to grab my citrus body wash. The tangy scent of lemon filled the steamy air as he poured some into his hands, rubbing them together to create a sudsy lather. His hands glided over my shoulders, down my back, and over my ass cheeks before slipping between my legs. He traced my swollen clit with his slick fingers and eased one inside me. I spread my legs apart and tilted my backside up, allowing him easier access. Propping my arms against the wall, I leaned against it.

"Baby," I whispered, losing myself in his touch.

He slid in another finger and my back arched.

"You like that?" he asked, nuzzling my neck. "You like me inside you, Gemma?"

"Yes," I whimpered.

"Sometimes I can't decide what I want the most," he said, trailing his tongue along my neck. "My mouth on your wet pussy or my dick buried deep inside you."

I groaned, his words sending pulsating heat through my body.

"Jesus, you're throbbing around my fingers. You like this, Gem? You like it when I talk to you like this?"

Between still being tipsy from my earlier drinks and his silky voice, I was putty in his hands. At this moment, he could do anything he wanted to.

"What do you want? Do you want my tongue

inside you or my dick? Tell me," he growled, squeezing my breast.

"Both," I moaned, pushing against his hand.

Hendrix turned me to face him, then grabbed the shower head and aimed it between my legs, rinsing away the soap. He positioned it back into the holder, then he kneeled.

Leaning against the wall for support, I gasped while he gently tugged at my clit with his teeth.

"Talk to me," he demanded.

"Hendrix," I said.

"Tell me." He flicked his tongue across my sensitive folds. I was so worked up, and yet so relaxed, my legs refused to hold me up. I sank down onto the wide, tile seat built along the length of the shower stall. He pushed my legs back, his gaze traveling over my core.

He leaned forward and kissed me deeply.

"Tell me what you want me to do to you, baby," he said, his words thick with desire.

Feeling brave, I grabbed his hair and leaned forward, nipping his ear.

"I want your tongue inside me, and I want you to fuck me until I scream your name." I released his hair.

"Jesus Christ," he said, holding his cock.

"You're going to make me come just talking like that."

He dipped his head between my legs and peered up at me with those startling blue eyes, our gazes connecting. I arched my back as he ran his tongue up my slit, slowly. He pushed my legs up, pinning my knees against my chest. I had the perfect view as his tongue claimed me, sliding in and out.

I ran my fingers through his soft, wet hair then held onto his shoulders, my nails digging into his warm skin as he fucked me with his mouth. Squirming in my seat, I fought the strong desire to climax. I didn't want it to end.

He moaned, bringing me to the edge, then stopped abruptly and stood. When he leaned in to kiss me, I gently grasped his erection and gave it a couple of long, slow strokes. I was hoping to undo him as much as he was making me unravel. With a deep growl, he grabbed my wrist, forcing me to let go and then he kneeled again, his tongue grazing my nub.

My eyes fluttered closed while he took me to the edge again, but this time he didn't stop. He sucked on my clit, pumping his finger in and out of me.

"Yeah, baby. Just like that," I gasped, my hands planting against the bench.

"Come for me, Gemma. I love the taste of you. Fucking come for me," he growled.

My hips thrust forward, and I ground my core against his mouth.

"Oh yeah," he said. "I can't wait to bury my dick inside you."

His words sent me into overdrive. I held my fist against my mouth to keep from screaming out when my entire body tensed, climaxing against him. Right as I finished, he pulled me up and spun me around. He eased inside me, his hands squeezing my tits.

"Oh, baby," I moaned.

He slammed every thick inch of himself into me. His mouth trailed hot kisses across my shoulders, and his arm encircled my waist, steadying me as he thrust inside me.

"Shit," he said, digging his fingers into my stomach. "I can't wait, babe."

With one more swift movement, our bodies seized with our release. Panting, I leaned my head against the shower wall. Happy and exhausted. Hendrix pulled out of me gently and turned me to face him.

"I love you so much," he said, kissing me. "I don't want you to think that because we have some fun and talk dirty to each other that I don't love you. If you told me it wasn't for you, I would be fine with it. I want us both to be comfortable exploring different things together, find out what we like and don't like. Most of all I want you to know how much you own my heart, whether we make love or fuck. I just want you to feel safe and happy with me, Gem."

"I do, Hendrix. I know you love me. Even when you had amnesia, you were on your way back to me." I kissed him gently. "Concerning the sex, it's a moment to moment thing, but I promise if I feel uncomfortable, I'll tell you. Likewise, if there's something new I want to try..." I giggled and gave him a wink.

His hands slid up my back, pulling me into him.

"You're my entire world, and I'll do anything I can to keep you safe and make you happy. I love you," he said, pressing his forehead against mine. I slipped my arms around his neck and kissed him, the hot spray of the water raining down on us.

Ten minutes later, we stepped out of the shower, washed, and rinsed.

"I'm exhausted," I said, putting on an over-sized T-shirt and clean panties. I tossed Hendrix one of the pairs of shorts he kept in my room for nights like this, and he stepped into them.

"Me too, you wore me out," he said, grinning. "But it was worth every minute. Hang on." My heart pitter-patted against my chest as I watched him saunter into the bathroom. The cabinet door clattered closed, and he returned with two towels. He made his way over to my side of the bed and shook the towel out, laying it on top of my pillow.

"Our hair is still wet."

"Thanks," I said. He had no idea how the simple things he did absolutely melted me.

I slipped under the blankets while he put the towel on his pillow and curled up next to me. Flipping the lamp off, I glanced at the clock. It was almost two in the morning. I snuggled up next to him, and he caressed my cheek, kissing the top of my head.

"Hey," he said.

Glancing up at him, I waited for him to continue.

"I'm meeting with John and Cade tomorrow night. I haven't seen them since I got home."

A wave of relief rushed over me. I was scheduled to train with Charles tomorrow.

"I bet they're excited to see you. What time are you guys hanging out?"

"I'll leave about nine. Cade has a late class, so we decided we would meet afterward. I'd invite you, but I think they want to hang out for a while. Are you okay with it?"

I propped myself up on my arm.

"Hendrix, you need your friends. I have Mac and Ada Lynn, and I totally understand that you'll need to hang out with the guys sometimes and I won't go with you. It's important we have friends outside of each other, too."

A pang of guilt jabbed at me. I wasn't too sure he would consider Charles a friend.

"You're sure?"

"Yes," I said, smiling. "Tell them I said hi and hope to see them soon."

"I will. And Friday night, I would like to take you out."

"Yeah?" I grinned up at him. Between all the shit that had happened during our time together, we'd not gone out on many actual dates.

"I would love that."

"Good. You might want to shop for a new dress with Mac."

"Oh, somewhere really nice, huh? I can't wait." I gave him a quick peck on the cheek and then drifted off to sleep, listening to the steady beat of his heart.

CHAPTER 25

The day whizzed by as Mac and I shopped. After trying on twenty different dresses, I bought a teal blue one that deepened in a V down my back. I hoped it was appropriate for our date Friday, but more than that, I hoped Hendrix liked it.

After dinner, I started a game of pinochle with Ada Lynn, Mac, and Franklin. Hendrix joined us for cards before he left to meet John and Cade.

"I gotta run, but it's been a great evening with everyone. I'll see you guys in the morning," he said, standing from the dining room table.

"Will you walk out with me?" he asked, extending his hand.

I took it and walked with him through the

kitchen and into the entryway. He opened the front door for me, and I stepped out into the crisp spring evening. A shiver shot through me and Hendrix pulled me in for a hug.

"I might be gone for a while, but I would like to sneak into your room when I'm home."

"I would like that. I'm getting used to you being next to me again."

"Me, too. In fact, I wondered what you might think of us moving back into my place. We need some privacy, and there are times I don't want to share you."

"I'd love to," I said, pushing up on my tiptoes and kissing him.

"I was hoping you'd say that. We'll need to talk to Dad and figure out what's best for Ada Lynn."

"Oh," I said, frowning. "I guess I figured she would live wherever I was."

"And she can, babe. I'm not saying she shouldn't, but let's talk about our options. She might be happier here. Dad loves having everyone around, so it might be good for both of them."

"And Mac?" I asked, realizing what he meant. Although I wanted to live alone with him, I needed to be near Ada Lynn and Mac. For some dumb reason, I'd just assumed we would all continue to live together forever.

"Hey, don't stress. We don't have to move at all yet. If you're happy here, then Franklin is cool with everyone staying. We'll continue like we have been. I just figured I would run it by you."

"I understand, and I want to live alone with you, but I guess I'd not thought about it. I mean, you had amnesia when we all came to Spokane this time, so I haven't moved past the idea of you regaining your memories. I guess in my mind, we were staying here forever. That's silly isn't it?"

"No babe, it's not. You've lost your family, and I'm in no rush to pull you away from Ada Lynn. Honestly, I just want to be able to run around naked together."

I laughed and smacked his arm playfully.

"Let's wait a bit, then we can talk about it again. How does that sound?" he asked, his fingers gently stroking my cheek.

"I love you, Hendrix Harrington." I kissed him again, my heart overwhelmed with his patience. He'd been nothing but supportive and gentle with me.

"I love you, too. You're my forever," he whispered in my ear.

"And you're my always. Be safe and hurry back home to me."

He kissed my forehead, and I waited outside while he climbed into his new Lexus and drove away.

Chewing on my bottom lip, I let myself back in the house and checked the time. I still had an hour before I met with Charles. Not only was moving into Hendrix's house now weighing on my mind, but I also needed to talk to Charles about telling Hendrix that he was training me.

I peeked into the dining room, but the group had split up. I meandered to Ada Lynn's room, only to find her door closed and the light off. Climbing the stairs, my brain ran through every scenario of us moving and where Mac and Ada Lynn would stay. I'd grown accustomed to us all in the same house, but I knew Hendrix was right and we couldn't stay forever. Eventually, I suspected his tour would pick back up, too. Then I'd be faced with traveling with him or remaining behind.

My chest tightened with the idea, but I shoved it to the side. I didn't have to figure it all out tonight.

Reaching my bedroom door, I hesitated for a

moment, then padded down the hall to Mac's room, but she wasn't there. Where had she gone?

I ran my hand along the wall while I went back to my room and flopped on the bed. A wave of loneliness crashed down on me, and I found myself struggling to not burst into tears. For so many years, my life had remained unchanged. Stagnant. And now, I'd give anything to settle down for a while. I was tired of moving, too. My chest ached as my thoughts drifted to my Mom. I wondered what she would think of my life now. Would she be proud of me, or ashamed that I was living with Hendrix? Kyle had shoved his religious beliefs down our throats, and I would never have the chance to ask Mom what she believed. She might have rolled over in her grave if she knew I was having sex before marriage. But I would never know.

A tear snuck down my cheek, and I wiped it away angrily. If it hadn't been for Kyle, I'd be able to pick up the phone and call Mom. The bastard had gotten what he deserved. I hated him. He'd ruined us all.

Glancing at the clock, I realized I needed to get ready to meet Charles. At least I was in a pissy mood now, which meant I could work it out on him.

I changed into my workout clothes and made my way to the gym. Charles wasn't there yet, so I stretched. Even though we'd only trained a handful of times, I noticed my body was growing stronger and more limber.

"Evening," Charles said, his voice deep and husky.

"Hey," I said. "How's it going? I feel like I haven't seen you much unless you're driving everyone around or some shit."

"You've seen me twice a week like always," he said, his tone sharp. His gaze traveled over my body and my cheeks warmed. Was he thinking about catching Hendrix and I in the swimming pool the other night?

"Yeah, I guess so." I ignored his attitude. I never knew which Charles I was going to get from one minute to the next, anyway.

"Let's get started."

I nodded, and this time, when he stepped forward and swung, I ducked and planted a punch to his gut.

"Good," he said, tucking his arms into his body. He lunged at me again, but I didn't move in time, and I took the full-on brunt of his weight. I toppled to the floor with him on top of me. The air whooshed from my lungs while he pinned me down on the mat. Flashbacks of Carl on top of me with his hands wrapped around my neck pulsed through my mind. Fear traveled through me as I struggled to catch my breath and shove down the panic that threatened to overwhelm me every time Charles pinned me down. I'd conquered so much, but this was my trigger. Dammit! I thought I was pushing through.

"Hey, what the fuck? Get off her!" Hendrix yelled, charging Charles, and knocking him off me. The second Charles was on the floor, I scurried backward.

"Hendrix!" I yelled, jumping up. I ran to him and grabbed his arm. He'd pinned Charles down, his fist poised in the air.

"It's not what you think," I said, my voice pleading with him. His eyes cut over to me as he stood, backing up.

Charles jumped up quickly.

"What the hell is going on?" Hendrix asked, his tone curt.

I rubbed my face with both hands and looked at Charles. Anger flickered across his expression.

"I can't lie to him. I'm so sorry," I said to Charles, my voice barely hovering above a whisper.

Frowning, I turned to Hendrix. I was about to

break my promise to Charles, and I hated myself for it. But I couldn't lie to Hendrix, either. He already thought Charles had attacked me, so at this point, there wasn't much to lose.

"I was going to tell you, but I needed to talk to Charles since it involved him, too."

Hendrix's eyes flashed with anger.

"He's been training me, Hendrix." I dared a glance at Charles, his posture rigid. "I asked him when you still had amnesia. I'd planned on asking you, but then you lost your memory. He was the only person I could turn to. I can't live my life in terror, wondering who will come after me next. Charles was there the night Carl attacked me at our house in Louisiana. Somehow, I managed to get Carl off me, but Charles saved me."

Hendrix's shoulders sagged under the weight of my words. "I should have been there, I'm so sorry."

"Don't," I said, holding up my hand to stop him from going down that road. "Charles and I swore we would keep our sessions quiet. Not only did I have to beg him to teach me, but we also didn't think Franklin would approve. Charles risked his job to help me, Hendrix. He's on our side."

Hendrix glared at Charles while he assessed the situation.

"Charles, I won't tell Dad. You're doing the right thing," Hendrix muttered. "A part of me wants to thank you for taking care of Gemma, and another part of me wants to beat the hell out of you for pinning her down like that."

I gently pulled on Hendrix's arm and turned him toward me.

"He's not hurting me, baby. He's teaching me how to save my own life. No one can be with me all of the time. Brandon..."

Charles hissed at the mention of Brandon's name, and I could have sworn I heard him mutter, *Fucker better not mess with our girl again.*

"Charles doesn't like him either. So when I told him Brandon had nearly raped me last year, he agreed to work with me."

Hendrix let out a sigh.

"Man, you're safe. I'm not saying shit to anyone. Just, moving forward, I need to train with you at the same time so I can make sure she's alright."

"No. I'm sorry, that won't work." I folded my arms over my chest and tapped my toe against the mat. "You'll get angry and mad at him, and he won't train me right. You have to trust me. You have to trust that if it gets to be too much, I'll talk to Charles. Right now, I'm fine. I get triggered sometimes, but I've been okay."

My focus bounced between Hendrix and Charles.

"Charles? It's your call. If you don't want to continue or if you're worried about your job, I'll understand. But Hendrix won't say anything."

His forehead creased. "I'm in if Hendrix trusts me. I can't risk any complications or drama while I'm on duty, though, so it's either a hundred percent support or I'm out."

"Fair enough," Hendrix said, rubbing his jawline. "We're good. Go ahead and train." Hendrix planted a kiss on my cheek and waltzed out of the gym.

"Fuck," I spat. "That's not how that was supposed to happen."

"Life never goes the way we anticipate," he said, stepping toward me. "It's why you have to be ready for anything."

I nodded. "Thanks for not bailing on me. I appreciate you more than you'll ever know."

His eyes softened for a moment.

"Let's work on the bag for the rest of the night."

I nodded and followed him over to it, my

mind not entirely focused. My attention had left with Hendrix, and even though he said he was fine with our training, concern nudged at me. I needed to know he was really on board with this. It must have fucked with him to see Charles pin me down and not understand what was going on. If the situation had been reversed, I would have beat the hell out of someone.

Forty minutes later, I ran through the house and up the stairs to Hendrix's room. Wiping the sweat from my forehead, I tapped on his door.

"Yeah," he muttered.

I opened it slowly and peered inside. He was sprawled out on his bed, his hands behind his head.

"Hey."

"Hey." Sadness flickered across his face, and I stepped in and closed the door behind me.

"What happened, anyway? I thought you were going to hang out with the guys tonight."

"John had to go help his mom. Her kitchen faucet broke, and it sprayed water everywhere."

"Oh. That sucks." I looked directly at him. "Are you mad at me?"

"What?" Hendrix asked, jumping off the bed. "Why would you think that?"

"Because I hadn't told you about Charles, and

then you walked in on us like that. I'm sorry. Please don't be upset with me. I love you so much, and when you didn't have your memories, and Carl attacked me, and Brandon...I...I..." My shoulders shook while the tears came rushing out.

"Babe, no." Hendrix pulled me against him, his arms wrapping around me. "I'm not upset with you at all. I'm actually really proud of you. Charles trains hard, and if you're handling it okay...Babe, you've come such a long way."

"Really?" I squeaked.

Hendrix leaned down and kissed me.

"I'm so proud of you," he said, smoothing my hair away from my face. "I'm sorry I wasn't there for you, but I'm glad you had someone."

"You're not mad at him, either?"

Hendrix dropped his arms and took my hand.

"Gem, don't take this wrong, but you've not had a lot of experience with guys. And I love that about you, but it also means you don't always re-alize when one is into you."

"What?" I screeched. "No, he's a total jerk," I said, my forehead scrunching in confusion. "I never know if he's going to be an asshole or a real-life human being. He doesn't even help me off the floor, he just..." I stopped myself. This wasn't proving my point to Hendrix at all.

"I don't think he would ever cross the line, but I highly suspect when he's in the shower, he's thinking about you."

My cheeks flamed red. Why would Hendrix say something like that? I buried my face in my hands and sucked in a breath.

"No. You're wrong. Charles is my friend. He was there...dammit, Hendrix, he burst through the door right after I hit Carl in the head with your living room lamp. If he hadn't come in when he did..." I couldn't finish my sentence. "We shared that horrible moment together. No one else went through it with me. He saved my life, and we connected over it. It's the only reason I asked him to help me. And now you're telling me he likes me?"

Hendrix stepped away from me, his jaw tensing.

I rubbed my temples. This could not be happening.

"Hendrix..." My attention fell to the floor, my chest tightening. "Up until now, every man in my life has raped me, beaten me, or forced their rules and beliefs on me." My gaze traveled back to his face. "The thought of Charles looking at me in that way...sexually attracted to me, brings up the fears I've worked so hard to leave behind. You're the only man I've ever been with who has loved me. And you've shown me sex is a truly beautiful act of love, and that it can feel good. You've helped heal my heart in that way. But I've never even had a guy for a friend until Charles, and I don't know if I can trust in that friendship anymore. How can I be sure he's got my best interest in mind and won't turn on me like the other men?"

"I didn't mean to upset you, but a dude knows when another dude wants their girlfriend. I was just trying to point it out."

"I understand that, but right now I need to shower." I turned on my heel and left Hendrix standing alone in the middle of his room.

Hurrying to my room, I closed the door and pulled off my sweaty workout top and yoga pants. I flung them into the hamper and turned on the shower. Leaning my forehead against the door, my shoulders heaved, and hot tears slipped down my cheeks. Hendrix hadn't meant to upset me, but the idea of some other guy wanting me in that way terrified me. I'd been scared enough when I'd asked Charles for help, and now every time he pinned me on the floor, I was going to worry he'd take it farther and hurt me like Carl had. The logical part of my mind argued he'd never do something like that—he wanted to kill Brandon for even trying—but the other part of me wanted to run. How would I feel safe with him again?

I opened the glass door and allowed the hot water to wash over me. Sinking down onto the seat, I let myself cry. It hadn't just been about Charles tonight, but the loss of both Mom and Kyle. Earlier, I'd wondered if I would ever want to leave the comfort of living here, having a family again. But now...maybe it was best if Hendrix and I lived somewhere else. I just didn't know what would happen with Ada Lynn.

My attention snapped up with the click of the glass door opening. Hendrix stepped in the shower with me, naked.

"Gem, I'm so sorry. I was a total dick."

I stood and flung myself into his arms. He'd gotten it. He'd realized that what he'd said about some guy thinking about me and getting off had sent me over the edge.

"He would never hurt you. If I had any concern at all, I would never have agreed to let you train alone with him."

"I know you wouldn't, so I just need to let that

sink in. If he was going to hurt me...he's had plenty of chances already. I need to trust that however he feels about me, the bottom line is, he's my friend, and he won't cross that line. He's teaching me to take care of myself, right?" I asked, looking up at him.

"Yeah, and if you can't trust him yet, then trust me, babe. I would never put you in that situation."

He smoothed my hair and held me tightly against him. Eventually, I cried myself out and we turned off the water.

We dried off and crawled into my bed. He immediately wrapped me in his arms, and I draped one leg over him. After some time, my mind quieted down and I fell asleep.

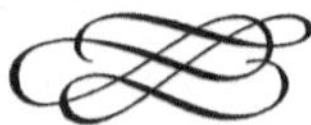

CHAPTER 26

The next evening, Mac helped me prepare for my date. She straightened my hair and applied my makeup just like she did the night Hendrix had taken me to Franklin's event. At that time, I was so nervous I was afraid I'd puke. This time, I was almost giddy with excitement.

"What are you doing tonight?" I asked, eyeing her in the bathroom vanity mirror while she finished the back of my hair.

"I don't know, maybe I'll figure out something." She gave me a half shrug.

"You've been quiet all evening. Are you alright?" I turned around on the bench and faced her, searching her for clues about what was going on.

"I'm fine. You go out on this date and have an amazing time. But do me a favor and keep the moaning and groaning down to a dull roar, will ya?"

"Shit," I'm so sorry. "I thought we were quiet."

"Only the dead can't hear you," Mac said, her eyebrow arching.

"Ugh. Not good. I'll let him know. Does Franklin suspect we're sleeping in the same room at night?"

Mac pursed her lips together. "Probably, but he won't do anything about it. He knew you two were living together before you had to leave Louisiana."

"Oh, yeah. I could see Hendrix telling him. I mean, that's what you do, right? Tell your parents when you're moving in together?"

"Yeah," Mac said gently.

The doorbell rang, and I frowned.

"Are you expecting anyone?" I asked Mac.

"Nope."

We hopped up, and I grabbed my phone off the bathroom counter. Hurrying down the stairs, we giggled while I passed her up and flung open the door.

"You're stunning," Hendrix said, his focus traveling over my body. "These are for you." He handed me a dozen red roses. I buried my nose in the bouquet, took a deep breath, and smiled at him. Charles was standing next to the limo waiting for us. Even though we hadn't discussed it further last night, we were on the same page. I knew deep down inside, Charles would never hurt me. I'd just freaked out after Hendrix explained he believed there was more than friendship on Charles's part. Plus, there's no way Hendrix would have agreed to let him train me if he'd been concerned about my safety.

"No one's ever given me flowers before, thank you. Would you like to come in?" I asked, batting my eyelashes at him.

He smiled, and I melted on the spot.

He flicked open the button on his black suit jacket, revealing a white dress shirt and a teal blue tie that matched my dress.

I peeked at Mac who was standing behind me, grinning like a Cheshire cat.

"You helped him with the tie?" I asked, smiling at her.

"Yup." She leaned against the banister and smiled at Hendrix. "It sure as shit is nice to have you back. Let me take the flowers, and you two have a great time." She took the flowers and practically skipped to the kitchen.

"Thanks, Mac," I called after her.

Hendrix placed his hand against my bare back.

"Your new dress is going to drive me crazy all night," he growled.

A spark of electricity shot through my body. He wasn't the only one looking forward to our clothes coming off.

Once we were settled in the limo and on our way, Hendrix popped the cork on a bottle of champagne and poured two glasses.

"Are you trying to take advantage of me tonight?" I giggled.

"At every opportunity I have," he said, grinning, and held his glass up. "To you, Gem. I love you more than life itself."

"To us," I whispered, kissed him, and tapped my glass against his. Hendrix had refused to reveal our destination to me, so when we pulled up in front of the Davenport Hotel, I was curious.

"Thanks, Charles. I'll text you right before we're done," Hendrix said, buttoning his jacket.

Charles nodded but never spoke. I'd forgotten how serious he was while on duty.

"What's here?" I asked, feeling a little light-headed from the champagne.

"The Symphony." I looked up at him, surprised, as the doormen ushered us inside.

A large crowd filled the lobby as well as the hallway leading to the concert hall. My focus darted around, taking in the luxurious surroundings. Large white columns were decorated with ornate gold trim and multiple crystal chandeliers seemed to drip from the marble ceiling.

"Let's locate our seats."

I held onto Hendrix as we weaved between the other people. After identifying our row and seats, we settled in. The room buzzed with excitement.

"I've never been to a symphony before, thank you." I grinned like a little kid and kissed him.

"I hope you like it. I've never asked if you like classical music, but I've always loved the symphony. I know we sing a very different style, but I would love to share this with you. As long as neither of us dies of boredom."

"Well, then the opera won't work." I laughed.

The room lights dimmed, and the curtains parted.

I laced my fingers through Hendrix's and relaxed into my seat as Beethoven's Third Piano Concerto began.

"OH. MY. GOD! THAT WAS AMAZING," I said, climbing back into the limo. "The flutes, the cellos, the violins." I grabbed his face and kissed him hard. "Thank you. It was breathtaking."

He chuckled and trailed his fingers down my cheek.

"I love to see you happy, and when you're around music, you light up. I could watch you for hours." He leaned back against the seat and stretched out his long, muscular legs in front of him.

The limo pulled away from the hotel and headed to Franklin's.

"Can Charles hear us back here?" I asked, nipping at his earlobe. "That music got me all hot and bothered." I moved my hand up Hendrix's thigh and squeezed.

He leaned over and hit a button on the console, the privacy glass rising.

"I'm all yours, babe," he said, kissing me.

My hand traveled up the inside of his thigh and cupped his erection while his fingers slid up the back of my legs to my ass cheeks. He brushed the thin material of my G-string and groaned.

"You're so wet," he murmured in my ear.

"I told you," I said, giggling and fumbling for the button and zipper on his slacks. Wrapping my hand around him, I stroked gently as he moaned against my mouth. He slipped his finger inside my G-string, making contact with my sensitive flesh while he trailed feather light kisses down my neck.

When I couldn't take any more teasing, I shifted my body and climbed onto his lap. With my knees on either side of his strong thighs, I guided him inside me. His eyes fluttered closed as I rocked against him. His fingers dug into my legs, urging me on while I slid up and down his shaft.

"I've thought about being with you back here so many times," he said, his gaze darkening.

"Yeah? Was I on top or did you have me beneath you?" I whispered in his ear.

"Both," he panted, thrusting deep inside me.

He slipped his hands around my back and flipped me onto the seat.

"Hendrix," I pleaded, digging my fingernails into the leather.

"Fuck," he muttered. "I have to taste you.

You're like an addiction, and I could have my face between your legs all damned day." He lowered himself onto the seat, and held my G-string to the side, his tongue swiping across my wet core. My hands fisted his hair.

"That's it, baby," I moaned, grinding against him, trying to ease the ache. He slid two fingers inside me, hitting the spot that made me forget everything else but him. I sat up, his blue eyes peering at me as I moved the skirt out of my way.

"Baby," I said breathlessly. "I really like to watch you."

He groaned against the inside of my thigh.

"I'll give you something to see then," he growled and ran his tongue across my wet folds up to my throbbing clit.

"Oh God," I groaned softly, my attention remaining on him while he did it again. I raised my hips up off the seat, my heel digging into the floorboard.

He buried his face between my legs and sucked me until I couldn't wait any longer. He flicked his tongue across my bud and swirled around it, his fingers pumping in and out of me. My eyes never left him once.

His fingers parted my folds, and he licked me

again. I grasped the back of his head, holding him to me.

"I'm going to come," I panted.

"That's it, that's my sweet girl."

My ass lifted off the seat as I released, his tongue never slowing down as my body trembled against him. He wiped his mouth off and pushed his hard cock inside me.

He paused, leaning down to kiss me gently.

"I love you."

"I love you too, baby." I ran my hands through his hair while he made love to me in the back of the limo. No matter what, I would remember this night for the rest of my life. He rolled his hips in a circular motion, setting me on fire. I grabbed his ass, tilting up to meet him. His pace quickened, and he moaned quietly in my ear as he came. Moments later, he collapsed on top of me. I played with the silky, soft strands of his hair while his head rested on my chest.

"Thank you," I said. "Thank you for giving me an amazing night."

He propped up on his elbow and kissed me. "I'm glad you had a good time." He slowly pulled out, tucked himself back in his slacks, and zipped up as I adjusted my G-string and dress.

"I think it smells like sex back here," I said, scrunching up my nose and giggling.

"I think you're right," he laughed, lowering the window. The fresh evening air rushed into the limo.

I leaned against him and sighed.

Just as we approached Franklin's property, a flicker of red caught my eye.

"Did you see that?" I asked, sitting up and frowning.

Hendrix lowered the window some more, and the limo eased to a stop.

"Hendrix, we have a problem," Charles said through the speaker.

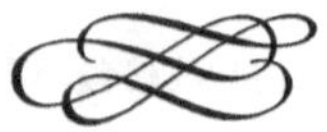

CHAPTER 27

"What's the matter?" Fear clutched at my chest. The limo had pulled into the circular drive and parked a short distance from the front of the house, next to a police car.

"Wait here," Charles said, exiting the limo before I could ask any more questions.

"Why aren't we pulling all the way in?" I asked, my pitch rising.

"I'm not sure yet. Let me see what's going on. I'll be right back," Hendrix said, giving me a quick kiss of reassurance before hopping out of the vehicle. The sound of his and Charles's voices drifted in the open window, but I couldn't make out anything they were saying. Charles had parked at an odd angle, making it difficult to see, too.

The high-pitched sound of an approaching siren broke the stillness of the night. My worst fears took shape when I looked out the back window of the car and saw an ambulance flying up the driveway and stop at the front doors.

"Hendrix!" I cried, jumping out of the back seat, my hands shaking with dread as I watched two men jump out of the ambulance and quickly enter the house.

"Babe," Hendrix said softly, embracing me.

He insisted we stay outside so as not to get in the way, but he refused to tell me any details. After what seemed like hours, the front door flung open, and Mac and Franklin appeared in the doorway. The EMTs followed, wheeling out a gurney. A sheet entirely covered the body.

"No! No! No!" I screamed, pushing against him as he circled his arms around me, holding me in place. I kicked against him, my shoes flying off and a gut-wrenching scream escaping me.

"Let me go! Let me go!" I wailed, the tears nearly blinding me.

Hendrix's hold on me relaxed, and I slipped out of his arms. The sharp sting of gravel bit into my bare feet as they pounded against the drive-way, my cries ringing through the air.

"Ma'am, you have to stay back," one of the EMTs ordered.

"Ada Lynn! Ada Lynn!" I reached my hand out toward the body. "Is it her?" I looked up into the paramedic's face. "Please. She's the only relative I have left, please tell me it's not her."

"I'll handle this," Franklin said from behind me. He whirled me around and held me tightly against him.

"I'm so sorry, Gemma. Ada Lynn is gone."

The only reason I didn't crumple to the ground was Franklin's firm grip on me. My entire world fell out from beneath my feet. She was gone. The one person who had loved me uncon-ditionally and stayed by my side no matter what had happened.

I watched, grief-stricken, while they loaded her body into the ambulance and shut the doors.

"We need to get her inside, Dad," Hendrix said from behind me, carrying my shoes. Franklin let go of me and Hendrix swept me into his arms. He carried me passed Mac and into the house. Placing me on the couch, he grabbed a blanket and covered me with it.

"Gemma," he said gently. "Are you with me?"

I glanced up at him, my chest aching. "She's gone," I mumbled, crying. "Why did she have to leave me now?" My shoulders shook with my sobs as Mac and Franklin gathered in the living room with us. Mac sniffled and wiped her tears away.

"I'm sorry, bestie," Mac said, sniffling. Franklin wrapped his arm around her and pulled her close.

"What happened?" I asked, sitting up.

"She didn't show up for our card game tonight, so I sent Mac to check on her."

My cry stuck in my throat. "Mac found her?"

"I...I...thought she was asleep at first, then I realized she wasn't breathing." Mac's tears flowed freely.

"She just passed away in her sleep?" I looked over at Franklin.

"Yes, she went peacefully. Gemma, she didn't have a lot of time left."

"What do you mean?" I frowned, my body tensing. "She had a stent put in, and her doctor said she was fine."

"She didn't want to tell you. There were some other heart issues, but she opted out of the surgery."

"What?" I said, flinging the blanket off me.

Hendrix reached for me, but I'd moved out of his grasp and jumped up from the couch.

"You knew?" I screamed at Franklin, stalking toward him. "Why didn't you tell me?" I demanded, getting in his face.

"Gemma," Hendrix said, wrapping his arm around my waist and hauling me backward.

"You knew, and you didn't say a fucking word? I hate you!"

Pain filled Franklin's expression. "Gemma, don't. Please. I didn't have any choice. Ada Lynn hired me as her attorney, to take care of her affairs. It wasn't my expertise, but she said she didn't trust anyone else to wrap up the loose ends and make sure you were taken care of."

"How could you?" I pleaded. "Why would she keep this from me?" I choked on a sob.

Franklin released Mac and took a step toward me.

"Don't. Don't touch me," I said, sinking into Hendrix. "Just don't..."

Even though I heard their voices, I could no longer understand what they were saying. Hendrix carried me up to bed and handed me a pill and a glass of water. I didn't even question him.

"Don't worry, Gem. I'm not going anywhere."

"That's what they all said," I stared at him

blankly. His face was the last thing I remembered before I drifted off into a dreamless sleep.

THE RED GLOW of the alarm clock let me know it was a little after four in the morning. Hendrix lay next to me, sleeping soundly.

I peered through the darkness and tiptoed out of my bedroom. Pulling the door softly closed behind me, I descended the stairs and went to Ada Lynn's room. Or the room she used to live in. My heart dropped like a lead ball into my stomach while I slipped inside. The lemon scent of her shampoo and bath soap tickled my nose. Sinking onto her bed, I curled up with one of her pillows and stared into space. She was gone. My Ada Lynn was gone, and she'd ripped my heart out when she'd left me behind.

My tears fell onto her pillow, and my chest ached with loneliness. How could she have opted out of surgery? How could she not have told me? I would have stayed and taken care of her. She was the only real family I'd had over the years. How could she have left me, too?

I screamed into the pillow, my hands clenched into fists. Eventually, I drifted off to sleep again.

I HEARD the click of the bedroom door open and close, then soft footsteps on the carpet.

"Hendrix?" I croaked.

"Yeah, babe, I'm right here."

The bed dipped under his weight, and he gently squeezed my arm.

"Why didn't she tell me?" I asked, peering at him.

"I don't know, Gem. But I think maybe she didn't want you to worry."

I nodded, my mind not really grasping what he said.

"Are you hungry?"

"No," I whispered.

The sun had risen, daylight filtering through the gap in the blackout curtains.

"Will you stay with me until I fall back asleep?" I asked him.

"Yeah." He laid down and curled his body around me. "I love you," he assured me.

"You too. But my heart is so fucking broken right now."

"I know." He wrapped his arm around me and pulled me in tighter. "I'll never let you go. I'm always right here."

"Will you sing to me?"

He gently rested his head against my back and inhaled deeply.

"What do you want to hear?"

"You sang 'Forfeit Tomorrow' the first time I heard you." I peered up at him through swollen eyes.

"Gem, that song is so sad. Isn't there another one?" His fingers stroked my cheek while worry flickered across his face.

"Then one of Billy's. I don't care which one."

He nuzzled my hair and began to sing "Until the Hurting is Gone." The sound of his voice vibrated through my body, reaching deep inside me. And for a flicker of a moment, I imagined Ada Lynn smiling. It was almost as though she'd joined us one more time just to hear him sing.

I snuggled against him and drifted off to sleep again.

IT WAS dark again when I woke up. Hendrix was still next to me like he'd promised. I suspected he'd only left my side to go to the bathroom.

I sat up, careful not to wake him. My entire

body ached from being in bed for so long, and I had a headache from crying for hours.

"Hey," Hendrix said, rubbing my back. "How are you feeling?"

I glanced over my shoulder at him. He was exhausted. Ada Lynn's death had impacted all of us. I hung my head down, my shoulders sagging forward.

"I don't know," I said, honestly. "I just don't know anymore. Every time I think this is it, this is what finally breaks me, I somehow manage to get back up again. But then something else happens, and I'm knocked down again. Eventually I won't have anyone else in my life. Everyone I love will have left me behind."

"I know it looks like that right now, but it's not true. You've had a lot of loss in a short time frame. Anyone would feel the way you're feeling. It's going to take some time, Gem. But you have Mac, Franklin, and me right next to you. I'll be there every step of the way. Every one of us has lost someone, and we all loved Ada Lynn."

"I know," I hiccupped. "I'm so angry at Franklin, but I'm also so grateful he allowed her to live here with us before she..." I covered my face with my hands and cried. "He knew when he planned the Seattle Space Needle dinner," I said. "And when he said he wanted us to stay here even after you had your memories back...he knew. He was keeping me close to Ada Lynn," I sniffled.

"Yeah, he was. He told me everything after you fell asleep. He's wrecked, babe. It's brought up shit about Kendra, and he really cared for Ada Lynn. We all did. She was family. He did the best he could under shitty circumstances. After we all got here and she realized you both were staying, she hired him to help her with a burial site and cremation. She had a few other loose ends to tie up for you, but..."

"Did Franklin take money from her?" I asked, frowning.

"No, he did it pro bono and had a friend who specializes in wills and trusts double check the papers for him. He just wanted to help her."

Something inside me settled down, and I finally realized how difficult this had been on Franklin. Holding onto a secret this big had to have crushed him.

"Do you think you can eat? Everyone's worried sick about you, and if you're up to it, I think they need to see you."

"Yeah." I nodded. I stood, my legs screaming in protest. "How did our perfect night go to shit so fast?"

He flipped on the lamp and the room lit up. My gaze traveled around the space, eyeing the wingback reading chair and thick furry blanket she had used. An empty drinking glass sat on the nightstand next to her reading glasses.

"She loved it here, Hendrix. She'd never even left Louisiana until we came up here. She loved this house, she loved you and Mac..." My voice trailed off while Hendrix walked over and wrapped his arms around me.

"I don't know how to make it easier for you, but I love you."

He kissed my forehead and then led me into the kitchen. Mac sat at the bar, picking at her food.

"Bestie!" She hopped off her chair and ran toward me, hugging me gently. "I've been worried sick about you. At least you're awake. I know you're not okay, I mean how could you be? But when you lost your shit, I didn't know if you would be able to come back from this big of a loss after everything else. And Ada Lynn, ohmigosh. My heart..." She pulled away, her head hanging down. "Come eat."

She tugged on my arm and patted the seat next to her. Hendrix slipped out of the kitchen while Mac grabbed some leftover stir-fried rice and warmed it up.

"It's chicken so eat up. Well, as much as you can, anyway."

"How's Franklin?" I asked, picking at my rice.

"A fucking mess like we all are." She shoveled a large spoonful into her mouth, and I remembered that she ate when she was really stressed.

I took a bite and chewed slowly, my stomach growling for more.

"That's a good sign," she said, nodding toward my belly.

Mac talked nonstop while we ate, but I needed the distraction for now. It reminded me of when we'd first met. I'd called Ada Lynn and told her about my chatty new roommate who was driving me crazy. We'd laughed so hard when I'd imitated how fast she talked. And now she was my best friend, and I was living in her house with her family.

Franklin entered the kitchen, his eyes bloodshot.

"Hey," I said, glancing at him shyly. "I'm sorry I screamed at you." Even under the circumstances, I was ashamed of my behavior.

"It's fine. Don't give it another thought." He leaned against the kitchen counter, folding his arms over his chest. "When you're ready, Ada Lynn left you a letter." He cleared his throat, his eyes welling with tears.

"Now works," I said, hopping off the stool, my heart in my throat. I needed to know what she had to say.

Wordlessly, I followed Franklin through the living room and back to his office. He unlocked a cabinet and pulled out a file.

"Here," he said, handing a white envelope to me. I stared at my name, scrawled across the front in Ada Lynn's tight handwriting.

"I'll give you some privacy," he said, making his way to the door.

"It's alright. I'm going to go upstairs."

He nodded and patted my back as I walked past him. I made my way through the living room, my ears perking up with the sound of Charles's and Hendrix's voices. My head snapped in their direction while they huddled near the front door. Charles caught sight of me, his chin tilting up slightly. I guess it was his way of saying he was there if I needed anything. My mouth tightened into a thin line, and I walked up the stairs and into my bedroom.

I sat down on the bed and flipped the envelope over. There was no way my heart was ready for this, but I tore it open, anyway.

Dear Gemma,

I imagine you're rather upset with me for not telling you about my heart, but my blue-eyed girl, you've come so far, and I couldn't let you give up your future for an old woman. I've lived my life, now it's time that you live yours. Hold onto everything that is precious and everything that is pure, and it will guide you through this life no matter what you face. Love with all that you have inside you and allow that beautiful light to shine through. And promise me you won't forget your music. Your voice touches so many, my dear, Gemma.

You've found a new family, and I couldn't be happier. I see how Hendrix looks at you. That boy is stupid in love with you, and it makes me grin like an idiot just thinking about it. Don't let him go. That kind of love only comes once in a lifetime.

I hope you'll always remember our time together on the front porch of my house in Louisiana. You own it now, so you sell it or live in it, whatever makes your heart happy. I do hope you finish college. Take Mac with you whatever you do. She needs you as much as you need her. Friends like her are a rare find, so keep her close to your heart. But please don't feed her any pie.

My sweet Gemma. You'll never know how much I love you. You were the light in a lonely old woman's soul. Just remember, you deserve to be happy. Live your life, be free, and know that even on the other side, I'll carry you in my heart forever.

With love,

Ada Lynn

Clutching the letter to my chest, I broke down and cried.

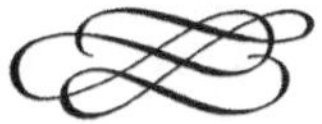

CHAPTER 28

The next week was filled with burial arrangements and legal issues. Ada Lynn had most of it in place, but Franklin sat me down and asked if I'd considered what I wanted to do with not only my childhood home but Ada Lynn's, too.

"You own three houses now," he reminded me.

I frowned. "Three?"

"When Hendrix bought the house across the street, he sold it to Ada Lynn, and she left it to you in her will. It's also paid for."

"I'd forgotten about that," I said, pulling on a loose string of my shirt. "I don't know yet. When do I have to decide?"

"Well at some point you'll need to go through

their belongings and decide what you'll keep and what you'll donate. I suspect some of your mother's belongings are in your other home."

I nodded. "Yeah, I would like to get a few things, but I'm not ready to walk in there yet."

"I understand. I'll have Marcus drop by and check on all three homes once a week for us until you're ready."

"That would help a lot. I don't want anyone breaking in or anything."

"I agree. I'll also have him forward all the mail. I'll help you notify everyone about Ada Lynn's passing."

I nodded. "I guess in Louisiana, I'd almost be rich owning three homes outright."

"She did right by you."

"She did. Thank you for all you've done for us. I'll never be able to repay you."

"Take care of my son, it's all I ask. He deserves to be happy. You both do."

I FOUND Hendrix in the game room where he was blowing the hell out of some army tanks in a video game. He paused it and set the controller down on the table when he saw me.

I walked over to him and slipped my arms around his neck, placing my head on his chest.

He wrapped his arms around me, and we stood still for a while. Finally, I looked up at him.

"I'm ready to go home," I whispered. "There's no reason to stay with Franklin unless you need to."

"Are you sure?" he asked, running his hand over my hair.

"I'm sure. We just need to figure out where Mac will stay."

"What do *you* want?" he asked, cupping my chin with his hand.

I stepped back, grabbed his hand, and sat down on the couch.

"Kyle used to ask me that when I was younger, but I always answered with what I knew he wanted me to say. I've never honestly considered what I wanted until you came into my life." I offered him a sad smile. "And now I don't have Ada Lynn or my parents to answer to. It truly is up to me, and it's a weird feeling."

"I get it."

"So I'm going to tell you what I really want if that's okay?"

"Always, Gemma."

"I want to go home and build a life with you. I

want to plan our future. I want to write music with you and sing again. I want to have Mac over on weekends and drink and laugh. I want to have BBQ's and dance around the house naked with you. I want to fall asleep in your arms and wake up every day to your smile. I want you, Hendrix Harrington."

Love and affection filled his eyes as he leaned over and kissed me.

"And I'll give you every bit of that and more. Let's go tell everyone we're going home."

It wasn't easy telling my best bestie that I wanted time alone with Hendrix, but she understood.

"It's going to be so weird without you guys here, but I've decided to stay with Franklin for now. I'm registered for classes, and I'll drive back and forth. It's really nice having a dad in my life. I'm sorry if that makes you sad."

"No, Mac. I want the best for you, and I'm so grateful Franklin turned his life around. He was missing out on really amazing kids."

"Ahh, thanks." She flashed me a toothy smile and then sighed. "Shit sure has changed since we first met, huh? Who knew you'd be bopping my brother and on your way to becoming my sister-in-law?"

"Not me," I said and giggled. "You'll be with us on the weekends too, don't forget. I've just flipped full-time roomies is all." I paused. "Are you sure you're feeling alright about the change?" A part of me wanted her to go with us, but I ached for the alone time with Hendrix. Mac was right, the year together hadn't allowed us to really settle down into being a normal couple. I longed for that more than ever, and so did he.

"Yeah, I think it's exactly what you and Hendrix need," Mac said, smiling softly.

AFTER MY TALK WITH MAC, I sauntered downstairs. There was one more person I wanted to talk to. I pulled my phone out of my pocket and tapped out a quick text. His reply came almost immediately.

I stepped out of the kitchen door and walked down the pathway. Charles was waiting for me by the garages.

I gave him a small wave as I approached.

"You're going to miss me," I said, giving him a sad smile.

"Why is that?" he asked, adjusting his sunglasses.

"Hendrix and I are going back home, to his house here in Spokane. We're leaving this afternoon. And before you start getting all sappy about how much you'll miss training me, blah blah blah," I said, whacking him on the arm. "Don't. We'll be over all the time."

"I'll try to contain my overwhelming emotions." Neither his tone or expression changed with his words.

I grinned and looked out over the property. The sun glinted off the green tree leaves and spilled across the open acreage. You could see for miles up here.

"I'll never forget what you risked for me, Charles. I just wanted to tell you thank you, and I'll miss you." I said softly. "You've been a good friend to me. A bit of an asshole, but a friend. I don't have many of those, so I try to tell the ones I have I appreciate them. You never know when it's all going to be over."

Charles folded his hands in front of him and leaned against the side of the garage.

"How are you doing about Ada Lynn?" he

asked, removing his sunglasses. His brown eyes softened while he held my gaze.

"It's hard. Every day is hard. But, she told me to live my life, and it's what I plan on doing."

He nodded and slid his sunglasses back on.

"I gotta go, but I didn't want to leave without telling you goodbye. And don't forget, we were a good team together when we took down Carl. If you ever need back up, I'm a phone call away."

I couldn't believe it, but he actually smiled. A real, genuine smile.

"See you soon," I said, then walked back in the direction of the house. I looked over my shoulder. His focus was on me until I made it to the door.

My heart ached with all of the goodbyes. Some of them were only for a few days, and others I'd had to say goodbye to for a lifetime. I found myself walking toward Ada Lynn's room, tears streaming down my cheeks.

"I think it will be easier for you, not having to see her room every day," Hendrix said, approaching from behind me.

"I know, but it hurts like hell leaving it behind."

He planted a kiss on the top of my head and took my hand.

"Are you ready? I think Dad is waiting to tell

you bye."

I nodded, and we walked through the house and to the front door.

"Gemma," Franklin said. "Thank you for taking care of my kids."

"I think it's the other way around, or maybe fate brought us together at the right moment, and we all saved each other." I dropped Hendrix's hand and hugged Franklin. "I'll never forget how good you were to Ada Lynn. I'll always love you for that," I whispered. Franklin's arms tightened around me, then we let each other go.

"We'll see you in a few days, Dad. Good luck with Mac," Hendrix said, grinning.

The guys chuckled together, and Hendrix took my hand and led me to the Lexus. We hadn't brought much with us and Hendrix had loaded our suitcases in the car earlier. He held the door open, giving me a quick kiss before I got into my seat. I peeked up, Charles was still in the same place I'd left him.

"I'll be right back," Hendrix said.

I watched him approach Charles, and they shook hands. Although we were only moving across town, it felt like a million miles away from everything that was safe. But I was ready to have Hendrix to myself and write some new music.

CHAPTER 29

The weeks flew by while Hendrix and I settled into our new life together. May had come and gone, and I looked forward to spending the summer on the river. The truck had shown up with our belongings from Louisiana, too. Apparently Franklin hadn't called for them until he knew we had planned to move back home. I think he would have kept us with him forever if he could have.

Mac had been over every weekend, which gave her and Franklin a break from each other, but from what I could tell, they were a good match.

The weather was beautiful, and this particular Saturday, Hendrix invited Franklin to come along with Mac for dinner. We sat on the back patio, watching the sunlight gleam off the rushing water as Hendrix grilled burgers.

"This is my first summer here, and I'm excited, but I wish Ada Lynn were here, too." Grief weighed me down briefly, and I focused on what I had in front of me. Family.

"I know. We all do," Franklin said, sipping on his non-alcoholic beer and staring out over the water. A light breeze swayed the tops of the Aspen trees, and the leaves rustled together softly.

"The humidity in Louisiana was nuts. I'm glad it's not like that here."

"We need to go rafting!" Mac chirped, clapping her hands together.

Hendrix grinned and took a drink of his beer. It had been a while since I'd seen him touch one. I stuck with a Coke Zero, and so did Mac.

"Well, you guys have fun," Franklin said, chuckling.

"Hendrix?" Mac asked, cocking an eyebrow at him.

"What about next weekend?" he asked, flipping the burgers.

Mac paused, thinking. "I'm open Saturday. Gemma, have you ever gone?" Mac asked, jumping up and down in her seat. Her excitement was infectious.

"Nope, but it looks like I am next weekend," I replied, grinning.

Mac laughed and chattered on about every rafting trip she'd ever taken. She had us laughing so hard my belly ached.

A few hours later, we said goodnight to Franklin, and Mac stayed over. Somehow, we ended up hanging out in the kitchen just like the first night I'd stayed here.

"Whew! That was fun, and I can't wait until next weekend," Mac said, propping up her feet on the kitchen counter.

Hendrix smacked at her feet.

"There's a no feet on the furniture policy, Mac."

"Sorry, I'm just excited about the trip, and I wasn't thinking."

"It sounds like fun. I'll need a life jacket, though. Where can I buy one?" I asked.

"Nah, we've got all of that already. We had friends go with us when we were growing up, so we have all the equipment. Except I'll want to grab those waterproof baggy thingies," Mac said.

Hendrix and I both frowned at her.

"Ya know, you keep your ID and phone in

them. Like they're totally waterproof so when you capsize out of the boat, your phone lands in the water but it still works. You might not work too well if you get banged around, but your phone will," she said, laughing.

My eyes widened, and I gave Hendrix a startled look.

"Mac, you're scaring Gem. You might want to keep the danger part under wraps for now."

"It's sort of out there now isn't it? She can't take it back, so you two need to tell me everything I need to know."

Hendrix stood behind me, rubbing my tense shoulders. In my mind, it was more frightening not to know the possibilities. If I understood the dangers, I could at least attempt to plan for the worst-case scenario. Maybe that was sad, but life had thrown me more shit than I thought I could handle.

Mac explained all the water safety rules to me, and what to do in case we tipped over. Plus we would be together. My nerves settled down after we talked everything through. I just needed multiple backup plans or exit strategies.

"Should we show her?" Hendrix asked, kissing my neck.

"Show me what?" Mac said, her eyebrow arching.

"Hmm, yeah. I don't know. Should we?" I looked at her, scrunching my nose.

"Whuut? Tell me, tell me." Her fingers drummed on the countertop while we messed with her.

"Come on," Hendrix said, laughing.

Mac hopped off her chair and followed us out of the kitchen and down to the end of the hall.

"Whoa," she said. "There wasn't a door here before, just a wall."

"Yup," Hendrix said, opening it and flipping on the light switch to the music studio. "We had this added on."

Mac stepped in and gasped, her mouth gaping open.

"I take it you like it?" I asked from behind her. One thing I loved about Mac was how childlike she could be, especially with fun surprises.

"Does this mean?" she asked, bouncing on her tiptoes.

"We already have," I said.

"Deets please," she ordered, plunking down in one of the chairs.

"Gem and I had talked about writing and singing

together again before we left Louisiana, so I had the studio plans made up. They had actually begun to build it, but then the tornado hit and I was … well, you know. The project was put on hold when I had amnesia, but it was finally finished this week.

"And have you two been hard at work in here?" Mac asked.

"Yeah, it's been amazing," Hendrix said, his soft gaze falling on me.

I smiled at him, my heart fluttering against my chest. The more we were together, the more I loved him.

Hendrix and I walked over to the console and sat down. He flipped some switches, and the music flowed through the speakers.

"We don't have a title yet," he explained while our song filled the studio.

Mac listened intently, remaining quiet.

"Man, you two blend so effortlessly," she said, rubbing her face. "It's crazy. It's almost like you two were born for each other."

"Does that mean you like it?" I asked, my nerves tingling with anticipation.

"I fucking love it, but I'm a bit biased, too. I mean, you guys could sing Kumbaya, and I would think it was the best ever."

I barked out a laugh.

"We're working on something more upbeat, too," Hendrix added.

"I'm so glad you guys are back in the studio. I don't know why you didn't do this in the first place instead of renting space at the college, Hendrix."

"At the time, I wasn't sure if my career was going to move forward, and it didn't make a lot of sense to put money into a home studio unless it was going to be long term."

Mac's expression froze. "Wait, are you going to tour again? And if so, will Gemma go, too?" Her voice squeaked with each question, her anxiety apparent.

"We haven't figured it all out yet. But I promise you'll be the first to know what our plans will be. We have schedules to work out, I've enrolled in classes again for next term, and...there's a lot to consider," I said.

"Don't get me wrong, I want this for you as well, but I'll be here by myself and...fuck." She twirled her braided pigtail around her finger. "What am I going to do without either of you? I mean, most of the time I've had at least one of you."

I glanced at Hendrix and he nodded.

"Well, we figured if we do go on tour, you

would come with us for part of it. We could ask Franklin to fly you in and meet us. We would have a tour bus with John and Cade, so one more person wouldn't make a difference. I suspect Franklin will want your college classes to come first, though."

A smile eased across Mac's face. "I will work my ass off in school in order to meet you guys. That could work, right? I mean, there's summer, and Christmas, and spring break, too."

"We'll figure it out, Mac. I promise. You won't be left behind."

Mac jumped up from her seat and flung her arms around me.

"Gemma, if anyone deserves their dreams to come true, it's you. I'm so proud of you. You're the best bestie ever, and I love you."

"I love you, too Mac," I said, returning her embrace. "But," I pulled away from her and rested my hands on her shoulders, "you need to understand that none of this would have happened if you hadn't stuck by me. You're such a huge part of why I'm here. There's not a day that goes by that I don't think about how much I love you and how important you are in my life."

Mac sniffled and wiped the tears away that had slipped down her cheeks. "Thanks, bestie."

Mac hurried to Hendrix and hugged him, too. "Love ya, bro. If you ever break my bestie's heart, you can say goodbye to your left nut. I don't want to be an aunt, anyway."

Hendrix laughed and flicked her pigtail.

"Love you too, sis. Someday, you're going to find the right guy who will love you for exactly who you are."

The color drained from her cheeks while her focus bounced between Hendrix and me.

"About that," she said, sinking into the chair.

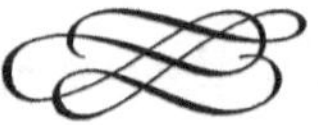

CHAPTER 30

"Jeremiah has been texting me. I don't know what it means, but he said he was sorry for being a dick and wants to visit me here. I'm not sure how Franklin will deal with any of it, but I'm considering seeing him. And marriage hasn't come up once. Now that I've had some time to take a step back, I realize I was jumping in way too fast. Plus, if he has hang-ups about money, then it just won't work. But shit went down, and he reacted, and I reacted, and we never had the opportunity to talk it through."

I bit my lip, making myself think before I spoke. At this point, I wasn't sure what I thought about Jeremiah other than he'd hurt my best friend.

"Is he still going to enlist?" I asked, my pulse racing with the idea she would most likely relocate with him if they got back together.

"He's put it on hold right now as we try and figure things out."

"Mac, we've always been straight with each other. My guess is he researched our family and found out how rich Dad really is. I'm not sure I trust his motives at this point," Hendrix said, folding his arms across his chest.

I loved when he was protective of his sister.

"I know. I've considered it, too. A part of me misses him, and the other part is still hot pissed that he even broke up with me like that. And of all the times to fuck with my heart, too. I was barely holding on while you were in a coma, bro." She closed her eyes and took a deep breath. "I'm just being honest with you guys about what's going on."

"I hope you know you can talk to either or both of us about anything," Hendrix added.

"I do."

Stifling a yawn, I glanced at the clock on my phone. It was after midnight.

"I swear the last few weeks have been the most

normal I've ever had in my life, but I'm exhausted all of the time."

"Life, girl. Life fucking wore you out. You should take advantage of the quiet and rest when you need to. You lost Kyle, your mom, and Ada Lynn within months of each other. Hell, I would be in bed depressed as hell and sleeping all the time. And don't get me wrong, I'm super happy you're not, but be good to yourself. You deserve some downtime. Read a good book, drink, have amazing sex, jump on the bed, go to a concert, or whatever helps your heart heal. Losing someone is tough but losing three..." Mac's words trailed off. "I'm glad you're here, and you finally have the chance to start a good life."

"You're right," I mumbled, grief stirring deep inside me with her words. "Writing music and singing again has really helped. It's been my life raft."

"Mine too," Hendrix said. "Mac and music saved my ass from going down a seriously dark road after Kendra."

"Mac saves everyone," I said, smiling at her.

"Aww, shucks," she said, fanning herself. "It's all in a day's work."

We laughed and headed out of the studio.

"I'm going to get some sleep," I said to Mac.

"I'll see you in the morning."

"I'll be up in a few minutes, babe," Hendrix said, kissing me.

I nodded and then made my way up the stairs into our bedroom. Now that I had some of my belongings from Louisiana, the house did feel more like ours instead of just Hendrix's. The first week we'd spent here, he'd gone to great lengths to help me unpack and took me shopping. I picked out a few pictures for the living room and bedroom, but not many. Hendrix had hired an interior designer when he bought the house, and I really did love what she'd done.

The most important things I had were pictures of Mom and Ada Lynn. Franklin had taken pictures of us together at Ada Lynn's birthday dinner in Seattle, and Hendrix had surprised me with framed professional images. He'd hung them up in the hallway, so every time I passed by, I knew Mom and Ada Lynn were still with me. Other days, I would walk by and break down crying. It was an emotional rollercoaster, but between Mac, Hendrix, Franklin, and my music, I was somehow able to move forward. Each of them was an intricate part of my heart healing.

I changed into my sleep shirt and crawled into bed, Hendrix's woodsy cologne lingered on his pillow. I grabbed it and took a deep breath. Even though we spent a lot of time together, I missed him when he wasn't next to me. He kept me grounded on the days I thought I would break apart from the grief.

Bone weary exhaustion seeped inside me and, I drifted off to sleep.

"BABE," Hendrix's voice broke through my sleep. "I need my pillow."

I peered at him, and a slow smile eased across my lips.

"What time is it?" I asked, yawning and handing him his pillow.

"It's almost two-thirty."

"Is Mac alright? I'm not sure I like the Jeremiah situation, but it's not like I have a say."

"We talked a lot about him tonight. I think she's really scared, Gem. He hurt her, and now she's worried he's after Dad's money."

I rolled over and propped my head up on my arm, staring into his piercing blue eyes.

"You didn't tell me you were rich for a while, and even then you didn't tell me how much money you came from. When Mac told me about the private plane, and I saw it...that's when it clicked, and I got it."

"I'm sorry. I've had a lot of girls come after me because of it, and not one of them genuinely cared about me as a person. I totally get where Mac is coming from. Plus, you were different. I knew it the first time I saw you behind the library."

"Hendrix, I love you for you. If you sing, fine, if you're rich or poor...it doesn't matter to me. I just want to be by your side, and we'll figure out life together. I've been dirt poor, and now I have some money. I prefer not to be poor again because it sucked, but I don't have to travel in a private plane to be happy, either. *You* are all I need." I said, leaning in and kissing him gently.

"I love you so much, Gem," he said, his fingers gently trailing down my cheek.

My hand wandered down his ripped abs and to his boxer briefs. I caressed him through the material, his erection almost instant.

"I love you, too," I whispered, against his mouth.

Our lips parted, his tongue caressing mine as his hand slid up my T-shirt to my breast. I tugged at his waistband, freed him, and stroked slowly. His hand trailed down my side and slipped between my thighs, a finger tracing my sensitive flesh through the material of my G-string. A soft moan escaped him when my hand tightened around him.

"I need you inside of me," I said.

He removed his underwear, and I rid myself of my clothes, tossing them to the floor. Hendrix disappeared beneath the blankets, his hot breath tickling my thighs. He pushed my knees apart, and his mouth landed on me. I groaned, my fingers digging into the bed mattress. Hendrix had full on spoiled me with oral sex, but he swore he couldn't keep his mouth off me, so I never argued.

His tongue licked my core agonizingly slow, and I squirmed beneath his touch. There was nothing rushed tonight, as we savored the sheer pleasure of each other. Heat swirled inside me, and I bucked my hips against him.

"Baby," I moaned. "Oh, God!" I yelled, my body shuddering against him.

His head popped out from underneath the blankets, a silly grin on his face.

"I'm pretty sure the entire neighborhood heard you, not to mention Mac down the hall."

"Dammit, I forgot she was here. And it's your damn fault, anyway," I said, smiling and smoothing his hair into place. "If you didn't make me come so hard I wouldn't have anything to yell about."

He chuckled and propped up on his arms, his body hovering over mine, and this time we stayed as quiet as we could.

Afterward, he kissed my forehead, our eyes locking.

"You are my forever and always will be."

My fingers traced over his jawline. "The song," I whispered. "What if it's called "My Forever"? I waited for his response.

"I love it almost as much as I love you," he said, grinning.

He gave me a quick kiss, pulled out of me, and sauntered off to the bathroom. A minute later, he returned with a warm washcloth and tenderly cleaned me off.

"Thanks," I said shyly. It was funny how we could make love or fuck, but then I was shy when he took the time to wash me off.

He tossed the rag into the bathroom and then slipped under the covers. I snuggled against him, my head on his chest. Every night I had the opportunity to listen to his heartbeat while I fell asleep was special, and it reminded me I had someone to live my life with.

CHAPTER 31

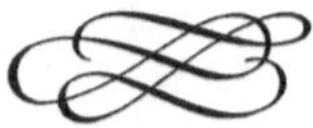

"Gemma?" Hendrix called for me.

"I'm in the kitchen," I answered. I finished loading the dishwasher, dried my hands off on a paper towel, and tossed it into the recycling bin.

Hendrix rushed in, a huge grin spreading across his handsome features. He picked me up and twirled me around. I giggled and kissed him while he set me down.

"Something has you excited. What's going on?"

"My manager just called. They want to start the tour again, but they want you, too."

"What?" I asked, my pulse two-timing. "They liked the new song?"

"They fucking loved it," he said, crushing my mouth with a kiss. "Say you'll tour with me, Gem. I've dreamed of this since the day I heard you sing. Let's do this. You can take whatever college classes you want, and...just say yes." His gaze fell on me. "I can't go without you. And I'm not saying that to manipulate your decision, but you're where I want to be, even if it means turning down the tour."

"Hendrix, you can't put me in that position. You're resting your career on my shoulders, and it's not fair."

"That's not what I meant," he said, taking a step back. "I would give up everything to be with you, that's all. I love the idea of performing, but I would have a hole in my heart the entire time we were apart."

Tension lingered in the space between us.

"It doesn't matter. None of this matters," I said, looking up at him. "I've already decided if the opportunity came up, I'd go with you. We'll tour together."

"Are you serious?" He wrapped his arms around me, searching my face.

"Yeah. I think it will be good." I took a deep breath and gave him a big smile. "I'm a bit dazed, but I'm super excited. The most important thing is that none of this comes between us. Promise me."

"Promise. It's what I was trying to say earlier, but I wasn't doing a very good job." He rolled his eyes and chuckled. "We should celebrate," he said nuzzling my neck.

"Yeah?" I asked, giggling.

Hendrix tugged my shorts and panties down, picked me up, and sat me on the kitchen counter.

"I know where I'm starting," he growled. He unbuttoned my shirt and flipped the front clasp open on my blue satin bra. My nipples immediately hardened against the air. He brought me closer to the edge, his focus never leaving me as his thumb brushed across my clit.

"We'll have to be quiet while on the road," he mentioned. "So, I plan on making you scream my name until we leave."

He leaned over and trailed kisses down my stomach, stopping before he reached my center. His eyes darkened as he peered up at me and ran his tongue along my throbbing core. He latched on to my bud and slipped a finger inside me. Just as I tilted my head back, getting lost in his touch, he stopped.

"Turn around and get on your hands and

knees," he ordered. I did as he wanted, my ass in the air.

"Jesus," he said, his fingers spreading me apart.

I whimpered with the contact of his mouth again.

"Mmm, so good," he said, sucking and licking me. "So wet." His fingers dug into my ass cheeks, pain and pleasure shooting through me. He pumped a finger in and out of me, groaning as I squirmed against him.

"This is my favorite, I could eat your pussy like this all damned day."

"Oh, God. Hendrix, don't stop," I pleaded, breathlessly.

Raw pleasure shot through me while he continued.

"Hendrix," I yelled. "You feel so good."

He ran his tongue across my clit repeatedly, my body jerking against him until I came so hard I thought I'd pass out.

"Scoot over," he said, hopping onto the counter with me. He got on his knees and pulled down his shorts, his erection bobbing free. He turned me in the opposite direction, and in one move he buried himself inside me.

"Aww, baby."

I shifted my hips and rocked against him, his

cock filling me. I knew exactly what he wanted, too. I glanced at him over my shoulder. He was intent on watching himself move in and out of me. My core pulsed around him. It turned me on even more that he liked to see.

"You like that baby? You like watching your big cock slide in and out of me, fucking me."

His brows rose in surprise. I'd finally found the courage to not be embarrassed and tell him what I wanted, plus I'd learned to gauge his mood on whether we were making love or playing.

"Gem," he groaned. "You're so fucking hot."

I grinned and closed my eyes, focusing on him moving in and out of me. He leaned over my back, his arm encircling my stomach, and slammed inside me.

"That's it, Hendrix. Harder," I panted. "Fuck me, baby." I braced myself against him while his body slapped against mine. He'd never taken me this hard, and I loved it.

His teeth sank lightly into my shoulder, and his arm shifted from my belly to between my legs. His fingers twirled my swollen bud, his pace picking up even more.

"Deeper," I said, begging.

"Fuck, you're going to make me come," Hendrix moaned. He pulled on my clit and pumped me as hard as he could, hitting every sensitive spot inside me.

"Are you ready?" he asked, breathless. "I'm going to come, but I need you with me. I need your tight little pussy to clench around my cock."

He lightly pinched my throbbing clit one more time and sent me over the edge while he drove his dick into me, his body shuddering as he came inside me.

His hot breath came in short bursts, and he rested his head against my back. My arms and legs trembled. He kissed a path down my back as he slowly pulled out and nipped my butt cheek. I collapsed on the counter.

"What did you do to me?" I asked, my voice cracking.

"Something we won't get to do on tour."

My lower lip jutted out.

"That part will suck. I've gotten spoiled living alone with you and having sex anywhere we want to."

He stepped into his shorts and kissed my cheek.

"We'll have a bed together with a door, but we'll have to be quiet. The rest of the guys get bunks, but it's my tour bus, so we get the room."

I sat up and stared at him.

"You own the tour bus?" I asked, surprised. "Where is it?"

"Well, Dad bought it for me before I got the house in Louisiana and started the tour. I rent a space at a bus and RV place that stores them and provides security. Dad made the payments when I had amnesia, but now that I'm better, I insisted on taking over the responsibility again. And he agreed. The house and car are one thing, but I have to pay my own way at some point. Plus I have my own money now, so I have to man up."

"It's sexy," I said, eyeing his muscled chest and ripped abs. "I like a guy who pays his own way."

"That's good because it's who I am." He kissed me, caressing my breast one last time before he pulled away.

"I need to make some business calls. You can listen if you want, but we'll be scheduling a meeting together, most likely tonight. We'll go over contracts and other necessary details then."

I scrunched up my nose.

"Thanks to you, I smell like sex, so if you don't need me yet, I'm going to go take a shower."

"Sounds good." He kissed the tip of my nose and then walked into the living room.

I peeled my bare ass off the countertop and immediately grabbed the Lysol cleaner. After a thorough scrubbing, I grinned and climbed two stairs at a time toward our bedroom. Even though I would miss the house, we would be back, and this was a chance of a lifetime. There was no way I could pass it up. But honestly, I would miss Mac the most. I'd be on a bus full of dudes, and an extra female part of the time would be super nice.

Stepping under the hot spray of the water, I pondered how the conversation with Mac and Franklin would go down. We'd mentioned our plans to Mac already, and she seemed on board with touring with us some of the time as long as her grades were good. There was no way I wanted to interfere with the ground rules Franklin had put in place for her, but I just didn't want her to feel like we'd left her behind. At this point, she spent every weekend with us, and it had worked perfectly. I had no idea how long we would be on the road, though, and I needed plans with my bestie in place.

WE MET with Hendrix's attorney, manager, and a music producer named Ricky at seven. Apparently an expensive meal was part of the meeting.

My nerves shifted into overdrive as the situation became more and more real.

Hendrix parked his car at the Davenport Hotel. He looked hot as hell wearing a deep blue dress shirt and black slacks. I'd opted for a dress from Nordstrom. Since it wasn't a flashy occasion, I wanted to present myself in a professional manner and opted for a black dress that complimented my figure but didn't showcase my assets in a sexy way. Plus I didn't want to attract unwanted attention from any of the men.

A sense of unease fluttered inside me as Hendrix opened my car door for me, extended his hand, and assisted me out of the car.

"I'm with you every step of the way. And Josiah is a damned good attorney. He'll review every bit of the paperwork, and if there's any bullshit clauses in place, he'll catch them. He and my dad go way back, so we're covered."

My hands trembled, and he grabbed them, kissing the inside of each palm.

"I wish Ada Lynn was here to see this."

He lifted my chin with his finger and smiled sadly.

"I know, babe. And this is just my opinion, but I don't think they ever leave us. I think she and your mom are with you every step of the way."

"Thanks," I said, brushing my lips against his.

We entered through the restaurant, and a handsome older man waved at us. I peered at Hendrix, my hand squeezing his.

"That's Josiah," he said.

The hostess approached us and led us to our table. Hendrix pulled out my chair before sitting down next to me.

I scanned everyone at the table, Charles's words ringing in my ears to always be aware of my surroundings. Even though I was with Hendrix, I still felt the heated gazes from his producer and manager. Apparently so did he, because he draped his arm over my shoulders.

"Let me be clear gentleman, I won't put up with any bullshit."

My back stiffened. I'd never heard Hendrix talk like this. He'd gone into full business mode, protecting his assets and future, which included me. I suspected Franklin's influence had something to do with it.

"No career is worth losing myself over, and I believe Gemma feels the same."

"I do," I chimed in, supporting Hendrix.

I peeked out of the corner of my eye, catching Josiah covering his grin. Whatever these two were up to, I would play along. From what I could tell, they were jerking the rug out from under anyone's feet before they even considered taking advantage of us.

The discussions continued while the men ordered alcohol, but I passed. I wanted to be alert and learn more about the business.

Several hours passed as negotiations, pay, tour schedule, songs, and more were discussed. What I hadn't realized was that they wanted me to sing in almost every song. Hendrix had already expressed his support with the change. It would leave him a few solo songs, and me, too. But overall, we were a team. Cade and John were also negotiated into the group again, plus they added a few backup singers.

My eyes bulged when the contract, including the amount we were to be paid, was placed in front of me. Thank God I'd had the insight to lower my head, allowing my hair to hide my shock. I'd never seen so many zeroes with my name next to it.

Hendrix squeezed my hand, and I glanced at him.

"I think it's good if you're comfortable with the dollar amount. We'll renegotiate after this tour, anyway," he whispered against my ear.

I nodded and watched Hendrix sign the papers, then I did the same. It was official. I was a paid professional singer.

AFTER WE ALL SAID GOODNIGHT, I sank into the car seat and buckled up, staring at Hendrix.

"Shit, that was intense, and my mind is still whirling."

He smiled at me as he maneuvered the Lexus away from the restaurant and toward home.

"Yeah, I've been through it once already, so I had some kind of an idea. Josiah took care of a lot for us. He's a super good guy. But..." he hesitated. "I almost backed out of the deal."

"What?" I asked, my brows knitting together in confusion. "You've wanted to tour again ever since you got your memories back. I don't understand."

He blew out a breath, and his intense gaze fell on me.

"The moment you walked into the room, our producer and manager looked at you like they wanted to...shit, I don't even want to say it out loud. It pissed me the fuck off. Yeah, you're beautiful, and men are going to look, but you're not a product to be handled, you're my girlfriend, and they know to keep their behavior in check. Then I realized you're going to be on stage with me. You'll have more guys coming onto you and offering sex than I will girls knocking on my dressing room door. I mean, we won't be a part of it, but some of the groups we're touring with, they party hard. Cocaine, heroin, meth, orgies, it's everywhere. I've had to learn really fast who I should spend my time with and who to steer clear of. That shit isn't who I am, or what I stand for, nor will it ever be. During my last tour, I stayed on the bus, wrote music and spent time by myself when all the parties started. Besides, I was already in love with you, so I had no interest in other women. Anyway, I had to back up for a minute and check myself at our meeting tonight. And I had to ask myself, was this really the best thing for you? For our future?"

My heart raced, I'd never considered the environment we would be in the middle of. I'd not spent any real time in the music industry at all.

"What changed your mind?" I asked softly.

"I saw how happy you were, Gem. Then I finally realized that this isn't just my dream, it's yours too, but all of that had been stolen from you when you were fourteen. But now, I'm actually able to help you make it happen. You've downplayed how much it all means to you, and I get why…every time you had something good happen, some fucked up shit would snatch it away from you. But that's all behind you. Behind us. You can dream again, babe. We really can do this together, and it's not my place to say you can't. It's my place to support you and stand next to you."

"Hendrix," I said, breathlessly. "I love you for wanting to protect me, but I love you more for helping me live. For so many years I wouldn't even allow myself to think about what a first date would be like, or my first kiss, or ever singing again. But you've given me all of that and more."

"I would give you the world if I could."

"Me, too." I paused, staring out the car window at downtown Spokane. No matter how many times I saw it, I loved the way the city lit up at night. Growing up in a small country town hadn't afforded a lot of beautiful scenery like this. "We only have two weeks before we go. When are we going to tell Mac? And how much does Franklin know?"

"If you don't mind, I would like to swing by his place and update him. He'll need to know the tour schedule, and he might have some words of wisdom concerning Mac."

"Should we call first?"

Hendrix nodded and pressed a button on his steering wheel.

"Call Franklin."

"Calling Franklin," the car replied.

"Ohh, so fancy," I said, giggling.

"Hey son," Franklin's voice boomed through the car.

"Hey, Dad. Gemma and I would like to stop by if you have a few minutes?"

"Yeah, that'll work. Mac's out with some friends tonight at a movie, but I'm here."

"We'll see you in about ten minutes, then."

Hendrix ended the call.

"Dammit, I wanted to see Mac. I'll text her to meet us at Franklin's."

"That would be good. We'll have her over more before we leave, but not too much. I need you naked and on every surface of our house before then. The door to our room on the bus is paper thin, so we'll have to be quiet. Until then, I want my name rolling off those beautiful lips of yours every chance we have."

I smiled, heat stirring between my legs. It didn't take me much to get me all hot and bothered these days.

HENDRIX RANG the doorbell when we arrived at Franklin's.

"It's a big house, and I know he has guns. I don't want to ever startle him by walking in."

My lips pursed. Guns. I'd grown up in the south where it was completely acceptable and a way of life, but I'd never even held one. I certainly wasn't sure how I felt about them.

"Come on in, kids," Franklin said, beaming at us. "You two look lovely. What's the big occasion?"

We followed Franklin into the family room, sat down, and Hendrix took my hand in his.

"We start the tour in two weeks."

"Wow, this is great news," Franklin said, clapping his hands together. "And you're on board, Gemma?"

"That's an understatement," I said, laughing. "I'm singing with Hendrix most of the time. There's some talk about some solos, too."

"They love her, Dad. She's officially part of the band."

"Congratulations, you two. I couldn't be happier for you."

Hendrix and Franklin began discussing business, and I excused myself. I'd been so nervous at the meeting, I'd barely drank anything, and my throat was parched.

My heels clicked against the marble floor as I wandered into the kitchen, grabbed some water, and downed it. My gaze drifted to the house down the hill. Stepping through the side door, I walked to the pool house. The familiar smell of chlorine filled my nose, and the clanking sound of weights caught my ear when I entered.

I poked my head around the corner and spotted Charles. He heaved, and bench pressed an ungodly amount of weights. Sweat covered his bare chest, and every muscle in his rock-hard body flexed with the effort. He set them down and sat up slowly. His deep brown eyes locked on me and surprise flickered across his face.

"We stopped by, and I figured I would see if you were around," I said, stepping forward.

"How are you?" he asked, reaching for the towel and wiping the sweat off his forehead.

"Good. We finished meeting with...well, I'm going on tour with Hendrix. But I'm singing with him, not just fangirling." I smiled, attempting a little bit of humor. I wasn't sure if Charles was in work mode or human mode.

"Congratulations, that's got to be exciting for both of you."

"Yeah, we'll be gone for several months, though. It will be an adjustment, but I think it's going to be a great experience."

"What about you? Any girls worth mentioning?" I asked, my brow arching. I crossed my arms over my chest and waited for his response. We'd never discussed his dating life.

"I don't have time for relationships."

"Makes sense. But you've been working for Franklin now for almost a year?" I asked.

"That's right, since last September."

"About the time I arrived in Spokane."

He nodded, his eyes softening briefly.

"It seems like a very lonesome kind of life," I said quietly, remembering the years I'd isolated myself from the world. "You're a great guy, Charles. I hope one day you'll find the same kind of happiness I found with Hendrix, but minus all the drama." I added, laughing softly.

A smile pulled at the corner of his mouth but was gone instantly. "I'm still under orders to protect you, Gemma. So as long as you're here, if you need me, you have my number."

"Thanks. Maybe we'll have a get-together, and

I can talk Franklin into letting you participate instead of work the party."

This time he gave me a real smile.

"Maybe."

"Well, I'd better go. I just wanted to say hi."

"Take care, Gemma," he said, his words carrying a hint of sadness.

I stared at him, then turned and walked away. Maybe Hendrix was right, and Charles really did have feelings for me. If that was the case, I didn't want to antagonize him with my presence. I'd been selfish in wanting to see him tonight.

Hurrying back to the main house, I chided myself for wanting to say goodbye to Charles. To me, he'd been a friend, and we'd bonded that horrible night Carl had attacked me, but maybe I was as naive as Hendrix had mentioned and I'd never seen Charles's attention shift into another direction. It didn't matter anymore, anyway. I was leaving in two weeks, and I highly doubted I would even see him again.

I headed to the kitchen in search of the grapes I knew Ruby always kept stocked in the fridge. Popping one in my mouth, I screamed as the back door burst open.

CHAPTER 32

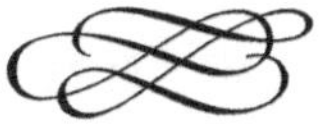

A fully dressed Charles flew past me and into the living room. I'd never seen him run except the night Carl had been in my house. I hurried after him as fast as my heels would allow me.

He rounded the corner toward Franklin's office, and as I followed closely behind him I scanned the living room for Hendrix, but I didn't see him. Where was he? Was he alright? Panic filled me with every step I took. Franklin's voice boomed down the hallway. As I entered the office, I immediately spotted Hendrix. Rushing to him, I stopped cold the moment I saw their expressions. Charles stood still, waiting for Franklin to finish a phone call.

I touched Hendrix on the arm, and he slowly turned to face me.

"What's wrong?" I whispered.

Hendrix pulled me in for a tight hug, his heart beating wildly in his chest.

"Dad's trying to gather more information, but...Brandon has Mac."

My knees buckled, and he swept me up in his arms. He carried me to the living room and sat me down on the sofa, kneeling down next to me.

"Babe, hang in there with me." His voice was laced with fear. "I need you right now. Gemma, please." He grabbed my hands and lay his head on my knees.

His words went straight to my heart. It didn't matter that I'd just lost Ada Lynn, he had too, and now he was terrified he'd lose another sister. No matter what, I needed to suck it up and be there for him. For Mac.

"I'm here," I said, stroking his hair. "What can you tell me?"

Hendrix lifted his head, his eyes locking with mine. The torment in his face nearly ripped me to pieces.

"All we know is that Brandon has Mac."

"What? Why would he want Mac?" A chill shot through me at the memories of his gruff and greedy hands groping my body. "He'd better not hurt her, I'll fucking dismantle him myself," I said, glaring.

"He texted Franklin from Mac's phone, but we don't know where he has her yet. Our investigation into Andrea and her motives led to Brandon. He's the link. And I think he's finally flipped out. But it goes much deeper than that. Dad is still investigating, we don't know everything yet."

"Is that what I'd catch you and Franklin whispering about sometimes?"

"Probably. Franklin wouldn't allow me to talk about it with anyone other than him. Charles was hired when Dad realized Andrea was only the tip of the iceberg, so he knows a few details, too."

"Is...is Charles with the FBI? And, how does he tie in?"

Hendrix sighed. "He's not with the FBI, he's one of the ex-military guys that work as private security, but what I didn't know is that the FBI contacted him right after you and I met. He's been helping with the case."

"Case? I don't understand," I said, grabbing his hands.

"I'll tell you when I know more. Franklin's working on it now. What I do know is that

Brandon is more dangerous than we ever realized. And now...now he has Mac."

Tears welled in his eyes as I gently tilted his chin up with my palm.

"You listen to me Hendrix Harrington. Mac is the toughest little cookie I've met in my entire life. Honest to God, I just might feel sorry for Brandon after she's done with him. Her mind whirls a million miles an hour, and she *will* find a way to either escape or contact us."

"Thank you," he said, kissing the inside of my palm. "I can't lose another sister, Gemma. I can't."

"Not another word like that. Mac isn't little, she's grown and smart as hell."

Hendrix stood slowly and ran his hands through his hair.

"Let's see what else Franklin found out."

I took his hand, and we walked back toward Franklin's office, but the door was closed.

"Dammit," he muttered.

"Who was he on the phone with?"

"The FBI," Hendrix muttered, leaning against the wall.

"What in the hell did you and Franklin stumble onto?"

Hendrix's jaw tensed, and he ran a hand along his well-trimmed beard. What was he not telling me? My chest ached with fear. I might have delivered a good pep talk to Hendrix, but inside, I was in an utter panic. Mac was my best friend, and I'd already lost half of the people I loved. I dropped my head and mentally vowed I'd hunt Brandon for the rest of my life if he harmed Mac.

Franklin's door opened, and he ushered us inside. Charles stood ramrod straight, his earpiece in place.

"Gemma, meet Pierce," Franklin nodded at Charles.

My eyes narrowed. He'd mentioned his name wasn't Charles, but he couldn't share what his actual name was with me?

"Hello, Pierce," I said stiffly.

"Since I'm waiting for the police to locate Brandon's car, I'll update you both. Before you and Hendrix met, some information came across my desk, and I started looking into it. It was an anonymous tip concerning the driver..." Franklin's voice trailed off. "The driver of the car that hit and killed my daughter, Kendra."

"What?" Hendrix asked, stunned. "Why didn't you say something?"

So Hendrix had been in the dark, too. I took his hand in mine. The Franklin I knew would keep his kids safe at any cost, even if it meant pissing them off. And right now, my gut instinct told me what he'd learned was fucking huge.

"Because I didn't want to get your hopes up, son."

I glanced over at Hendrix, his expression a jumble of emotions.

"What I began to unravel went well beyond Kendra, and I contacted the FBI with what I had. At that point, I hired Pierce. Not only was I worried about my family's safety, but my own. I shared this information with Connor, who became my go-to guy at the bureau."

I blanched. Franklin had a guy at the FBI?

Hendrix's leg bounced, but he remained quiet.

"Gemma, you were actually followed from Louisiana to Spokane. The bureau has a file on you."

"What?" I gasped, standing quickly.

"Dad, this better be goddamned good," Hendrix said, jumping out of his chair, his chest puffing up. He slid his arm around my waist protectively.

"It was because of your father, you've done nothing wrong, Gemma. I'm sorry I scared you. I'm really rattled and sick over Mac right now, so please, both of you, be patient with me." Franklin rubbed his face and inhaled deeply.

Hendrix and I sat back down, my heart hammering against my rib cage. The FBI had been tailing me?

"They wanted to make sure you weren't a participant in your father's activities."

I could feel the color drain from my cheeks. The mere idea turned my stomach. I would have never assisted that monster.

"And of course you had no idea. It didn't take long for them to realize you were just a young woman striking out on her own for the first time."

"That's why they never caught Brandon attacking me, they'd already moved on," I stated.

"Yes," Franklin said. "But Hendrix told me. Then, when Andrea accused my son of rape, I assumed Brandon was behind it, but I had no proof."

"But why would he do that to Hendrix? And why would he want Mac?"

Franklin's gaze bounced between Hendrix and me.

"Because not only were we closing in on the investigation concerning Andrea..." He paused, his face grim. "We discovered that it was Brandon's brother, Mathew, who killed Kendra."

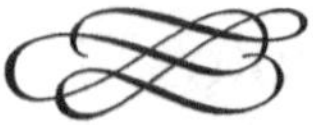

CHAPTER 33

Hendrix released a gut-wrenching yell that shattered my soul. I wasn't even sure what to do for him. He dropped to his knees, his shoulders shaking, his cries ripping through the room. Tears streamed down my cheeks, and I looked to Franklin for guidance. He nodded, and I dropped to the floor with Hendrix, cradling him in my arms. He clung to me while I stroked his hair, his face buried in my chest.

A few minutes passed as Hendrix gathered himself together. Franklin waited patiently, and Pierce never moved, but I knew he was paying attention to every word, every noise, every movement. I was grateful he was on our side. If anyone could get Mac, it would be him.

Hendrix stood, his shoulders slumped forward, and he walked out of the room.

"Franklin?" I asked. "I'm at a loss right now. What does he need from me?"

"He needs a minute. He knows Mac is a top priority. He'll be back."

I nodded, held onto my dress while I got up off the floor, and sank back into my chair. I silently cursed my dress and heels. Jeans and a T-shirt would have been more appropriate for the situation, and I wouldn't have had to worry about accidentally baring my ass to the room.

Staring out the window, I tried to figure out how my life had become such a tangled mess that the FBI were now involved. At first it was my family, and now it was Hendrix's.

"Did Brandon know?" Hendrix asked from the doorway of the office. "We were thirteen when it happened. Did he know his brother was a murderer?" His voice cracked with emotion, his hands fisting together.

"I don't think he knew at first. But when I approached the police last August concerning the anonymous information and my additional investigation into Kendra's accident, the case was reopened...I suspect he found out then."

Hendrix's head dropped, then his stone-cold gaze traveled back up to Franklin.

"Why didn't you tell me they reopened the case?" Hendrix roared, stepping toward his father.

I flinched as Pierce took a step and planted one hand on Hendrix's chest.

"Because I had to goddamn protect you!" Franklin yelled.

My mouth dropped. I'd never seen either of them like this.

"Protect me from what? Fucking liars? I can take Brandon. If you'd told me, I could have taken care of him a long time ago, and he would never have hurt Gemma or kidnapped Mac!"

Franklin's eyes narrowed.

"Son, my job is to take care of my kids and protect you from others and sometimes your-selves. I fucked up with Kendra, but I won't apol-ogize for trying to keep you and Mac safe. Now sit down or leave."

The same raw power that exuded from Hen-drix rolled off Franklin in waves. Complete si-lence filled the room as they stared at each other. Finally, Hendrix sat down next to me, and Pierce resumed his post.

Franklin sat on the edge of his desk and inhaled sharply.

"By this time, Gemma, Hendrix had shown an interest in you and Brandon knew it."

"The day at the library," I whispered. "When you stood up to him, and he spat on your shoes."

"I should have stopped him then, but I didn't. I figured he would move on to someone else," Hendrix said.

Franklin shook his head. "Brandon is a bully and worse, a rapist. Gemma was an easy target at the time. When he realized you were protective of Gemma, it became personal. Brandon was also aware that I had been instrumental in reopening the investigation concerning Kendra, and that his father was feeling the heat."

"What do you mean?" I wasn't sure I understood. "Why would his father be feeling heat?"

Franklin looked at us with sadness in his eyes. "Brandon's father covered up the hit and run."

"What?" I gulped. "The dean of the university covered up his son's hit and run?"

Franklin nodded. "If the cops arrested Mathew, they'd also go after his father. Brandon would lose everything—his family, his money, and his ability to get away with the shit he'd been doing to girls on and off campus."

I nodded, the pieces beginning to fit together.

"But there's more."

Hendrix took my hand. I wasn't sure how much more either of us could handle.

"Dean Montgomery," Franklin started, only to be interrupted by the chime of his cell phone ringing.

"This is Franklin," he answered. He frowned and ran his hand over his head. He shot a look at Pierce while he listened.

"We're on the way. Pierce, get the Mercedes ready for us."

Pierce left without a word as Hendrix and I waited for Franklin to update us.

"Get your phones, and let's go. The cops tracked Brandon's car and have located where he's holding Mac."

Hendrix jumped out of his seat and took my hand, pulling me behind him while we hurried out the front door and into the car.

"You said there was more," I said from the back seat to Franklin as Pierce pulled out of the driveway.

Franklin turned to us.

"I'm sorry, it's too difficult to talk in the car while you both are in the back seat. You'll have to wait until we get there. Then I promise I'll tell you everything."

TWENTY AGONIZING MINUTES LATER, Pierce parked the car and stepped out. Franklin opened my door, and Pierce grabbed Hendrix's. My mouth gaped open. Police cars, a SWAT van, and an ambulance surrounded an old warehouse. The building had no windows that I could see. Maybe there were some on the other side.

"She's in there?" I asked, my voice trembling. Hendrix and Pierce walked over to us.

"Yes, but we're to stay back, do you understand?" Franklin said to Hendrix and me.

I nodded, the reality of the situation becoming too real.

"Negotiations are underway," Pierce said.

"What does he want?" Hendrix asked. "Just give it to him, Dad. It can't possibly be more important than Mac."

I grabbed Hendrix's arm, staring at him.

"She's strong, baby," I said. "Hold onto that."

A shiver shot through me. My dress was sleeveless, and the night air was still chilly this time of year. Hendrix removed his suit jacket, placed it gently over my shoulders, and I snuggled up to him.

"Franklin, you mentioned there was more.

Since we're waiting at this point, just tell us the rest, please."

Franklin's gaze traveled to Pierce, and he gave a slight nod.

"When the police reopened Kendra's case, which now pointed to Brandon's brother, Mathew, they inadvertently stepped on the FBI's toes. You see, the FBI had been investigating the boys' father, Dillon Montgomery...dean of the university. By the time I'd learned who had killed my daughter, there was nothing I could do. The FBI's investigation trumped ours, and we had to stand down."

Hendrix dropped his arm and walked away, turned in a circle, and back to me. Anger flashing in his eyes. "Dad, what in the hell…?"

"Dillon Montgomery is from the founding family of the Dark Circle Society."

I frowned and looked at Hendrix. He shrugged. Neither of us were familiar with the name.

"His great-grandfather started the same so-ciety your father belonged to, Gemma. The same group that connects rapists with young women. The meetings and rapes are referred to as a swap."

My knees buckled with the revelation, and my

stomach churned. I scrambled away, tossing the contents of my stomach into the bushes. Violent tremors traveled through my body while Hendrix gathered my hair and held it for me.

"I've got you, babe."

I clutched at his arm, steadying myself. Wiping my mouth off with the back of my hand, I willed myself to stand up, and we returned to Franklin.

"I'm sorry, Gemma. I know it brings back horrific memories for you." He handed me a bottle of water, and I took a sip.

"Is Brandon a part of it? Of the society?" I asked.

"At one point he was, but apparently he couldn't control himself very well, and his behavior began to cause issues and draw unwanted attention. The last thing Dillon wanted was for his son to get arrested for rape. Just the possibility of it sent ripples through the society, so they banned him from any swaps until he could prove he was ready. He'd already been kicked out when you showed up, Gemma. There were already numerous reports of his sexual assaults on and off campus, but no proof. As the police closed in concerning his brother, instead of Brandon backing off, his activity escalated. It didn't take long before the FBI got wind of it, and without realizing it, he led them to his father's doorstep."

I barked out a laugh. "So his lack of control and stupidity gave the bureau what they needed?"

"That and more. Not only has Dillon Montgomery been the leader of the society for years, but he's also wanted for human trafficking and prostitution of women and underage girls."

My stomach churned, and I hurried toward the grass again. Tears streamed down my cheeks, not only for my best friend who was being held against her will by a complete monster, but for every woman who had lived through what I had or worse.

I straightened on shaky legs as Hendrix's arm slipped around me.

"Thanks." I leaned against him. "I hope they put a bullet in both of their heads," I hissed, my words laced with venom. "I hate them. I fucking hate them all." I wiped off my mouth, and we returned to Franklin and Pierce again.

"Sorry," I said, taking the water from Franklin's extended hand.

"There's nothing to apologize for."

"So Brandon went off the deep end when they arrested Dillon, and he went after you through Mac?" I asked.

"Well, he certainly went off the deep end, but Dillon is nowhere to be found. He disappeared into thin air and left his sons to pick up the pieces. From what I've been told, Brandon went home after classes, and his father was gone. He'd walked into an empty house, no furniture, no boxes, nothing. When he tried to contact Mathew, there was no answer, and that's when he lost it."

"I thought Mac was going to a movie tonight. Where would she have seen Brandon?" I asked.

"We suspect he waited for her to leave our house and grabbed her after the movie."

"I shouldn't have moved out. I know that fucker's car. If we'd still been there, I could have spotted him. Mac didn't know what he drove," Hendrix said, his voice full of regret.

"Don't blame yourself, Hendrix, you can't control an insane person. Sickness runs in that family. You don't run a society that sets up rape and sex trafficking unless you're seriously fucked up," Franklin stated.

My eyebrow shot up. I'd never heard Franklin drop the F-bomb before tonight. Maybe Mac had rubbed off on him. But I suspected he was barely holding his shit together beneath his calm attorney exterior.

"And, honestly, if they wanted Mac or anyone for that matter, they would have been able to set it up. These people are sneaky and devious, even the FBI had a difficult time nailing them down."

"Until Brandon?" I asked.

"Yeah."

"Is there anything else, Dad?" Hendrix asked, a hint of anger in his tone.

"The cops arrested Mathew, and he's being charged with Kendra's murder. It's why he didn't pick up his phone when Brandon called him today. He was being booked."

Hendrix dropped his head on my shoulder, and I turned into him, holding him tightly.

"Dillon had gone to great lengths to cover it all up. Mathew was on his way to a swap and was running late when he hit Kendra. There's typically only a small window for them to...to."

"Rape the girls," I stated, emotion thick in my voice. "I was on my way home from choir practice. It was a five-minute walk from school. I was almost home, actually. But now that I know the truth, if it hadn't happened then, Kyle would have set up another time, especially since I'd been a virgin."

Franklin's expression fell. "Sick bastard."

"Sir," Pierce stepped up. "Something is happening." He paused and held his hand over his earpiece. "Come with me."

"Oh God," I said under my breath. Hendrix flashed me a look, his face twisted with fear. We hurried forward and through several policemen. A barrier of cars wouldn't allow us to go any farther, but for the first time, we were close enough to see through the darkness. I searched around us, eyeing the cops that were crouched down and aiming their guns at the door of the building. Normally civilians weren't allowed near a hostage situation, but Franklin and Pierce had the connections, and it was Mac inside that building.

"Jesus," Hendrix said, seeing what I had. He clutched my hand, his body tense.

Pierce stopped in front of another uniformed officer, and we gathered around.

"Sir, this is Officer Lambert. He's in charge," Pierce explained.

"Franklin, we've spotted some activity inside through our thermal imaging cameras, and we just heard from Brandon."

"What does he want?" I asked, confused.

"You."

My stomach dropped.

"He'll trade Mac for Gemma." He paused and turned toward Franklin and Hendrix. "He said since you took his brother and father he's taking your girlfriend, Hendrix. And from what we've put together, and the time Mackenzie left your house, they've been in there for almost two hours. From what we've already learned, Brandon has a short fuse, and he could blow at any time."

I gasped. I was raped in minutes, what was he capable of doing to Mac in two hours?

"We sent a few men to scope out the area, and there are additional entrances. We have a few options. We can toss in smoke bombs and storm the place, or we can let Gemma go in. It would be less risky if we had a distraction and handled it that way."

Franklin frowned.

"And sir, the cameras were able to determine that Brandon has a gun," Lambert said.

I spun around and buried my face into Hendrix's chest, willing myself to not break down or scream.

"Goddammit," Franklin said.

I swallowed my emotions and turned around. Franklin's shoulders sagged, his head hanging down.

"I'll go. Brandon knew the moment he took Mac that I would be here. Offer me as a trade," I said. "And if he's serious and not bluffing, he'll agree and let Mac go."

"What? Fuck that," Hendrix growled.

"Gemma, no, you can't do that," Franklin said. Pierce stared straight at me, respect flickering across his face.

I stood tall and squared my shoulders.

"I know the society. My father, Kyle, was a part of it. He set up my rape. Plus, I was one of Brandon's targets. Not only am I a personal vendetta, but he swore one day he'd rape me. Tell him I'm here, and I'll trade myself for Mac. I'll go in," I said to Lambert.

Hendrix spun me around, facing him. "No, no, no," he said, fear filling his expression. "No."

"Baby, if anyone can get to him...I have the best chance."

Tears spilled down Hendrix's cheeks as he cupped my face and placed his forehead on mine.

"I can't let you," he said. "I know she's my sister, but I just can't."

"Hendrix," I said staring up into his beautiful blue eyes. "I love you more than life itself, but it's not your choice. You and Mac have given me more than I could have ever dreamed possible. If they agree, I'm going in," I said softly.

Hendrix's mouth crashed down on mine, and

I kissed him back with everything inside me. This man had taken a chance on me and breathed life back into my shattered heart more than once. I had what most girls only dreamed of. If it were over tonight, I would die a happy woman.

We released each other, and I took a deep breath.

"What do I need to do?" I asked Lambert, directly.

"Gemma, you might not come back out. We might lose you both, please, I'm begging you, don't go," Franklin pleaded, pulling me into his arms.

"You've given me so much. You took care of Ada Lynn and shared your son and daughter with me. Let me try, Franklin. It might not work at all. But I need to try."

"There are never any guarantees in situations like this, but I think it might work," Officer Lambert said. "I need to check on a few things first. Hang tight."

"Gemma," Pierce said, gently grabbing my arm. He pulled me over to the side and away from Franklin and Hendrix.

"If you're going in...if they agree to do this. You're not going in unarmed."

"I've never used a gun, Pierce. I don't..."

"I'm not talking about that."

For the next fifteen minutes, Pierce walked me through multiple strategies, including taking the gun from Brandon. My heart hammered a million miles an hour. Hendrix and Franklin stood to the side, watching intently.

"Let's do it," Officer Lambert called.

"Thank you, Pierce."

He squeezed my hand for a second and then let it go.

"Goddammit, you better come back," he said, his voice thick with emotion.

I flung my arms around him, catching him off guard.

"I will," I said. "Thanks for being a good friend." I let him go and hurried toward Hendrix and Franklin.

"We texted him that you were here, Gemma. It worked. He's agreed to the trade," Lambert said.

"Fuck," Hendrix said, pulling me to him and kissing the top of my forehead. "Please don't, baby. Please," he pleaded in my ear.

"I'll be back."

He kissed me again, unwilling to let me go.

"You're my forever," he whispered in my ear.

"And you're my always."

I hugged Franklin, then followed Lambert to a group of police officers.

"When he sees you thirty feet away from the door, he's agreed to walk Mac out. He'll have a gun trained on her. Do not talk to her. Do not touch her. I don't want to set him off any worse than he already is. He could easily open fire on both of you. I want you both back safely." I nodded and continued to listen as Lambert instructed me on what to do while his men slipped inside the back side of the building. My pulse hammered so hard, my head throbbed.

"Are you ready?" he asked.

I glanced over my shoulder to Hendrix. "I love you," I mouthed.

"I love you, too. Come back to me," he said in return.

I gave a small wave to Franklin and Pierce.

"Good luck," Lambert said. "You're one hell of a young woman. We need more of you, so make sure you come back to us."

"Thank you, sir."

In thirty feet, my entire future would be in the hands of a crazy and sick man...again. But this time, it was my choice.

Spotlights warmed my back as I walked to my destination. Hendrix's jacket still hung across my shoulders, and I pulled on it, imagining his arms around me.

The door of the warehouse flung open, and I gasped as Brandon held Mac tightly against him, a pistol to her temple. My eyes focused on her, waiting to get close enough to see if he had hurt her.

We were within steps of each other when he pushed her down on the ground and grabbed me. His gun positioned at my temple.

"I love you, Mac!" I called to her.

She scrambled backward and stood.

"Gemma!" She cried. "No!" A cop ran out and snatched her, pulling her to safety while Brandon walked us backward and into the warehouse.

He shoved me against the wall, his hand trembling as he trained the gun on me. My eyes closed, and I recalled the plan. I only had to keep him occupied for a few short minutes.

"I've waited a long time for you."

"Brandon," I said softly. "It's not too late."

"Shut the fuck up. You can't talk your way out of this one. I would have gladly grabbed you instead of Mac, but you were holed up with your fucking boyfriend, probably sucking his dick. Now it's my turn."

A sour taste filled my mouth while he rubbed his crotch against me.

They can smell your fear, Gemma. Pierce's words whispered through my mind. *This time...let him.*

"My dad...he was in the society, too."

Brandon's brow rose. "You know about that?" He sneered. "Man, it was the best set up. I popped more cherries than I knew what to do with. They were at my beck and call."

"Kyle, too. He swapped me with someone."

Brandon's face fell. "Your dad? What the fuck?" He took a step back, lowering the gun from my head, but still aiming at me.

"I know what it's like to be betrayed by a parent, Brandon. If I'd known...if I'd known, I wouldn't have ever fallen for Hendrix." I swallowed my lie, forcing myself to continue as Pierce had instructed me.

"Are you fucking with me right now?"

"If anyone understands the society and the betrayal you went through, I do. We could have helped each other. You never had to threaten me. I just didn't know we were the same."

"We're not the same," he said, holding the gun with both hands.

I held my breath and took a step closer to him, getting my back off the wall so I could move or duck if I needed to. There was no telling when he might snap.

"Kyle betrayed me, and he betrayed members in the society. He was found dead outside of our house in Louisiana. Brandon, if you provide the cops with any information, the society will come after you, too. You've already drawn a ton of attention to yourself and to your father when you took Mac." I took another step toward him, but he didn't back up. "I don't want you to go to jail. You and I, we got off on the wrong foot. I can give you anything you want."

His eyes narrowed, and his breathing quickened.

"Anything," I said to him. I was fucking crazy. This whole idea had been crazy. Then a calm flowed over me. If worse came to worst, I would be with Mom and Ada Lynn soon. If not, I would be with Mac and Hendrix.

I cautiously walked to him.

"Brandon," I coaxed, "lower the gun. Let me help you get out of here, so you're not arrested."

"Why? Why would you help me?"

"Because I understand what your father did to you, and while he's hiding to avoid being arrested, there are at least ten cop cars outside. Every one of them has a gun aimed at the door.

They're waiting for the right moment to take you out. I can help you."

Before I could take another step, he lunged at me, knocking me on my back. The air whooshed out of my lungs as he stepped forward, the gun in his hand hanging at his side. A sneer spread across his face.

"Fuck them, because I'm about to fuck you," he snarled.

It was then that I realized my plan had no hope of working, he was too far gone. Too evil. I'd offered myself up on a silver platter to him, and he still wanted to rape me.

Brandon took one more step toward me, and I shoved my three-inch spiked heel straight into his balls as hard as I could.

"Ahh! You bitch!" He doubled over, dropping the gun and clutching his junk. I kicked him in the thigh as he crumpled to the floor, blood seeping through the crotch of his jeans. No regular guy would get back up from that, but he wasn't normal.

I scrambled off the floor and ran for the gun. I'd told Pierce I'd never use one, but Brandon didn't know that. My fingers closed around the cold metal, and I whirled around just in time.

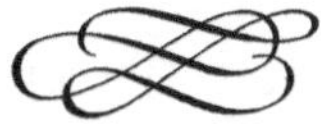

My entire body froze, and I stood rooted to the floor as Brandon charged at me. Images of Hendrix, Mac, Franklin, and Pierce flipped through my mind. I didn't want to die, and if Brandon reached me, he would kill me. More than anything else in this world, I wanted to walk out that door and run into Hendrix's arms. Mac was safe, and my dreams were finally coming true.

With one squeeze, I pulled the trigger. Brandon's body lurched backward with the impact, and a scream ripped from my lungs. Blood seeped from his body, and a puddle had already started to accumulate on the floor. He wasn't moving. I had no idea where the bullet had hit him.

"Police!" The door flung open, and somehow my brain registered what I needed to do next, and I managed to hold up my hands in surrender.

"Drop the weapon," one of them shouted as multiple officers filed in.

I knelt down, set it on the floor, and kicked it away from me like I'd seen on the cop shows I'd watched with Kyle.

"Gemma!" Lambert ran in. "Are you okay?"

I nodded, my mind and body in shock.

"Talk to me," he said tilting my chin up to him. "They'll take care of Brandon, you talk to me."

"Hendrix's jacket is on the floor," I said, dazed.

"Did he hurt you?"

I shook my head.

"Let's get you out of here. Your family is worried sick."

He put his arm around my shoulder and guided me out of the warehouse and into the fresh air.

"Gemma!" Hendrix yelled from across the parking lot. "Gemma!"

The sound of his voice broke through my haze, and I took off running to him. He pulled me into his strong arms and picked me up, twirling me around.

"Baby, are you okay?" He asked, tears

streaming down his cheeks.

"Yeah," I said, peppering his face with kisses. "Just don't let me go, Hendrix. I don't know if I can keep my shit together."

"I've got you, and Mac is okay. He didn't hurt her."

My body trembled violently as he kissed me, my heart rate calming with his touch.

"Don't you ever do that to me again, and at the same time...thank you for saving my sister. I love you so fucking much. You're my forever."

"I love you too, Hendrix. And all I want is to go home with you," I whispered.

He set me down and wiped his tear-stained cheeks.

"The cops need to speak with you first, then I promise I'll take you home. Plus someone else wants to talk to you, too."

He took my hand and led me to the large group of people. I stopped while the EMT's loaded Brandon into the ambulance. His head wasn't covered with a sheet, and I could see the oxygen mask on his face.

"I didn't kill him," I said, my words catching in my throat.

"We'll find out what's going on. Come on babe."

Honestly, I wasn't sure how I felt about Brandon being alive. A part of me wanted to kill him, but the other part of me might not have been able to live with the fact I'd taken a life.

"Gemma!"

"Mac!" I cried. I dropped Hendrix's hand, and we grabbed each other, full on crying.

"Are you okay?" We both asked at the same time.

I laughed through my tears.

"What the fuck were you thinking?" she asked, wiping her face.

"That he wanted me, and I had three-inch-high heels on." I searched the area for Pierce. He'd told me how to use them to my advantage. If it weren't for him, I would have had zero chance of walking out of there alive.

"Did he hurt you, Mac?"

"No, he just scared me. He threatened to, but the only time he touched me was to force a rag in my mouth, tie me up, and toss me in the back of his trunk."

A cry escaped me, and I pulled her in for another hug. "I'm so sorry."

"I'll be alright. Knowing Franklin, he'll pay for therapy, and I can use my trauma as an excuse to drink," she said, laughing.

"Gemma," Franklin said, approaching me.

I ran into his open arms, clinging to him.

"I don't know how to thank you," he said against my hair.

"You don't have to. We're family."

By the time I'd talked to everyone important and gave my account to the police, not a single civilian had a dry eye. Even Pierce blinked rapidly a few times, attempting to keep his emotions in check.

It was nearly three in the morning when we arrived at Franklin's. Exhausted, but too wired to sleep, Franklin set the alarm system, and we all went upstairs to the game room. I slipped my tired feet out of my shoes, spotting blood on the heel. Those would have to be thrown out, maybe even burned.

Hendrix leaned against the arm of the couch and patted the space between his legs. I sat down and scooted back against him gently. His arms wrapped around my waist, and he kissed my cheek.

Mac plopped down near my feet and rested her arm over my leg. Right now, we were doing anything to be near each other. Touch each other. Know we were safe.

Franklin walked over to the bar, and all of us

snapped to attention.

"Dad," Mac said, standing. "You're not making a drink, are you?"

He stopped mid-pour and stared at her.

"Did you just call me Dad?"

"Yeah, I did. But don't change the subject, who's the drink for?"

"You," he said handing it to her. The tension melted in the air as he handed her a vodka cranberry. "Hang on," he said. "There's two more coming."

"Three, please," I said. "One is for Pierce. We're home, and I wouldn't be here with all of you if it weren't for him. Again."

Pierce stood still, not acknowledging that I'd even spoken.

"Pierce, she's right. You're having a few drinks with us. Your off-duty, relax. It's been a fucked-up night."

Mac's mouth dropped open.

"Did you just drop the F-bomb?"

"I did," Franklin said and chuckled.

Hendrix's chest rumbled with his laughter, and I twisted toward him for a quick kiss.

"Have a seat with us, Pierce," Franklin ordered.

Mac brought Hendrix and me our drinks and

sat back down.

I sipped my cranberry and vodka and welcomed the tingle. Tonight, I wasn't concerned about Jungle Gemma. I was too exhausted, and all I wanted was to remain in Hendrix's arms.

"Until you two leave for your tour," Franklin began.

"What?" Mac said, spilling her drink in her lap. "Shit, sorry Dad. You guys got the tour?"

Pierce hopped up and grabbed a towel for her to mop up her lap with.

"Yeah, we leave in two weeks," I said, squeezing Hendrix's thigh. "We have the full schedule, so we can plan when you'll join us. Hopefully, Franklin will fly down with you, and we can all spend some time together."

A smile eased across his face. "That would be awesome. I would love to see you two perform, anyway."

"Sounds like a plan," Hendrix said.

"Until you two leave for the tour, I would like you to stay here."

Although I couldn't see him, I was pretty sure Hendrix had shaken his head no.

"Hang on son, hear me out. You can spend the days at your house, but at night, I would like everyone here. I'll be making a call tomorrow to hire extra security, too. Each one of you will have a bodyguard assigned to you."

"What?" Mac screeched.

I sat up and patted her arm.

"It's because they haven't been able to find Dillon, Brandon's father, Mac."

"None of this is up for discussion. You're a prime target as long as he's loose. In fact, Pierce will go on tour with you."

"Dad, seriously?" Hendrix asked. I sat up, my focus bouncing between Hendrix and Pierce. Tension filled the air. Pierce would be with us constantly. The only privacy we would have would be in the bedroom.

"I considered hiring someone else for you two, but Gemma feels safe with him, and he can continue to train both of you on the road."

"You know about that?" I asked.

"I always knew, Gemma. I trusted Pierce, and I understood why you talked to him about it. I was proud of you for getting some help."

"Did you tell him? I mean, you were the one that swore me to secrecy," I said, my tone slightly accusatory.

"I didn't have a clue he knew until after Brandon took Mac," Pierce replied, taking a long drink.

I sank back against my seat, my frustration settling down as the vodka did its job. Franklin was right. After tonight, I trusted Pierce implicitly. Even Hendrix trusted him, he just knew he had a thing for me.

Knowing when he'd lost the battle, Hendrix sank back into the couch. If he'd told Franklin Pierce cared about me, Franklin would fire him. For now, being able to trust him with our lives outweighed a harmless crush.

I suspected Hendrix came to the same conclusion, because he let it go and slipped his arm around me.

"I would love to have you guys here until you leave," Mac said, her voice laced with sadness.

"We'll see each other a minimum of once a month, and some of the time you'll travel with us. At least we hope so."

"Your grades come first, Mac, so if you want to join them on the road, I need Cs and better."

She groaned. "You're kind of being a ball buster tonight," she said, scrunching her nose up at him. "Plus I'm twenty, not twelve."

"Correct, which means you're capable of stepping up to the challenge without flipping me a bunch of attitude. Especially when I pay for it all."

My mouth formed an O. He'd just pulled the

money card on her.

"Only because I let you," she said, laughing. "My bestie has a bit of change in her pocket, too. She'd put me up."

Even though we all laughed, it was true. I'd always be there for Mac.

Pierce stood and placed his glass in the bar sink.

"I'll get it later, Pierce. Thanks for having a drink with us." I flashed him a tired smile, and he gave me one back.

"I'm glad everyone is home safe and sound. I'm going to check the perimeter and then head down the hill."

"I'll go with you," Franklin said, standing. "You kids know where everything is. I'll see you in the morning," he said and left the room.

Seconds later, he walked back in, his hands shoved deep in his pockets.

"I love you all very much." He walked back out as we stared after him in silence.

I blinked the tears from my eyes and reached for Mac and Hendrix's hand.

"This is how shit's gonna happen," Mac said. "We're throwing down together tonight. I can't handle sleeping alone. That bastard will give me nightmares for years. So you two figure it out. We can either sleep in one of the beds, or we can pile up the blankets and pillows in here on the floor and watch a movie.

"That sounds fun," I said. "Baby?" I asked Hendrix.

"Yeah, I think I need you both close to me, too. I wasn't sure which one of you I was going to lose tonight, or maybe both," he said, his voice trailing off. A heaviness settled in the room, pressing down on us as we attempted to make sense of an insane situation.

"First I need a shower. Brandon's stench is stuck in my nose," I said, breaking the silence.

"Me too," Mac said.

"We'll meet back in here then." We all stood, staring at each other. I wasn't sure about them, but I was a little surprised to still be alive.

THE HOT SPRAY streamed down my body while Hendrix kissed me.

"Are you really alright?" he asked, worry filling his handsome features.

"I don't know, but right now I am. Somedays, I think that's as good as it will get. Just moment to moment."

"I thought I'd lost you tonight, Gem. I've never felt pain like that before. Not even with Kendra."

"I'm so sorry. I took a huge gamble, but it paid off."

"I can't lose you," he said, choking on his words.

"You have me, all of me," I said, jumping up into his arms, wrapping my legs around his waist. He slid inside me and kissed me again, but this one was different. This kiss was full of fear and desperation. We'd almost lost each other tonight. Everything good we'd found—our love, it had nearly all come to a tragic end.

I grabbed his wet hair as he slowly made love to me. He sank down onto the seat, his hands running up and down my back.

Tears streamed down my face as I gave everything to the man who had dared to take a chance on me from the beginning. He saw through my walls and straight into my heart. His faith in me had set me free, and I would forever belong to him. He was the light in my soul, the very air I breathed.

Forty minutes later, we joined Mac in the game room. She'd already piled a million blankets on the floor, and our pillows were all situated. I positioned myself in the middle of them.

"This is my first threesome, so take it easy on me," I said, giggling.

"Ohmigosh, you're killing me over here. And even though Hendrix is my stepbrother, that shit's fucking wrong."

Hendrix chuckled. "No worries, Mac. I fully support your thought process."

"Shit. I guess we'll have to reschedule the rafting trip. I don't know about you two, but after tonight, I'm toast. I'm not sure I'll even get out of bed tomorrow unless I have to pee or eat."

"I think we're right there with you. Unfortunately, tonight won't fade away for a long time," I replied.

"Love you guys," Hendrix said, his grasp on my hand tightening.

"Yeah, whatever, I guess you guys are alright. I mean I can put up with you if Dad makes me," Mac said, then we all laughed.

We snuggled into the blankets and Mac turned on *The Breakfast Club*.

"I've not seen this," I said.

"So fucking good. They're all opposites who would never have become friends if fate hadn't thrown them together. Just like us."

I pulled the covers up over me and grabbed Mac's hand too.

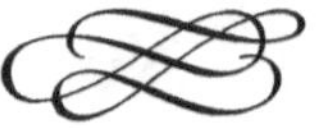

CHAPTER 35

The next two weeks flew by. I spent every minute, I could alone with Hendrix, but by seven in the evening, we were back home with Franklin and Mac for dinner.

"Are you guys ready for tomorrow? I think I'm a little nervous myself," Franklin said, folding his napkin and placing it on his empty dinner plate.

"I'm nervous anyway, but the fact that our first show is in Louisiana set me back a little," I said.

"Yeah, no shit, but at least it's summer, and I can go with you," Mac chimed in.

"I know," I said. "It helps."

"I sure as hell didn't want to go back, but raising money to help rebuild after the tornado...well, I couldn't turn it down. Plus, Billy and Citizen Shade will also perform. The lineup is insane, and we're going to share a stage with them," Hendrix said, leaning back in his chair.

"I'll even be there, so if a tornado moves in, we're all going together," Franklin added.

We all stared at him.

"Sorry, guess my daughter is wearing off on me," he said, winking at Mac.

We'd agreed to perform in Shreveport, then we would all fly back after three days. The next day Hendrix and I would hop on the tour bus with Cade, John, and Pierce, then we would drive to California.

Ruby fluttered into the dining room and removed our plates.

"Thanks, Ruby, the alfredo was amazing."

"You're welcome. I sure will miss you two."

I smiled at her. "You, too."

"Since we're not truly parting with you for a few days, I think Gem and I are going to turn in early," Hendrix said.

Mac snickered, and Hendrix kicked her under the table.

"Dude! Not cool," she said, rubbing her shin.

I laughed and hugged Franklin goodnight. Hendrix took my hand and led me up the stairs.

He closed my door behind him and kissed me.

"How are you doing?"

"Honestly? I'm scared. Everything about this trip is huge."

"I know babe, but I support you a hundred times over. I'm so proud of you. This next step, what you're doing…"

I placed my finger against his lips, silencing him.

"Make love to me, Hendrix."

He picked me up, carried me to our bed, and gave me a night I would remember for the rest of my life.

CHAPTER 36

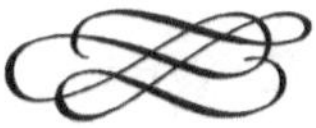

"Hello, Louisiana!" I said into the microphone. The audience roared in response. My legs wobbled beneath me, but I took a deep breath and remembered why I was here. This was also the first time I'd been on stage alone, and it was terrifying.

"A few months ago, I was on the stage singing just minutes before the tornado ripped through Baton Rouge. People were wounded and killed, but tonight...tonight, we stand united as your city is rebuilt."

The crowd roared and cheered. I hung my head down and took a shaky breath.

"There's another reason I'm here tonight," I said, quietly. "When I was fourteen years old..." I glanced over to the right side of the stage at Hendrix, Mac, and Franklin. "When I was fourteen, I was brutally raped."

The room fell silent instantly.

"My entire life was stolen from me. Not only had I been raped, but weeks later, I found out I was pregnant." The intensity of the moment speared my heart, and I stepped away from the microphone.

"You can do it, bestie!" Mac shouted.

I smiled at her and resumed my place.

"I carried my son and then gave him up for adoption. And I know I'm not the only woman here tonight that has been assaulted or raped."

The stadium held fifteen thousand people, and we'd packed the house. Silence filled the entire auditorium, emotion thick in the air.

"So tonight, twenty percent of your ticket sales will help fund and start a center for rape survivors right here in Louisiana."

The crowd roared at an ear-splitting level.

"I'll personally oversee this project, and with your support, I hope to see it grow across the country. The center will offer counseling, self-defense training, and temporary housing. If a woman is pregnant from her assault, and she chooses to give the baby up for adoption like I did, there will be a free service to help place the baby in a safe and loving home."

Tears of happiness streamed down my cheeks, and the crowd went wild. I'd never imagined my decision to invest in this project would catch fire, but here I was, surrounded by an overwhelming amount of love and support.

I closed my eyes briefly and focused on the audience again.

"I won't lie, it's been a hell of a journey. I lived for five years as a shut-in. Terror struck my heart anytime I even considered leaving my house. But one woman stood beside me, believed in me, and helped give me the courage to not only leave but also attend college in Spokane, Washington. Her name was Ada Lynn, and she left this earth a few months ago. The foundation will be named after her." I paused. "Once I arrived in Spokane, Washington, my life changed drastically, and I met a boy."

Cheers rang through the air.

"As you can imagine, after being raped and hiding for years, he terrified me. But day after day, he showed up and loved me until I could breathe again. He's the love of my life, but you all know him as Hendrix Harrington."

I stepped away from the mic and flashed a

smile at my boyfriend who stood side stage. I waited for the audience to settle down again.

"This song is for him," I said, the spotlight going out in a blink.

"You," I sang a capella, a single soft light shining on me. "are the reason..." I stood on the stage, vulnerable, baring my soul in front of thousands of people while I laid my heart at Hendrix's feet. My nerves diminished into the background as I continued to sing. I finished the song on a whistle note, and the thunder of the applause overloaded my senses. The next thing I knew, Hendrix had rushed over to me, picked me up, and twirled me around, kissing me passionately. He placed me down and ran up to the microphone.

"Ladies and gentlemen, my amazing girlfriend, Gemma Thompson!" He kissed me again then hurried over to the piano and sat down. "Shit, I'm the luckiest man alive," he said to the crowd, winking at me.

Then, he began our song "Couldn't Love You More," and I joined him. Our voices blended together effortlessly. And as always, everything and everyone else faded away except for us.

Several songs and twenty minutes later, we

bowed, and Hendrix grabbed my hand. We waved to the audience while we exited.

"Oh. My. Fucking. God!" Mac screamed, hugging me and Hendrix. "You were so fucking awesome; there wasn't a dry eye in this place."

"The two of you are spectacular together," Franklin said, pulling me in for a hug.

"I'm so glad you're here," I said.

"Son," Franklin wrapped Hendrix in a bear hug. "I'm so proud of you."

"Thanks, Dad. Thanks for making this happen."

"Hey, man. Fantastic performance," Billy Raffoul said, approaching Hendrix and slapping him on the back. "You too," he said, hugging me. My brows shot up in surprise, and Mac giggled.

"I'm glad you're alright. I lost track of everyone after the tornado. It's good to see you again," I said to Billy.

"Yeah, that was some crazy shit. I'm glad our boy is back to normal. He made national headlines with his amnesia."

"I did?" Hendrix said, shocked.

"Yeah dude, people love you. You've got a voice like none other, and the two of you together... Shit, people are gonna go home tonight and make a lot of babies."

My cheeks flamed red with his words.

"I'll catch you guys after the show. I still want to talk business, but right now I'm up." Billy grabbed his guitar and made his way on stage.

Hendrix stood behind me, linking his arms around my waist while we watched Billy perform.

"I love you," he said in my ear.

I turned to him and kissed him. It was crazy to think that this was just our beginning.

CHAPTER 37

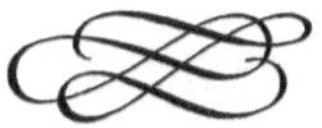

The air in June was muggy and hot as hell. I already missed Spokane.

"You ready?" Hendrix asked.

"I think so." I peered out of the car window at my childhood home. I hadn't been ready to clean out Kyle's or Ada Lynn's house, so I'd hired people to pack up their belongings. I'd deal with it later.

A burgundy colored Hyundai pulled up next to us.

"That's her," I said, my heart skipping a beat as I studied the dark-haired beauty behind the wheel.

"I'll let you meet her, first."

Pierce peered into the rearview mirror at me, his way of letting me know he was there for me.

I opened the car door and stepped out.

"Olivia?" I asked, approaching a strikingly beautiful woman my age. Her large hazel eyes landed on me, surveying me. I waited until she seemed comfortable. I understood completely.

"Gemma?" she asked, her voice steady.

"Hi," I smiled. "I'm so glad you could meet with me."

"I was shocked when you found me. I...I had no idea Kyle had a daughter."

I totally pulled a Mac and embraced her.

"I'm so sorry for what my father did to you," I said in her ear.

"Oh my God, and Carl too," she said, returning my hug. I stepped away, taking a deep breath.

"Are you alright? After..."

"I'm scarred, but step-by-step I've taken my life back," she said.

"Me, too. I didn't leave the house for years, terrified that Carl...would find me again."

"My uncle was evil. And I'm so sorry, but so was your father."

"I know. But he's dead and Carl is in prison for life. Now I just want to help anyone else the society harmed. And when I found out you were a psychologist, I hoped you'd be open to running the Ada Lynn Foundation of Hope."

"I was thrilled. I already work with rape victims."

I took her hand in mine like we'd known each other all our lives. In a way, we had. Through our shared tragedy, we were immediately bonded for life.

"Let me introduce you to my boyfriend, then I'll go over my vision with you."

I opened the door for Hendrix, and he stepped out of the car.

"Hendrix Harrington?" she asked, a bit breathless.

I laughed, and Hendrix's face lit up with a huge smile.

"Thank you for meeting with Gemma." He extended his hand to her, and she shook it, a bit awestruck.

"Shit, you're *the* Gemma Thompson," she said, her eyes widening. "I was at the concert you performed at. Holy wow, you two are amazing, and here I am talking business with you."

"Yeah, that's me. Us," I said, taking Hendrix's hand in mine.

"This is my second dream, Olivia. I hope you'll

be a part of it as we both continue to heal and live a full life."

Over the next hour, I walked Olivia through my childhood home and explained to her everything I wanted to do. Then we walked her across the street and showed her the new house she would live in if she took the job.

Pierce had already checked out the inside and cleared us to enter. I smiled at him as Hendrix led the way into what had been our first house together. My heart stopped when I stepped inside. The memories of Ada Lynn and us outweighed the attack from Carl.

"This will be part of the compensation for the job...the house plus pay. Your job will be incredibly difficult, so I want to make sure you're taken care of," I said. Her eyes grew wide with disbelief. "Plus, I'll cover your personal counseling. I'm a strong believer in a counselor having a therapist."

"I'm in," Olivia said, smiling. "What's next?"

We sat at the dining room table where I'd had dinners with Ada Lynn, and might have turned the table into a Jungle Gemma playground once or twice. My chest tightened, my heart longing for Ada Lynn.

After we hammered out the details, funding,

and responsibilities, Olivia left, and Hendrix and I were left alone in the house.

"It feels like a lifetime ago," I said.

"I know. Sometimes I miss being here."

"Really?" I asked, standing and walking over to him. "Why?"

"It was our first place together. I lost you and won you all right here."

"Baby, you always had my heart," I said, placing my forehead against his.

A loud engine fired up, pulling me from our conversation. I glanced at the clock on my phone.

"I guess it's time," I said, standing.

Hendrix took my hand, and we made our way through the house. I mentally said goodbye as we closed the door behind us, and hurried down the steps.

We stood in the middle of the street, holding hands, and staring ahead of us. The bulldozer knocked over the fence and slowly made its way toward my childhood home. Anger, terror, and pain flowed through me as the powerful machine knocked down the porch. The porch where Hendrix had slept all night, waiting for me.

I stared speechless as my entire past was turned into rubble. The bulldozer ran over the pieces that were left of my house and then turned in the direction of Ada Lynn's. I said goodbye to my second home while the walls tumbled down.

Hendrix pulled me against him, and we watched the houses disappear. The contractors would be out in the next few days to begin building the Ada Lynn Foundation of Hope, the center for rape victims. Everything old had tumbled to the ground to be replaced with the new.

"It's done," I said, turning to him.

"I'm so proud of you, Gemma."

"I couldn't have done it without you," I said, kissing him. "And now the house that held a criminal will now be a place of healing. I'm so happy Olivia agreed to run the center."

"And I'm happy you two found each other."

"I know. Life has been full of surprises, but you've been the best one."

"You're my forever, Gemma Thompson," Hendrix said, kissing me tenderly.

"And you're my always, Hendrix Harrington."

FALL IN LOVE with the lead guitarist in August Clover. Click here for Love & Consequences with Mackenzie and Cade! Click Here!

. . .

FOR EXCLUSIVE LOVE & RUIN BONUS SCENES sign up for my newsletter. https://www.authorjaowenby.com/newsletter

*** *Looking for the next book in the series? Here's the series order.*

The Love & Ruin Series
Love & Ruin
Love & Deception
Love & Redemption
Love & Consequences, a standalone novel
Love & Corruption, a standalone novel
Love & Revelations, a Valentine's Day novella
Love & Seduction, a standalone novel

<u>Love & Vengeance, a standalone novel</u>
<u>Love & Vengeance in Hendrix's POV</u>

You can also join my Facebook group, J.A. Owenby's One Page At A Time, for exclusive giveaways and sneak peeks of future books.

I appreciate your help in spreading the word online as well as telling a friend. Reviews help readers find books they love, so please leave a review on your favorite book site.

Love and Redemption

J.A. OWENBY

Edited by: Deb Markanton

Cover Art by: iheartcoverdesigns

Photographer: CJC Photography

First Edition

ISBN-13: 978-1-949414-22-6

Gain access to previews of J.A. Owenby's novels before they're released and to take part in exclusive giveaways. www.jaowenby.com

ABOUT THE AUTHOR

J.A. Owenby lives in the beautiful Pacific Northwest with her husband and cat.

She also runs her own business as a professional resume writer and interview coach —she helps people find jobs they love.

J.A. is an avid reader of thrillers, romance, new adult, and young adult novels. She loves music, movies, and good wine. And call her crazy, but she loves the rainy Pacific Northwest; she gets her best story ideas while listening to the rain pattering against the windows in front of the fireplace.

You can follow the progress of her upcoming novel on Facebook at Author J.A. Owenby and on Twitter @jaowenby.

*Sign up for J.A. Owenby's Newsletter:
BookHip.com/CTZMWZ*

*Like J.A. Owenby's Facebook:
https://www.facebook.com/JAOwenby*

*J.A Owenby's One Page At A Time reader group:
https://www.facebook.com/groups/JAOwenby*